Annelies Ismail

and Mona Gabriel

My Husband is Egyptian

Annelies Ismail
and Mona Gabriel

My Husband is Egyptian

15 Women tell their Stories

Order this book online at www.trafford.com
or email orders@trafford.com

Most Trafford titles are also available at major online book retailers.

This book was published in Germany under the title: Mein Mann ist Ägypter
by Glaré Verlag, Germany.
Translation with friendly permission of Glaré Verlag

Note for Librarians: A cataloguing record for this book is available from Library and Archives Canada at www.collectionscanada.ca/amicus/index-e.html

Contributors:
Translation: Alana and Harald Bordewieck
Editors: Susan LeVangia and Suzanne Abdel-Aal
Cover art: Helga Mehl

Printed in Victoria, BC, Canada.

ISBN: 978-1-4251-9131-3 (Soft)
ISBN: 978-1-4251-9133-7 (e-book)

Trafford rev. date: 7/16/2009

www.trafford.com

North America & international
toll-free: 1 888 232 4444 (USA & Canada)
phone: 250 383 6864 • fax: 250 383 6804 • email: info@trafford.com

Table of Contents:

Prologue

The idea for this book came to me in 2006 when I became acquainted with some German, Swiss, and Austrian women, as well as women of other nationalities in Alexandria, Egypt. They are all married to Egyptians and some of them have been living in Egypt for many years. They told me their very personal stories. All of these stories are true. I changed only some of the names upon request. For many it is a story of the love of their lives, sometimes even love at first sight. I myself have been married to an Egyptian since 1965. We lived together most of the time in Germany and a few years in the United States and France. Our life has been interesting, varied and sometimes difficult, too. But as all these women told me their stories, words failed me more than once. Many of them raised their children in Egypt under, at times, difficult conditions. They lived in an unfamiliar environment with a very difficult language to learn. They live in a mixed marriage of culture and religion, mostly a Muslim husband and a Christian wife. They have exemplified with their lives that one can overcome much with love and tolerance. Of course, there are cases where the family fell apart. But I think that any woman who undertakes such a risk brings with her special capabilities, the readiness to master difficulties and the determination not to give up everything at the slightest problem. All the women I interviewed agree that their unusual circumstances have enriched their lives. Only very few said to me that they regretted their decision.

This book is dedicated to all of these courageous women.

My special thanks go to my husband, Moniem Ismail. Right from the beginning he encouraged and supported me in this project. His constructive criticism helped me write the stories in a logical and understandable way.

My daughter, Mona Gabriel, worked with me to put the stories into a fluent, readable form in the original German version. This is our first collaboration; perhaps it will not be the last.

Annelies Ismail　　　　Alexandria, February 2009

Chapter One
Betty I. Sometimes the Road to Egypt Runs through England

I met Betty for the first time in Agamy during an afternoon with other German women. Out of curiosity I asked her a few questions about her life. She spontaneously told me her love story and I was immediately fascinated with her experiences in Egypt and with Egyptians. Much surprised me although I myself have been married to an Egyptian for over 40 years. I could not get her story out of my mind, and I asked her permission to write it down. She quickly agreed. After many further conversations and interesting stories, the idea for this book was born.

Betty is rather tall and stands very straight, although she walks somewhat cautiously after her two knee operations. At 79 she is the oldest of the women who told me their stories. Nonetheless she still seems very spry. Sometimes she falters while narrating and often I have to ask my question again.

Here is her story as we reconstructed it together:

Actually my path to Egypt was probably predestined. I had just turned 12 when I went with a friend to a fortuneteller. After some „hmms" and „ahs" this wise woman stated even then: „You will live under palm trees!" Of course I did not take it seriously and forgot about it right away. And now in the end it actually has turned out that way anyway!

I was born in Hamburg in 1928. My father died young, when I was still a little girl. In 1943, while the bombing left the city in rubble and ashes, my mother lay in the hospital with leukemia.

She had to be moved as quickly as possible. During that transfer she contracted pneumonia and died shortly thereafter. At only fifteen I was already an orphan and in the middle of a war. I did have an aunt, but she too had a very hard time during the war. Her husband had already been killed in action and her two sons, too, so that she barely knew how she would manage. I could not really count on her support.

Nevertheless, I succeeded somehow in completing my training as a nursery school teacher. Afterwards I went for an internship near Jesteburg in the Lunenburg Heath country.

One day I went to Hamburg and found out that in the meantime my brother had given up our apartment. He moved - the neighbors told me curtly. So I stood in front of the locked door and did not know where to go. I did meet him later, but we did not have much contact after that. So now I was entirely on my own and had no place to stay in Hamburg any more.

Fortunately, I quickly felt at home in Jesteburg. I became acquainted with Lili, who became my best friend. Actually her real name was Elisabeth like mine. But she was called Lili and I Betty, so there were no mix-ups. Lili lived with her Aunt Else who took me in, too and quickly grew very fond of me. Soon I belonged to the family and Aunt Else became a "surrogate mother" to me. We remained close friends until she died at 92.

In 1947 - I was just 19 years old - Lili and I opened a nursery school in Jesteburg together. At that time the State provided no subsidies. That meant we had to pay all the expenses of running our business ourselves. The parents paid us ten Reichsmark for each child. In retrospect that was a very nice time in the village. Everyone knew us and really liked Aunt Lili and Aunt Betty. Of course, there was not much available to eat, but the farmers had enough and no one had to starve.

Then in 1948 came the currency reform and all at once everything was different. From one day to the next, people did not have money any more, and no one could afford nursery school. Soon we had hardly any children to take care of and then we had to close altogether.

What now? There was no work for us in Germany, and we had to make a living somehow. In England there was work; nannies and aides in sanatoriums were in demand. Lili put her name on a list, and shortly thereafter she found a position in England. She helped out on a farm as a nanny. Of course we stayed in touch, and soon she wrote me that I should come, too. She had even found work for me.

So I made my way to England in 1949. I went by ship from Hamburg to Hull. I do not remember much in detail except for the crossing, which was awful. Almost everyone was seasick, me too, of course. It was after all my first trip by sea. On top of everything else, I was all alone. When I arrived in England, I felt as sick as a dog. There I was supposed to continue on by train through Darlington to Newcastle. I had never traveled outside of Germany, and I knew only school English aside from a few private lessons I took practically at the last minute before my departure. When I finally got settled on the right train, I felt rather forlorn. I could hardly make myself understood, so I watched my fellow travelers. Two women were knitting scarves or pullovers from thick wool. But the technique they used was entirely different than the way we do it. It looked very confusing. I had never seen knitting like that. My courage flagged, and little by little I began to feel really desperate: all alone, without adequate language skills and now they even knit differently...! All of a sudden I felt very inexperienced. Everything was new and strange for me.

When the train arrived in Newcastle, the next unpleasant surprise was waiting for me. Lili had promised to pick me up, but she was not there. After I had looked around for a while, an Indian man addressed me in English. At least I understood enough to realize he was my new employer. He packed me along with my luggage into his car and talked continuously. I did not understand a word. At some point he finally paused, and I asked him, „Where is Elisabeth?" Only then did he notice that I had not understood him at all. He had, as a matter of fact, just been telling me in great detail why Lili could not come. We both had a good laugh about that. When we arrived at his house, he introduced me to his wife and two children. His wife was English, but I did not understand her any better than him.

I had been traveling for five days and had eaten

hardly anything. Finally we had supper. It was a type of cold salad: red beets, tomato, cucumber and some cold meat, all with mayonnaise. I found this very strange and did not like the way it tasted at all. After the long journey I was really starving and had hoped for a nice hot soup. Unfortunately nothing like that was to be seen.

They showed me my room, and I soon went to sleep. The next morning the master of the house showed me how to make a fire in the fireplace. From then on that was always one of my duties. In addition, I helped with the housework and watched the children. That sounds easy but was quite difficult at times. As a matter of fact, the two children often acted very stubbornly on purpose and maintained that they simply did not understand me. I found them rather naughty and the mother treated me in a condescending manner.

The farm where Lili worked was quite a ways away. In spite of the distance, we met of course on our first mutual day off. We took the bus into Newcastle. I jumped on the bus as I was used to doing. Lili was very embarrassed. She flailed her arms around wildly and shouted: „Get off there, will you get off now! Here you have to stand in line (the famous British queue). If you do that, I'll never go out with you again." I learned very quickly. We spent the whole day in Newcastle. I was so happy to see her! We had a whole lot to tell each other, and I was happy that I could speak German again. I went back alone on the bus—after I had stood in the queue like a good girl, of course.

Soon I no longer had any serious difficulties with the English language. But there were a few funny misunderstandings. One evening the lady of the house was expecting visitors. Shortly before their arrival, she had to go out with her bike to buy a few things and wanted me to start cooking. So she asked me: „Can you make ships?" Well, of course I can, I answered in a confident voice. Then I went to the kitchen and carved ships, that is ships from potatoes. When it comes to crafts, I am really talented; therefore, I made really nice single-masted sailboats, two-masters, etc. I did not really understand entirely why I was doing it, but I did not always understand everything anyway. Then the lady of the house returned from shopping. She brought her shopping bags into the kitchen and asked casually, „Did you make the ships?" „Yes here are the ships", I answered and proudly showed her my little armada. She burst out laughing. Later she told everyone she met, even on the telephone, „Betty made ships." (Note: Chips in British English are French fries; in American English, chips are potato chips or in British, crisps.)

Another time I was supposed to fry fish in batter. She asked me specifically if I knew how to do that. „Yes" I answered; after all, that could not be so hard. Unfortunately I had understood „butter". She had barely left the kitchen when I got to work. First I could not find any butter. Then I found three packages way back in the refrigerator. Whenever she cooked, everything was fried in a lot of fat, so I would do the same. When she came home and evaluated the results of my culinary arts, she was somewhat indignant. At that time butter was still rationed, and I had used up the entire month's supply.

All in all I did not feel really comfortable with these people. The children did not obey me, and the lady of the house seemed to hold a grudge against me just under the surface. So I was very glad when a German friend, who also worked as a nanny, got me a position with a new family.

My next stop in England was with the family of a doctor. He was a lung specialist and his wife was a nurse. I was given a nice room and for the first time in a long time, I felt really good. I grew very fond of the children. I could have stayed in this household a long time. However, after two years I became restless. I was now 22 years old and stood on my own two feet. But originally I had imagined a much different life for myself.

I decided first to return to Germany and visited Aunt Else in Jesteburg and after that a friend in Hamburg. Because I was so used to it, I of course got in line to board the train. It left without me right in front of my eyes! Here you did not do it that way; instead everyone simply jumped on whenever and wherever it suited him. It took a little while, but soon I got used to it again. Nevertheless I did not really feel at home in Hamburg any more. Naturally, I wrote Lili in England and told her how I was doing in Germany. Her answer came immediately by return mail: I should simply return to England.

This time I went to a widow with two children. This widow had several boyfriends at the same time (today we would say affairs) who often came to visit. I did not like that at all; my morals were very conservative. But I have to admit that she was always very nice to me. Her children were really dear, too. I had a pretty room in her house and my only responsibility was the children.

In 1953 I decided that I wanted to achieve more in life than to take care of other people's children. I began training to become a nurse. Of course, I had to take an exam in English first, but I passed it without any problems as my English was quite good by now. So now I was a nursing student– a student nurse we called it then. I lived with many other student nurses in a nurses' residence. We slept in dormitory rooms with several beds to a room, and whenever we did not want to eat in the hospital cafeteria, we could cook up something in the dorm's common kitchen. I quickly adjusted and felt comfortable living in the nursing community. My best friend was Trudi, also a German.

After a day's work in the hospital, I almost always wanted to get out in the fresh air. Trudi often accompanied me, and we could get to Hyde Park in a short time by bus. We liked to go for walks there, to enjoy the fresh air and talk with each other. Sometimes we listened to the orators at „Speakers Corner". They talked about everything possible under the sun: God, the world, politics or other topics. Only the Royal Family was off limits. You were not allowed to talk about them and certainly never to poke fun at them.

One evening Trudi was too tired to go with me, so I took off alone. I went to Hyde Park and went for a walk. At some point I dug a cigarette out of my coat pocket but I could not find any matches. At that time I still smoked as all the nurses did, actually. I looked around to see if someone nearby was about to light up. Soon an opportunity arose and I asked, „May I have a light?" A man approached me with his lighter and I lit my cigarette. He kept the lighter open a rather long time. He wanted to look at me longer he later told me. We began to talk. He told me he came from South America, which I found a bit strange. I thought right away that he was Egyptian. I had already seen a few Egyptians, as doctors from Egypt worked at the hospital. He said that he had been here only a few days, that he was all alone and rather lonely. Now I could really understand that because I had often felt lonely, too. I told him that I came from Germany and so we talked for quite a while until I had to go home. Finally we arranged to meet again the next day in Hyde Park.

I had not decided for sure if I really wanted to meet him again. I wanted to leave the decision up to chance. I went to the bus stop in the evening as planned and thought, „I'll take the first bus that comes. If it goes to Hyde Park, then I'll meet him there. If it goes somewhere else, I'll just go wherever it takes me." The bus came and sure enough it was the line to Hyde Park. Therefore I went to our agreed meeting place. And there he stood waiting for me...

From then on we met almost every day, as often as I could make it. Of course he had to confess at some point that he came from Egypt and not South America. Why he told me otherwise at first, I do not know to this day. Maybe he was just joking. His name was Ibrahim. We got along very well; we talked and talked. As soon as the third day he asked me if I would marry him and go to Egypt with him. I was surprised and of course said, "No." I could not imagine going so far away to such a strange and foreign land. Although England had seemed nearly just as foreign to me only a few years ago, I felt almost at home there in the meantime. But Ibrahim did not give up so quickly. Every evening he asked me again and I always answered, " No." It went this way for several weeks: we met, went for a walk and talked. And every time he asked if I would marry him, I again said, "No." Once during that time I even went with him to his hotel. I do not remember what I was thinking, because naturally Ibrahim tried to make advances. That did not help his cause because I refused him, but we kept meeting. Everything remained the same as before.

I wanted to use my upcoming yearly vacation time to visit Lili in at the farm Newcastle. The last evening before my vacation I met Ibrahim in the park as always, and we went for a walk. Afterwards he accompanied me to the bus and we said good- bye as we always did. „Bye, bye", I said. „Bye, bye", he answered. I remember that we waved to each other. I knew that he would soon travel back to Alexandria. His business in England was done; he had to go back to Egypt to take care of his shop. He bought and sold used electrical appliances. At that time there were hardly any new appliances to be bought. Everything was scarce. In England Ibrahim had bought various items that were not available in Egypt and in addition had learned about new technologies. He was finished with his business and now he had to go back to Egypt. We would not see each other any more. I knew all of that, but it seemed unreal to me anyway.

I went back by bus to the dormitory. I had already packed up my belongings because I had to give up my room for the time I was on vacation. For this last night before my vacation, I was allowed to sleep in Trudi's bed because she had night duty that night. Her boyfriend was a very nice Englishman and besides he had a car. The next morning she and her boyfriend wanted to take me to the train station. I entered Trudi's room and sat on the bed. Sleep was out of the question. Therefore, I sat at the table and wrote a letter to „him". Afterwards I tore the letter into little pieces and cried. I began again and wrote a second letter. Then I cried again. It was awful. Then finally and quite suddenly it became clear to me that I would never see him again! Ibrahim was something very special--of that I was sure. He was decent and honest and I would miss him so much!

When Trudi came off duty the next morning, she had to look only briefly at my face and then she knew. I sobbed again or maybe I was still sobbing. She advised me that I definitely had to meet with him once again. But I was very uncertain whether or not I should. In the last weeks I had refused him so many times that now my own sense of pride stood in the way. But Trudi persuaded me. Actually I have her to thank that in the end I decided in favor of love.

First we wanted to go to the train station to check the departure time of my train. Then we wanted to go to his hotel once more. If Ibrahim was already gone, then it was not meant to be. But what if he was still there? What then?

When we arrived, I was very agitated and feeling a little ragged from the night before. With my heart pounding I went to him in his room. He had not left yet. I had to open the door wide and go into the room before I could see him. Ibrahim lay completely dressed on the bed. All the same he, too, looked rather bleary-eyed. Maybe he had even cried, too. The only thing he said to me then was, „Are you coming?" „Yes", I answered simply. At once everything was clear. Everything was decided.

All my former, so carefully wrought plans changed practically overnight. First of all I cancelled my trip. And then we had to get our papers together to get married. As a foreigner I had to present certificates at different places; it was a lot of running around. Finally after several nerve-wracking weeks, we got married at the London City Hall. Afterwards we ate in a nice restaurant in London, and my friends Lili und Trudi were of course there, too. It was a very happy day for us.

Next we got busy organizing our trip from England to Egypt. Around Christmas it was finally time, and we boarded a ship in Dover that would take us to Port Said in Egypt. The passage took five days, but to me it seemed an eternity. To dispel the boredom we would sometimes play games. I can still remember very clearly one of those games: One had to gather all sorts of objects, among other things a sprig of mistletoe. Then it happened. An Englishman caught me under the mistletoe. True to English custom he kissed me. Ibrahim did not find that at all funny. On the contrary, he got very upset about it and was very jealous. It was our first serious difference of opinion. From then on I was always very careful that something like should not happen again because in such matters Egyptians have no sense of humor.

After five days at sea, I was glad to be on dry land at Port Said. On top of that there was all the excitement. Egypt was supposed to become my new home, but I had only a vague idea of what actually awaited me there. The port was a confusing bustle of activity back and forth. Strange that anyone could find his way in such chaos. One of Ibrahim's nephews picked us up, and we lived with him in a small apartment for the first few days. During those days I saw for the first time women clothed entirely in black. First I thought they were nuns. Ibrahim explained that they most likely came from the country. There black was the traditional dress of women. On the other hand, almost none of the women wore headscarves in the city at that time. That came much later.

Finally we drove to Alexandria where Ibrahim had an apartment. His parents had already died and both his sisters were married. The older sister had been married for a longer time and had many children. It was one of her sons who had picked us up in Port Said. The other sister was only recently married. Ibrahim had to make sure his sisters were married first before he could think of committing himself to a relationship. That is still customary in Egypt today.

At first we lived in Ibrahim's apartment in Alexandria. But Ibrahim really wanted to build a house and looked around for a buildable plot. Finally he bought a piece of land near Sidi Bishr (part of Alexandria). Today there are many houses in that area, but then it was only desert. Between the sea and our house was only sand. Besides ourselves a few other families lived there, almost all foreigners. And farther out in the desert lived the Bedouins. We built a modest house with three rooms, kitchen and bath. After only six months we were able to move in and set up house. I remember our garden with special fondness. We had soil brought in and planted trees, shrubs, and flowers. Soon daisies and geraniums blossomed and many other flowers, too. Everything grew here; of course only if you watered regularly! We planted four eucalyptus trees, and were amazed how quickly they shot up. Soon we could sit in the shade under the trees and it smelled wonderfully of eucalyptus and of flowers. Our garden was really beautiful and is one of my nicest memories.

Sometimes we went to the Bedouins and were invited into their tents. They shared their food with us and we were allowed to participate in their celebrations. There were drums, singing, and rhythmic dancing, sometimes with a big stick. It was simply wonderful. They were not doing it for the tourists. It was their own very traditional way of celebrating. I was able to witness their customs up close, an unforgettable experience.

At the beginning of my time in Egypt, it was not only the language that was difficult. There was much I did not know, and the details of Egyptian customs revealed themselves only slowly to me. Ibrahim went shopping with me, and I tried to note everything the best I could. I learned the Arabic signs in the market. Finally the big day came and I set off alone to the greengrocer. I pointed to the eggplants, tomatoes and onions, bargained with the price and in the end everything I needed actually turned up in my basket. I was proud and as happy as a small child that I had met this challenge so well. As a reward the merchant handed me a red rose.

Then I went home and began to prepare the food. When Ibrahim got home, I was still very happy about my new capabilities and joyfully showed him all that I had bought and cooked. Of course Ibrahim immediately discovered the red rose and asked where I got it from. „From the greengrocer", I answered spontaneously and without thinking about it. Big mistake--because Ibrahim got very upset again and forbade me to go there ever again. He calmed down only when I had promised him not to do so. He was very jealous. I really understood to what degree only much later. Whenever he went out, the doors and garden gates had to be securely locked. When I was alone, I was not allowed to let anyone in. In Egypt one regards a woman alone as always offering temptation. That is the general impression. At the very least she can lose her good reputation. For example, when a woman stands around alone anywhere, people think she is looking for „customers". For that reason, whenever women move along the street alone, they do so with downcast eyes. They walk as quickly and purposefully as possible, so that no one gets the wrong idea. It is just the way society is here. A man's jealousy always serves in this respect as protection for the woman.

One day we invited Ibrahim's family to our home. Something came up at short notice, and Ibrahim had to go to work. That should be no problem, I thought to myself. After all, by now I got along quite well on my own. I carefully thought over what I wanted to serve and left to buy the necessary ingredients. Then I got busy with the preparations, cleaned the house, cooked and baked. When they knocked on the door, everything was prepared and a good meal was on the table. One after another all the relatives wandered in. Everyone had come. They greeted each other exuberantly and asked back and forth: „How are you?" again and again as is customary here. Usually the answer is „Good, with God's help". I had set the table in the garden. It was a nice day: not too hot and not too windy. Everybody sat down and I proudly carried out the bowls of delicacies. I offered something to each one of them, and each took a tiny portion. I thought that they were really eating much too little. Therefore, I offered everything again. And then again a third time. When no one took any more, I carried all the platters and bowls into the kitchen again and made tea. For dessert there were homemade pastries. They did not eat many of them either. People began to say good-bye, and everyone went home.

When Ibrahim came home that evening, he asked me, of course, how it went for me. Actually quite well I told him; only that no one had eaten very much. „Did you put the food on their plates?" Ibrahim asked right away. I had not done that. After all in Germany that is not customary. That it was expected here I knew, but in the excitement and under the stress of making a good impression, I had completely forgotten. Now the whole family thought for sure that I was stingy. Luckily later on we were easily able to explain the misunderstanding. From then on everyone knew when you were invited to Betty's, you had to serve yourself. They did not hold it against me but considered it more an odd foreign custom. I, on the other hand, have never been able to get used to always getting a plate piled high at other people's houses. First of all I had trouble with cutting my food and with eating it when my plate was too full. And secondly I was accustomed from Germany to having to clear my plate; with Egyptian portions that was simply not possible. Customs are different everywhere. When one has been living here longer, one gets used to it.

In 1954 our son Tarek was born. When the contractions started, we were at a picnic in Shatby on the beach. Ibrahim's sister and her family were also there. After the picnic Ibrahim wanted to drive me back to Sidi Bishr. But nothing came of that; instead he took me directly to the hospital in Shatby. I went to the maternity ward; of course men were not allowed in. Between contractions I walked back and forth -- to the horror of the nurses who insisted that I had to lie down. But I knew better. During my training in the hospital I had witnessed several deliveries. The birth and delivery proceeded just fine and then the nurse brought me my son who was completely wrapped up in cloths. First of all I took the package completely apart; I wanted to know for sure whether or not everything was really OK. Only after I had unpeeled the tiny Tarek from all the layers was I content: our son was perfect.

The next year I brought our second son into the world. We named him Khalid. Now I really had my hands full since we did not have any household help. I did all the housework myself. Whoever has had two children in diapers at the same time can imagine how much work that means. Moreover there were no Pampers. The diapers were washed and sterilized with boiling water on the stove. Let alone all the other wash. At least Ibrahim usually relieved me of most of the shopping. On his way home from work, he would stop at the grocer's or butcher's and buy me whatever I needed. It was a stressful time but indeed a very beautiful one. Ibrahim was a good husband and father.

In the beginning I spoke mostly English with Ibrahim because he did not know German, and I did not yet know Arabic. I had been diligently learning Arabic since our arrival in Port Said and with time I was able to express myself better and better in this strange language. Later on we spoke mostly Arabic with each other. At first I spoke English with my children. I thought they ought to be able to really communicate with my husband. Not until they were older did I speak German with them, and today all my children speak very good German in addition to Arabic and English.

As with many other families, my husband went to work in the morning and often did not come home until late. He ran a small shop that bought and sold electrical appliances. Mostly he bought appliances that were broken, repaired them and sold them again, for example, kerosene stoves or refrigerators. At that time there was hardly anything available to buy; therefore, practically everything was repaired and used again as long as it could be. Ibrahim always had a lot of work and the shop earned enough for us to live well. Soon we could even afford to buy a car.

The variety of choices for groceries was quite good. I was not very spoiled from Germany or England. Of course I was not familiar with much of the produce, like Betingan (eggplant) or Bamia (okra), and spices like Kamun (cumin) were unknown to me, but I managed quite well. Ibrahim's younger sister helped me find my way and little by little taught me how to cook the Egyptian way. Egyptian cuisine is really delicious. I really love the many tasty spices. Ibrahim liked German cuisine very much, too. Although during those years provisions were in general not very plentiful, my husband was able to get whatever we needed. There were always plenty of fruits and vegetables anyway. The wide beach of Sidi Bishr was our favorite place to go during that time. The children were still small, but even then they already loved the sand and the sea. We walked over the sand, crossed the tram tracks and continued through the sand to the sea. When the children could not yet walk, we packed them in a carry-all and carried them there because, of course, we did not have a stroller. They did not yet have anything like that in Egypt. We went swimming and the children played in the sand. Those were wonderful excursions for us and we were very happy. Today Sidi Bishr is very developed with apartment houses and there is very little open shoreline. The few strips of sand are mostly private beaches.

We spent a lot of time in our beautiful garden. We did not need a country club such as they have today. We had it just as nice at home where the children could play and run around. When we were sitting outside at the weekend, friends and relatives often came by. Egyptians like to visit frequently. All the visitors expected to be served, of course, so I always had a lot to do. Sometimes we went in to the city to a nice park or the zoo. It was a big treat for the children when afterwards we went to „Ahmed Taieb" restaurant and ate Ful and Tameya (called also Falafel) there (please see Appendix A). Soon the waiters there knew us and we were treated especially well. The children were always welcome. And I was especially happy of course because I did not have to cook!

We socialized a lot with our close neighbors. There were the Bedouins, but in addition, Greeks and a family from Malta in our neighborhood. And of course Egyptians. One of them had a shop in Alexandria. Every morning he drove his donkey cart to his shop. This donkey fascinated our son, Khalid, and just like any small child, he wished for an animal like it, too. Every day he asked Ibrahim, if he could have a donkey like that. My husband never said No but instead always answered „Insha Allah" which means „God willing". Eventually Khalid could no longer be put off with this answer. He became angry and howled: „I don't want an Insha Allah donkey; I want a real donkey". Only then did he comprehend that he would not be getting a donkey.

The time flew by and soon it was time for us to think about the education of our children. First both boys went to a French nursery school. That seemed to us to be the best solution. Later we sent them to an Egyptian school. At that time people told us that children who went to foreign schools could not get far later in Egypt. Whether or not that is true, I do not know, but for our children, anyway, things went well at this school.

In 1962 our son, Nabil was born and in 1972 we had a daughter, Hanja. Well, now our little house was really too small and so we built a second house on the same piece of land. When we had guests, they could spend the night there, and when the children got bigger, they had their bedrooms there.

Ibrahim was a very good father. He liked to spend time with his children, played with them, and was devoted to them. He was a dear husband, too. I did not make a mistake that day in England. My decision to go with him has been entirely the right one. To this day I am thankful to Trudi that she persuaded me and that I gave in at last. Trudi, by the way, later returned to Germany and got married there. We kept in touch a long time, and she visited me once in Egypt.

In 1971 the street where our store was located was closed because pipes were being laid. In Egypt something like that can take a long time—months and even years. Well now there was no thru traffic any more and the customers did not come. Business got worse and worse and finally Ibrahim had to give up the shop. All of a sudden we had no income. As there was no work for Ibrahim in Alexandria, I decided to go to Germany in 1972 to work there. Hanja was still a baby at the time so I took her with me. The boys stayed with Ibrahim in Egypt. I found a position at a nursery school and earned money for the whole family. After six months my husband came with the two younger sons. The eldest could not come because he had to fulfill his military service.

We were very frugal with money, and after one year we were able to return together to Egypt. The time in

Germany naturally changed Ibrahim, too. He had to deal with the fact that I, as a woman, went to work and earned our money. Because it was not so unusual in Germany, he finally got used to the idea.

When we were back in Egypt, I started to cook for some wealthy families. In particular I cooked and baked for parties and receptions. The high quality of my cooking got around quickly. I also baked cakes and jelly doughnuts (so called „Berliner") which I then sold at the German school.

My eldest, Tarek, after graduating from high school in the college track, went to a trade school; the second son, Khalid, attended business college. When it came down to actually finding a job, they both wanted to work in Germany. At first Ibrahim agreed, but later he suffered a great deal from the separation from the two boys. Of course both of them come sometimes to visit in Egypt, but their lives are in Germany. Tarek is married and has two sons. He works for a big company in Germany. Khalid is not married and runs a restaurant in Hamburg. By the way, the very first stop for my sons was at Aunt Else's in Jesteburg. They lived with her at first, and she helped them find work. She was really like a much loved relative to all of us.

Ibrahim died of a heart attack in 1982. It was a terrible blow for me. We always got along so well and to this day I miss him very much. When he died, both Tarek und Khalid immediately offered to return to Egypt to be with me. They thought I would need them here, that the family should be together after such a blow. But I did not want that. They have a good life in Germany, and every few years they take a vacation here in Egypt.

Shortly after my arrival in Egypt in 1954 I got in touch with other Germans. When a German group formed in 1991, I was there right from the beginning. I met many nice women there, including some who were also married to Egyptians like me. That gave us a lot in common. Now we meet regularly for a day out, or privately for coffee, and once a month at the Goethe Institute. This network gives me support; I never feel alone and I keep my connection to Germany.

My youngest son, Nabil, lives in Alexandria. He is married and has two children. My daughter, Hanja, lives in Alexandria as well. She, too, is married and has two children: her older son is ten years old; her younger son is one and a half. I see Hanja a lot and can take care of the little one sometimes. I especially enjoy those hours, and so life goes on.

In 2006 I was in Europe for three months in the summer. I went to Germany, Austria and England. The children were actually not in favor of my taking such a big trip alone. But it was very important to me to see certain people once again. I visited my friend, Lili, in England, and other friends in Germany. I do not have any relatives any more, at least not any with whom I keep in touch. Perhaps that was my last big trip. It was very nice to see so many things again.

But nevertheless one thing is clear: home for me is here in Alexandria, where I have spent so many happy years. When I first left Germany, I had neither homeland nor family. Today Egypt is my homeland.

Chapter Two
Elisabeth H. The Love of My Life

Elisabeth's story is different from all the others. I deliberated for a long time over whether to include it here. After Elisabeth agreed, I wanted to tell her story because we both think it contains many truths. Some of it relates specifically to Egypt, but much of it could have happened in any other country. Elisabeth faced an overwhelmingly difficult situation, yet after all the tragedy it still ended happily for her. It is amazing to me how well Elisabeth took control of her life in Egypt after the occurrences described here. Elisabeth told me her story openly and honestly, but one could tell it was not easy for her to talk about it.

I met my husband to be, Sherif, in Mainz in 1962. I was 24 years old, worked for a lawyer, and had moved from home into a furnished room in Mainz. Sherif lived in Mainz at his cousin's. In Egypt he had studied philosophy and originally had wanted to become a teacher. It is probably not easy for philosophers anywhere to find a job and so Sherif's search for a job in Egypt remained unsuccessful. But he had to earn money somehow and find something he could live on. He had a cousin who lived in Germany and who found him a position at Daimler. It was not so difficult then, so Sherif came to Germany. This cousin had been engaged for some time to my girlfriend, Katrin. Obviously, we met the new cousin from Egypt soon after his arrival. We went out to eat, and at the very first meeting it clicked between Sherif and me. We fell head over heels in love. From the very first moment there was no doubt that we belonged together. At first, of course, we could only meet up and go out together. Sherif visited me only once in my furnished room, and when my landlady got wind of it, I was given notice to leave immediately. There was nothing left for us to do but to get married as quickly as possible.

Before we did that, of course, Sherif had to meet my parents, but fortunately they liked him right away. To be sure, they were concerned that I wanted to marry a man from such an unfamiliar country, but they soon realized he was a decent guy.

After only three months we got married in a civil ceremony at the marriage bureau. There was a small celebration in a pizzeria. We had invited only a few friends and I told my parents only after it was all over. Perhaps I was not so sure after all how they would react. But later to make up for it we held a really big celebration at my parents' house in the village. I come from a big family in Northern Hessen and had seven older siblings -- six brothers and one sister. At our celebration there it was accordingly as festive and tumultuous as our wedding celebration in Mainz had been quiet.

My father was a post office clerk and a house painter and decorator. He was very musical and played several instruments: violin, clarinet, trumpet, and more. I was glad that my whole family accepted Sherif right away. My nephews and nieces were quite taken with their new uncle from Egypt. Unfortunately, almost all of my siblings have already died. Only my sister in North Hessen is still living. She is eight years older than I am.

After the wedding, Sherif and I moved into an apartment in Mombach. Sherif worked now at MAN in the paint shop, and because he applied himself and worked hard, he was soon promoted to supervisor. He made a very good living and we lacked for nothing. I continued to work as before. After just one year our daughter Nadine was born (1963), and from then on I stayed at home with the baby. We led the very typical life of a young family, enjoying the early years with just the three of us and occasionally visiting my parents. Sherif fitted in very well with my big family, got along with everyone, and everyone liked him. My mother was considerate of his dietary restrictions in her cooking: from that moment on pork was no longer served when we visited. For us that was not taken for granted because people in the country did their own slaughtering and pork was a mainstay of the diet However, even as a child, I did not like pork, and so for me it was no big loss.

We were doing very well. Sherif liked to stay home and was a good father. We had enough money and were quite content with our life. But then Sherif became homesick for Egypt. Most Egyptians are very attached to their homeland, and at some point long to go back. They do not like to emigrate, and when they do go to another country, in the course of time, they usually return. Sherif went to great trouble to make the thought of living in Egypt appealing to me and painted a very pretty picture of everything. His parents would be there; his whole family. They all lived in the same village, and guaranteed, he would make a living there, too. He wanted most of all to work independently, and he was sure that he could succeed at that there, too. In no way did he prepare me for what I would experience; I had no idea of the real conditions in Egypt. Young and naive as I was, I believed his every word. Nonetheless, it took a few years before he convinced me.

In 1966 the time had finally come. I gave away almost all my things: linens, furniture, warm clothes. I did not know of course that soon I would desperately need all those things. My friend, Katrin, had been living in Egypt for a while in the same village. When she learned that I wanted to come, she was thrilled and really worked on convincing me. She did not warn me of the conditions in Egypt either. Maybe she was less sensitive than I was, or just looking forward to having a friend from Germany by her side. Katrin still lives in Mansura today, and we still keep in touch sporadically. But to this day I do not understand why she did not warn me.

Sherif bought a Mercedes diesel, and I took my car with me, too, an Opel. Sherif did not even have a driver's license. We wanted to sell the Mercedes in Egypt, even though there were no diesel passenger cars there; in fact, they were still not allowed. But once we arrived, we succeeded in selling the car to -- of all people -- someone in the government.

We arrived in Alexandria at the port and were picked up by the whole family. My first impression of Egypt amounted to a minor culture shock. It was very hot, crowded and chaotic, and on top of all that, I could not understand the language. With my blond hair I was stared at like a wonder of the world. The people, though, were very nice and open with me. We went to Sherbien, a small village in the Nile Delta. But it had little in common with a village in Germany. When we arrived there, hungry and exhausted from our long journey, I was at first at a loss for words. The people lived in the simplest conditions. There was no electricity and we had running water only at night. Refrigerator, washing machine, all those things that at home in Germany belong in general to the standard of living—there was nothing of the sort. I was dumbfounded. I found it very difficult to acclimatize; everything was so primitive and unfamiliar. The heat got to me, along with the mosquitoes that constantly descended on me in a swarm. The dog of the house, a mixed breed, was the only thing I liked and I made friends with him right away. So at least I did have something to take my mind off things.

Our car had to be registered and so we drove to Cairo. For those few days we stayed with one of my husband's cousins. But then Nadine got sick; she had the measles. It was a very stressful time, and we could not return to the village in Sherbien until six weeks later.

My mother-in-law was very kind to me. She noticed right away that I was not doing well and that the daily routine in Sherbien really got to me. Every day she baked fresh bread for me and tried to cheer me up somehow. When she talked to me, she always spoke in a very loud voice. Most likely she thought that I would understand her better that way. I asked Sherif to tell her to speak in a normal voice, please, and after that things went better. My husband's parents owned their own land and farmed. They did not farm the land themselves but had tenant farmers. My father-in-law was quite tall (6′ 2″) (1,84 m) and strong. He weighed two hundred twenty pounds;

my mother-in-law on the other hand was short and slender.

Throughout his whole life Sherif was grateful to his father for making it possible for him to go to school and afterwards to study at the university. He was the first one in his family to go to college. The others had fewer possibilities than he had; most of them stayed in Sherbien and lived the life of simple farmers.

So we lived in the village and I learned to manage with very little luxury. After a few unsuccessful attempts and with a lot of persistence, I learned to cook on a simple small gas stove with one burner. There were only basic ingredients available: flour, lard and eggs, no helpful processed foods or mixes. At least I had not given away my cookbook and my Dr. Oetker (note: the equivalent of Betty Crocker) book on baking. For baking cakes I used a pot made of aluminum that was closed on top and sat on the stove - no oven. My simple cakes were met with enthusiasm by the family because Egyptians love sweets and they had never tasted anything like them before. Over time I got used to the way of life although I missed many things from Germany. Sherif on the other hand was very happy to be in his homeland again. I thought if he is happy, I will find a way to make the best of it, too. I believed it would work out.

Sherif had, of course, not given up his dream of independence. Now it was time to get started. Selling the Mercedes had brought us a nice little sum of seed money. Sherif bought land and imported cows from Holland. He thought it would be easy to make a good profit from the milk. What he did not think of was that he needed a working infrastructure to process and sell the milk. In the end Sherif sold the calves, too, and finally the whole herd was broken up. Thus our first foray into independence ended rather miserably.

In Sherbien itself one could not go shopping at all; there were no stores of any kind. To stock up on supplies we always had to drive to Mansura, the next large town. For a long time, well into the 70's, many groceries like sugar and oil or clarified butter were still rationed, although farm products like fruit, vegetables, potatoes, eggs and flour were always available in the village. We ate meat only on Thursdays and Fridays because Thursday was slaughtering day. As we did not have a refrigerator, we were very limited in what we could store.

For a change of pace, we rented an apartment in Gamasa on the Mediterranean; it is located between Alexandria and Port Said. Friends of ours already lived there. It was only about ten miles (16 km) from Sherbien. The apartment had only two rooms, but it had electricity and running water. In Gamasa I had everything that I needed: refrigerator, electric stove, a shower and everything that I had so taken for granted in Germany. Finally I could cook and bake in a halfway „normal" way. We used that apartment as a summer place for many years, and I have many happy memories of Gamasa. I quickly made friends with nice people from Belgium and England. We swam in the sea almost every day, an incredible indulgence for all of us. Especially in the summer it was much more livable there than in Sherbien. Sometimes my parents-in-law and the rest of the family visited us in Gamasa. My mother-in-law went in the water with all her clothes on and dived for mussels. Afterwards she found a quiet spot, far from me, and consumed her catch raw. She knew by then that I did not like fish and was disgusted by it. I could swim in Gamasa in my bathing suit without inhibitions just like all the others. Today Egyptian women go swimming only fully clothed. These concerns with outer appearance have changed greatly since then and not necessarily for the better. For three years we lived the majority of the time in the village and in the summer by the sea.

In 1968 our daughter Nevien was born in Mansura. When the contractions started, we were visiting at one of my sisters-in-law; however, the home birth went well, and I was relieved to have again brought into the world a healthy girl. Like all mothers in Egypt, I nursed my children a long time. There was no other choice because there was no baby food anywhere in the country.

The business with the cows had not been a success, and gradually Sherif grew restless again. He played with the idea of going back to Germany. I was up for it immediately. I found life in Egypt very trying and really wanted to live in my own country. Sherif had already bought his father a piece of land out of gratitude, because he had done so much for him and had financed his schooling and college education. My mother-in-law asked us to take one of Sherif's brothers with us to Germany. At first I was against it, because it seemed too much of a responsibility to me. Finally I agreed, and Sherif and his brother, Jussef, got their visas for Germany through me.

So in 1969 we were in Germany again. At first we lived with my parents. Sherif got in touch with his old company, MAN, in Mombach and was able to start there right away. There was a shortage of good workers, and they were very happy that he had returned. Right after our arrival in Germany many people offered their help, even the pastor. Everyone was very helpful and obliging, but actually it was not at all necessary, because everything was quite easy. Soon after Sherif started work we rented an apartment in Mombach. My brother-in-law, Jussef, obtained his work permit in two months and was able to start working right away at Sherif's firm. So the men went to work; I stayed at home with the children. Nadine was already in school. Everything was very normal except for the fact that my brother-in-law was part of the household, too. Our apartment was expensive, but nevertheless we managed. I took for granted that Jussef should contribute to the expenses, too; after all he lived with us under the same roof and ate what I cooked for all of us. But when I asked him about it, my husband got very upset. According to Egyptian custom, such a request is a „disgrace" because one does not accept money from relatives -- never mind ask for it. I absolutely did not understand that. After all Jussef earned very good money and had hardly any expenses. But it did not help to argue against it; it stayed that way and we had to support him as long as he lived with us. After a year he started to look for his own apartment in Mainz.

Sherif still did not have a driver's license, although

we had a car. Now and then we visited my parents in their village in North Hessen, about 155 miles (250 km) away. My husband never went out in Germany; he liked best to spend his time with the family. His brother, Jussef, however, was very much in touch with other Egyptians and was out and about a lot.

Then Sherif became seriously ill. During his examination, the doctor determined that a kidney stone was somehow stuck and could not pass. Sherif had to be operated on immediately and afterwards he had adhesions and needed a second operation. Thank God everything went well. He recovered from the ordeal and regained his good health.

Sherif was a Muslim, but mostly out of tradition. He was very tolerant of my ways; I was always allowed to wear what I wanted even in Egypt. I never wore a headscarf and I do not do so today either.

After only three years in Germany, in 1972, homesickness for Egypt plagued Sherif again. We had saved some money, so we did not return empty handed. We packed up our belongings and set out. This time I was better prepared and knew what awaited me. Sherif wanted to try again to establish his own business and to this end bought two trucks in Germany. I really wanted to move to Alexandria by the sea. No way did I want to live again in Sherbien, and Mansura, the nearest city to the village, was simply too dirty. For me the only possible place to live was Alexandria. At first we stayed with friends in Alexandria and started looking for an apartment. We liked one very much and quickly made an agreement with the landlord. After only one night we fled our newly found home. The whole apartment was full of bugs, and by morning all four of us were bitten everywhere. Luckily, we did not have a lease yet. In Egypt they do things differently from Germany and so there were no problems when we did not take the apartment. It actually took quite a while until we found something suitable, where we could feel good about it. Until that time we lived once again in the village in Sherbien.

Finally we found a furnished apartment in Sidi Bishr,

a district in Alexandria. Alexandria had a German school, and Nadine was accepted immediately. Nevertheless, she had to learn Arabic first, because the German school there ends not only with the German college preparatory diploma (Abitur) but also with the Egyptian high school diploma. So Nadine had private lessons in Arabic and caught up quickly. Nevien went to preschool. Every day I drove the children to their school, mornings there and afternoons back again. I did that for all of my children all those years. I drove from our apartment along the „Corniche", the street by the sea, to the school. The traffic was not nearly as heavy as it is today; there were fewer cars and one moved right along.

In December we traveled once again to Germany to close my brother-in-law Jussef's apartment. Sherif had also ordered two trucks that we had to pick up and send by ship. Nadine had no desire to come with us and stayed in Alexandria with a girlfriend. The three of us, Sherif, Nevien and I set off. We reached the port of Alexandria again on January 16th. On that day there was an awful storm on the Egyptian coast and our ship ran aground on sand. The bow canted; it was really very frightening. The ship was evacuated and soldiers packed us into lifeboats using rope ladders. It was terribly cold and we had to leave all of our things on board. We could take only one small bag with us. Later we did get everything back, but of course it was all completely soaked.

Well, now Sherif had his trucks and together with his brother Jussef he established a trucking business. Later he bought Jussef out and continued working on his own. He employed as many as ten workers; truck drivers and office staff to develop and expand the company. The company's site was on a former chicken farm, which Sherif bought and cleared of the buildings. Actually the land still belonged to the city, but he could build his offices, a repair shop, and garages on it. This time things worked better for his dream of independence and the business flourished. Now both of us flew regularly to Germany to buy trucks, which were then transported to Egypt over the Mediterranean.

In 1974 I became pregnant again and our third daughter came into the world in the summer of 1975. We moved again and then once more and rented for some time in Loran. Later my husband bought the apartment house under the names of our daughters. We had the building completely renovated and this time the right way. We had a carpenter come especially from Germany. He lived in the apartment house along with his whole family and supervised the renovations. His children went to the German school with our children, so we could relieve each other a little bit with the driving. Sherif often went to Germany alone now. Our supplier was located in Ulm, and because we did not always want to stay at a hotel, we bought an apartment there. In the following years we often used that apartment as a vacation place in the summer.

My brother Michael moved from Germany to Alexandria and worked with my husband in the business. That meant a reliable representative was always around when Sherif was not there. Naturally Michael lived with us as well. I took care of the household and the children and had more than enough to do. That is why I never worked in the business. In 1979 our son Ahmed was born.

There were difficulties with the German carpenter until we finally had to fire him in 1981. He went back to Germany without settling his debts to us. Anyway we had our nice apartment on the seventh floor.

In 1982, when Anwar El Sadat died, business took a turn for the worse and gradually everything went downhill. All over the country there was a sense of great uncertainty. Sherif still had a lot of work, but much of it was clearly beyond his capability. Suddenly there were constant difficulties with payment. Once he sold three trucks to a customer but the man paid only partially in cash and for the rest he issued promissory notes. When my husband went to collect on the mature notes, they bounced and we did not get a penny. There was no legal recourse for us to get our money.

The situation and the worries it brought with it really got to Sherif, even if one did not notice at first glance. He became depressed, but I realized it only much later. Depression is an illness to be taken seriously, and the doctor to whom I took Sherif prescribed drugs. Although Sherif did take the pills, they did not help at all. He could not sleep at night anymore; it got worse and worse. I also went with him to a doctor in Germany whom we had known for years. But my husband was not honest with him; instead he put on an act. His condition embarrassed him, so he did not tell the doctor what was really wrong. I dared not interfere. If I had spoken to the doctor myself, Sherif would surely have become very angry.

For the first time in my life, I was afraid. I did not know exactly what I feared, but one thing was certain: I could not go on like this. Once in Sherif's briefcase I found contracts from Germany for thirty motor coaches. But we did not have that kind of money—I knew that for sure. I tried to talk to him, but it was all in vain. He just explained that the first bus would soon be delivered; after all he had enough room. But in the meantime we did not have any employees any more, and how did he think he would rebuild the business without people and without capital? It was completely impossible and flew in the face of reason. Apparently Michael had been let in on this business. I was desperate. I agonized over it and fought with myself, and in the end I succeeded in canceling the order for the busses. I provided a doctor's certificate that implied that my husband was ill. One bus was delivered anyway, but luckily we were able to sell it quickly.

One night Sherif had trouble sleeping again; he got up and tiptoed quietly out of the bedroom. I heard him going up the stairs to the roof. I was terrified, got up immediately and followed him. There he stood on the roof staring into the void. „If you had not come just now, I would have jumped", he said. This incident unsettled me even more, but I could think of nothing that I could do for him. With time I repressed the episode and thought no more about it. Somehow everything would turn out all right—that was my deluded hope.

A few weeks later he drove to Sherbien alone. There he tried for the first time to kill himself. He had acquired a caustic liquid which he drank. But one of his relatives found him in time, and he was brought to the hospital, where they immediately pumped his stomach. When the relatives called me, I rushed to the hospital. And I was not the only one. Everyone was there and wanted to help him. The problem with depression, though, is that a depressed person could not care less about the help others offer.

His mother had a serious talk with him: „You should be happy; you have a beautiful wife who loves you and you both have four beautiful, healthy children. Money is far from everything. Be content with your life". But he was not content. He felt like a failure and that despite all of his schooling and education he had come to nothing.

I assured him how much I loved him, and that I would always stand by him. „Together we can meet any challenge. The main thing is that you get healthy again!" But in the end all of our talk did not help a bit.

My brother Michael had been living with us for three years now. Actually he wanted to leave Egypt soon and return to Germany. But now he was afraid for me and decided to stay. „I cannot leave you here alone", he said. „If something happens..." I could not imagine that Sherif would ever do anything to me. After all we loved each other; he knew I always supported him, and my well-being was always his heart's desire. But Michael did not let himself be misled; he was seriously worried about me. „Some people who want to kill themselves take those they love the most with them", he explained. He stayed in Egypt. To this day I am still thankful for his persistence and concern.

Another three weeks passed before the horrible day came. At first it seemed to be a very normal day. It was quiet in the house. As always the children had come home from school, and we all had lunch together. My brother-in-law Jussef was there for a visit and after eating had lain down to sleep. Michael went out again because he wanted to repair something in our nearby office. I was busy with various things in the household. Then I noticed that Sherif was very restless. He could hardly sit still; instead he paced nervously up and down in the living room. Suddenly I saw that he held a big knife in his hand. His eyes seemed strangely out of focus. I was petrified. He stepped towards me, grabbed me, covered my mouth and tried to cut my throat. I defended myself instinctively, but no sound came out of my mouth. The knife cut into my right hand; all of a sudden I saw blood spurt from the wound on my throat. I turned ice cold, froze inwardly and thought only of my children. At that moment I was sure my life was over.

Just then my daughter Nevien came into the room. Her eyes widened and she screamed in panic „Papa, Papa". My brother was just coming in again at the front door. He could not set anything up at the office because of a power outage. He rushed immediately into the living room and screamed enraged: "You murderer. You have killed my sister". Now Sherif finally let go of me and raced to the balcony. He did not hesitate for a second. He jumped, landed on the roof of a car and died instantly. I still stood in the living room as if rooted there.

My brother saved me. He stopped the bleeding, carried me to the car with the help of our chauffeur and drove me to the nearest hospital. However, their emergency room was closed and we had to drive to another hospital. I was very lucky. The doctor on duty knew me; she taught at the German school, too. With great presence of mind, she immediately clamped the blood vessels, finally stopping the bleeding, and gave me blood transfusions. Of course I heard about it all only afterwards. I suffered from shock, had lost a lot of blood and kept fainting. Besides I was terribly worried about my children. Michael arranged for them to stay with neighbors in the same apartment house until I was on my feet again.

The hospital where I was treated was very basic. Considering the circumstances, in Germany they would have surely thrown up their hands in horror. Sometimes stray cats jumped over our beds. But the doctors and nurses there did the right thing at the right time and by doing so saved my life. I had to be operated on immediately and only later was transferred to another hospital.

The knife cuts on my hand were stitched and healed pretty well; only a few fingers have no feeling since then.

Sherif was buried the next day, as it is the custom in Egypt. I was still in the hospital, of course, and could not really grasp what had happened yet. All my friends came to visit me. They supported me very much; otherwise, I could not have got through it all. Actually I had a lot of good luck after that terrible day. Even people from whom I would never have expected it selflessly offered me their help and support.

They did not tell Sherif's mother how her son died. They said to her only that he was dead. She was already failing herself at the time; she had had several strokes and died six months later. But we did tell Sherif's father what really happened; he had to endure the truth.

I do not know how I survived the next few months. My two older daughters helped me live through this ordeal. They supported me, helped with the household, and took care of the younger children. The first few weeks I was numb and I only went through the motions of completing the daily routine. My brother stayed with me for a while. Then my sister came to Egypt and stayed for three months. And many friends and acquaintances helped me as well even if I cannot remember all the details.

I kept thinking angrily of Sherif. He had almost killed me, and what would have become of our children then? Now they no longer had a father. I had nightmares. I kept trying to imagine how I could have prevented this. Only years later did I understand how sick Sherif had been. He could no longer think clearly. What happened was horrible, but it was not my fault.

The most important thing now was my children. They needed me now more than ever. I had to be there for them; without them I would hardly have found the strength to keep on living. The events naturally upset them very much. My son Ahmed was only four, and did not really understand what a catastrophe it was, but all three of my daughters suffered a severe shock. It took years until they processed what had happened and could look to the future again. Nevien, the second eldest, had to witness everything with her own eyes. She was only fifteen years old at the time. She suffered from it for a long time.

After several weeks, when I could think halfway clearly again, I set about sifting through the family finances. Once again a big shock. We had accumulated mountains of debt at different banks. Besides, there were stocks that were not yet paid in full and dozens of checks and promissory notes.

Nadine was the only one of my children who was already legally an adult and therefore she could inherit directly. For the other three I had to have everything recorded without missing anything. I succeeded in transferring all the documents from Sherbien to the court that dealt with custody and guardians in Alexandria. I spent countless hours in the office of a court official; everything was recorded individually.

According to Egyptian law, after Sherif's death, the grandfather automatically became the children's guardian. When the grandfather then died, my brother-in-law tried to get guardianship. I did not think that was right; after all I was the mother of the children and therefore the guardianship belonged naturally to me. There was a rather unpleasant legal battle at the end of which I succeeded in having the guardianship of my children transferred to me. With that done, the entire settlement of our financial affairs was much easier.

All of our business documents had been registered in Mansura. Everything now had to be transferred to Alexandria. My knowledge of Arabic was limited, and the contact with all these government offices was anything but easy for me. I hoped my brother-in-law would help me; after all he had lived with us in Germany and we knew each other very well. He quickly agreed to take care of everything for me and I trusted him. Unfortunately it soon became clear that he was thinking only of himself and his own benefit. The whole family seemed all of a sudden to have sworn a pact against me and begrudged me my children and my financial independence.

For example, Jussef wanted one of our cars for himself, and turned to our chauffeur for help. The chauffeur pointed out to him in a friendly way what was written in the title. In fact I was registered as the owner; therefore, only I could decide who should get the car. Jussef had the chauffeur give him the papers and studied the entry with disbelief. When it became clear to him that he would not get the car, he flushed red with anger and could not make a sound. I have never forgotten his face at that moment. From then on I knew that I could not depend on him at all.

At least my brother Michael helped me, but he could not speak Arabic very well. And our chauffeur stood by me, too. Therefore, I was not all alone in confronting all the extensive formalities.

The first thing we had to do was to close the company and dissolve it. Dozens of trucks that had to be sold were still standing around on company property. Spare parts and machines were stored in the repair shop. Day and night a security firm guarded the company so that nothing would be stolen. All in all it took four long years until everything was finally sold. Our chauffeur helped me very much with all these transactions. Not only did he know the language but also he was very familiar with how business was conducted here in Egypt. He knew all of the customers personally, where they lived or where their businesses were located. And, what was most important, I could depend on him one hundred percent. He came from Sherbien like Sherif and had accompanied him on all his business. I think he was the only one who really knew Sherif well. His loyalty to his old friend lasted even beyond Sherif's death and it fortunately included me. To this day I am in touch with him. Occasionally he calls and asks how I am doing. Little by little I was able to collect on many of the checks and promissory notes. But to this day I have notes that are unfortunately completely worthless.

After another four years I was able to liquidate the company completely. The buildings were sold; the land belonged to the city. And once again I could not please my husband's family. They thought the purchase price was much too low. But they could not find a buyer who would have paid more. For every sale I always had to provide authorization from all the heirs. Pretty soon I knew Islamic inheritance law better than the officials and notaries. The family always interpreted everything to their advantage, and I had the feeling more than once that my own family was shortchanging me. I arranged to have the expenses that I had incurred deducted from the final sum of the inheritance. The land in Sherbien that my husband had bought was leased to a brother. Nevertheless we were often deceived in that they hid things from me and even forged my signature. Therefore the children were denied part of their rightful inheritance, and I could do nothing other than salvage what could be saved.

Finally, eight years after Sherif's death, calm was gradually restored. All the transactions were completed, and I could pay off all the debts, even the back taxes. I received a final statement, and with that everything was done. I was glad that it was over, even if not everything had worked out to my benefit. Now I could finally let go of the past and get a good night's sleep.

The money from Sherif's inheritance was enough to take good care of the children. All of them could go to college, and we could keep the apartment house in Loran as well. I bought an apartment in Agamy (near Alexandria on the beach), where we then spent our summers.

My brother-in-law Jussef died in 1989 in Germany. He was supposed to have heart surgery there. Three days before the scheduled operation he died. My father-in-law had already died in 1987.

In the meantime I have thought a great deal about my husband's death, how it came to be, and all that happened before. Today I believe that Sherif never learned how to deal rationally with his problems. His family cherished him very much. They were so proud of him because he was the first one to go to college. He was always praised; no one believed him capable of making mistakes. Therefore he could never accept his own mistakes. I know that together we could have managed everything that came after his death: the whole liquidation of the company and consolidation of our finances. I would always have stood by him, and we could have had a beautiful and fulfilling life with our children. How gladly I would have supported him in all his business dealings and with his problems. But he did not allow that. Maybe because he did not trust me; maybe, too, because he never wanted to admit he had problems. Instead, it made him ill.

Today I often think back, too, on the nice times we had together. We loved each other very much, and after all these years now I can finally think about him without hatred or anger.

I have grown very fond of Egypt over the years. Two of my children live in Egypt. One of my daughters is married in Alexandria and has two children. My son lives in Sharm el Sheikh. He is divorced and has a son who lives with his mother in Alexandria. So I have three grandchildren nearby. My two other daughters live in Germany and in the United States. Like almost all mothers I would like to see my children as often as possible, and so I travel every year at least once to Germany and once to the United States.

I had little contact with other German women over the years. I always had a lot to do with my family and little time for casual socializing. The two German women friends whom I have here in Egypt were a great help and source of support during my most difficult time. Only much later, by chance--ten years ago-- I happened to get in touch with the German women in Alexandria. That is a loosely knit group of friends who meet regularly to exchange experiences. Since my children are all grown up, I have more time for myself, too. To keep myself a little fit, I go regularly to the Sporting Club (note: a kind of country club) to run. There are many visits and return invitations among women friends. Today I like Alexandria very much and have become used to a lot of things that were difficult for me in the beginning. Sometimes it is not easy to be accepted in Egypt, especially as a woman from another country. But, especially if you can speak the language, most people here will treat you with respect.

My life has not gone in a very straight line and was for a long time very difficult. Today I am glad and proud that I had the strength to cope with great adversity for my children's sake. They are my great joy, the reward for all the struggles and setbacks endured. Next year I will be seventy, and I hope very much that I can experience many more beautiful years with my children and grandchildren.

Chapter Three
Heike B. The Fire in his Eyes

Heike is a petite woman with blue eyes and a long dark pony tail. Despite her 64 years she still has a youthful air. She is a little bit shy; she probably always has been. She comes to me accompanied by her best friend, Renate H., and tells me her story. She often falters and I have to question her again. What makes such a reserved young German woman go off with an Egyptian, leave everything she knows in her homeland and begin an entirely new life? That is a fascinating question for me. Was it the love of her life, simply curiosity or thirst for adventure? I will try to get to the bottom of this question. Here is Heike's story:

When I met my husband in 1960 in Hamburg, I was just 17—and very shy. It is actually astonishing that we even found each other.... I was still living with my parents, my mother and my stepfather. My father had died in the war (WW II), but I still had a brother. My mother had remarried after the war, and from that union I have a half-sister. I was in the middle of my training as a furrier. Many people today no longer know what that occupation is. It is like a tailor for furs and fur accessories.

It was at a club that I first saw Fawzi. The look in his eyes hit me like fire. He asked me to dance and looked deeply into my eyes. Instinctively, I tried to avoid his eyes. It was useless. He kept turning my head back towards him so that I had to look at him. Of course at the time, I did not know that he was Egyptian. He wanted to meet me again, but I did not go, although I thought about him a great deal. But I was so young and so inexperienced; it was all too much for me. Nevertheless, my heart had already caught fire.

Fawzi was 21 at the time and studying medicine in Hamburg. Soon after our first encounter, I met him by chance on the street. This time I could not escape so easily. Our eyes met and from that moment on, we have never let go of each other. Now everything went very fast. We were very much in love and never wanted to separate again. I quickly realized that Fawzi was very jealous– but without any reason. I did not understand it for a long time, and it took years until I could halfway get used to it. I was very sincere in my feelings and very in love. So his jealously caught me completely off guard, and of course, it was entirely groundless. Today Fawzi is still very jealous, but over the years I have learned to deal with it.

As I said, we were sure from the first moment and we wanted to get married soon. At first my mother was against the marriage. Naturally, she was worried whether or not I had really thought everything through, etc. My stepfather, though, agreed right away and supported me. Together we were able to change my mother's mind. So Fawzi and I got married in 1960 in a civil ceremony at the marriage bureau in Hamburg. By 1961 our son Farid had already been born.

In 1962 we went to Egypt for the first time on vacation. We left our son with my parents. My husband's family lived in Mansura, which is on the Nile around 180 km/110 miles from Alexandria. I met Fawzi's family on this trip. But they were not supposed to know that we were married. In fact, my husband was supposed to marry a relative; that arrangement had already been decided years ago. In Egypt it is still customary even today that the parents arrange engagements and Fawzi himself was not sure how his parents would react to our marriage. Therefore, I slept in one of the sisters-in-law's room and was considered just a good friend to my husband. What the family might have thought of this arrangement, I do not know. But at some point we had to come out with the truth anyway. Fawzi told them everything, and I still remember that he had tears in his eyes as he told them. He had great respect for his parents and did not want to disappoint them in any way. We told them about our son and showed them all the photos we had brought along of little Farid. Faced with a fait accompli, Fawzi's parents made the best of the situation: after they had digested the unexpected news, they accepted me very warmheartedly into the family. We enjoyed our last few days of vacation and afterwards went back to Germany.

Fawzi continued to study medicine in Hamburg; I worked in my field as a furrier. My mother took care of our son part-time. We all liked that arrangement. Fawzi and I had an apartment and we were actually quite content.

Unfortunately Fawzi did not make any real progress with his studies. On the one hand that had to do with the language, of course, but in addition the higher education system in Germany is structured entirely differently from Egypt. That's why we decided after a time that he would be better off continuing his studies in Egypt.

In 1966 we packed our suitcases and moved to Egypt. We traveled to Venice in a Mercedes and then by ship to Alexandria. The Mercedes was registered in my name, and we imported it officially into Egypt. But it took a long time until we got through customs. We had to go to Cairo several times to take care of all the paperwork. Then we sold the car in Egypt. The money was supposed to secure our livelihood for the time being. Many foreigners did the same at that time, because it was a simple, risk-free way to earn money. The import duties into Egypt were very high, which drove the prices up. As a foreigner, one was exempt from customs and could therefore sell the cars in Egypt at a good price with a nice little profit.

In the beginning it was rather difficult for me in Egypt. We lived with Fawzi's parents, and everyone tried hard to make it pleasant for me, but it still took a long time until I got used to everything. Fawzi's family was very warmhearted. My husband had ten siblings, but of course they spoke only Arabic. My father-in-law was a cotton trader. He often drove to Alexandria on business. At that time the stock exchange was still in Alexandria, and cotton was traded there. He was really very nice to me. For example he bought butter and jam for me, because at first I just could not get used to a breakfast of Ful (fava beans). You have to have grown up with it—although it is supposed to be very healthy and really does keep you satisfied all day. My father-in-law also sat with me in the living room and practiced Arabic with me. I learned my first words from him: chair, table, bread, water. With a great deal of patience, he taught me one word after the other and kept repeating them until I knew them.

My parents-in-law's apartment was simple like all the apartments then. The maids slept in the kitchen on the floor. That was common then. The hygiene conditions left something to be desired; it was crawling everywhere with cockroaches and fleas. One had to be very careful not to catch anything. Of course the bathroom did not meet the standard I was accustomed to in Germany either. All of that was very difficult for me, but I was young, and sooner or later I got used to everything. However, I was very glad when we finally moved into a rented apartment in Alexandria. We had sold the car and bought ourselves furniture from the money. There was even some left over, and we lived on that money for quite a while.

Fawzi went to the university again in Alexandria; now he was studying dentistry. As for me, I was a housewife and a mother. At that time there were no German newspapers or magazines to be bought anywhere. Of course there was no television either. I felt very lonely and cut off from my homeland. I missed interacting with people every day; I had no one with whom I could talk. I spent most of the time cleaning, maybe because the dirt in Egypt really got on my nerves. First I had to thoroughly clean the apartment. The climate in Alexandria is sometimes damp and often very windy. So every day you fought anew against the sand and dampness. At that time Renate H. was my only friend; our husbands knew each other from Hamburg. In time I became acquainted with other German women through her. My big boy started school and went to an English school. The school bus picked him up in the morning and brought him back around 2 pm.

In 1968 our second son, Sherif, was born. At that time we had a maid living with us. She was a little girl from the country; she was only ten years old and helped me with all the housework. We did the wash by hand in the bathroom; there was no washing machine. The laundry was boiled in a big pot on the stove in the kitchen; the diapers, too; and of course, the white socks for the school uniform. It was all very laborious. The girl had her own little room at our place and got the same food that we ate, too. When she first came to us, I had to wash and delouse her; otherwise, she would have dragged all the bugs into the apartment. She stayed several years. Afterwards I had a housekeeper who came once a week for 25 years. Her name was Fatma and she was very reliable. Today it is much harder to get good help. The people are not as reliable anymore and then maybe from one day to the next you are standing there all alone.

When we came to Egypt in 1966, provisions were still very meager. Many of the groceries were rationed, and for some items one had to stand in line for hours in 'Gameias' (Gameia is a local covered community market). Every family had a food stamp book with stamps which were often not enough. For example, flour, oil, sugar and clarified butter were rationed. Sometimes there was canned fish or corned beef, too. You got meat and poultry only on certain days. I spent a lot of time waiting in line and just had to make do with whatever groceries I got. However you could always get fruit and vegetables. We experienced the war with Israel, in 1967, only peripherally. We had to darken the apartment every night as all the houses had to be dark in order not to be seen from the air. Once we heard that the airport in Alexandria had been closed. We did not hear much more about the altercations.

It was the era of Gamal Abdel Nasser. Nasser had sealed Egypt off politically from the West and sympathized openly with the Soviet Union. Any opposition was violently repressed. Fawzi continued to attend university and had friends there. Many of them came from other countries; he had especially a lot of contact with some foreign students because they got along so well. Of course, some of these young people had political ideas and convictions that contradicted the system under Nasser. Fawzi himself was never politically active; what was important to him was to finish his degree quickly. In spite of that, he, too, somehow became a target for the Egyptian secret police. Without our noticing it, the doorman of our building was spying on us. There was no reason at all to mistrust us; we lived a very typical life. Maybe one of Fawzi's friends did something; we do not know to this day. Some were already politically active then.

In the middle of the night, in 1970, there was suddenly a violent pounding on our door. We almost fell out of bed in fright. Fawzi opened the door; I had to get dressed first. They said I should quickly pack a suitcase for my husband. But I refused. There must have been some kind of mistake! Surely Fawzi would come home the next day at the latest anyway, so I thought. They took him with them, as he was, in pajamas without anything. He spent the first night at the police station. The whole night the men stood on the few chairs available because the whole room was crawling with bugs. The conditions must have been terrible, and no one dared shut an eye that night. Then they blindfolded them and brought them to a train. No one told them what they were accused of or where the train was taking them. Fawzi was brought to Cairo to the citadel and put into solitary confinement. He had to endure it there a whole long month.

I could not have any kind of contact with him and was completely alone. I did not know if or when Fawzi would come back again. No one could find out what had happened to him or when he would be freed. It was a terrible feeling that I would not wish on my worst enemy. Fawzi did not talk much about his time in prison. To keep his sanity, he washed his clothes every day, just to have something to do. He always had the feeling that someone was watching him through some holes in the wall. Time crept by endlessly, like slow motion. Every day he was questioned. When he finally returned a month later, he was not the same person as before, he had changed somehow. He wanted to forget his arrest and imprisonment as quickly as possible, but I noticed immediately that he was no longer as unselfconscious and easy-going as he had been previously. Our doorman disappeared quite suddenly, and we never saw him again.

In 1970 Fawzi took his exams at the University of Alexandria. He was now a dentist and had to work first for the Egyptian State for a very small monthly salary: 30 pounds or, calculated at today's rate, $6. Even at that time, it was not nearly enough to live on. Fortunately the family supported us; otherwise, we could not have survived. The money from the sale of the Mercedes had gradually been used up. We did have enough to live on, but it was not nearly enough to open a practice. We considered over and over again what we could do to become financially independent. Germany—that was our first thought. In April, 1974, I traveled alone to my parents; my husband and the children stayed in Alexandria. I worked again as a furrier and at the same time looked for a job for my husband. Six months later Fawzi followed and got a job at the land surveyor's office. True, he was not working as a dentist, but he earned good money anyway. I went back to the children in Alexandria. For several years we lived "at opposite ends" like that: I, in Egypt with the children, Fawzi in Germany. We could not earn a living any other way. Later on Fawzi found work as a dentist in Germany, too, mostly covering for other dentists. We were able to put aside something from his salary so that Fawzi could someday open his own practice in Egypt. But that was still a long way away. We always spent the summer vacation together in Germany, and we all especially enjoyed those few weeks. Finally we were all together! But then after the vacation it was back to Egypt for the children and me. The children went to school again, and I had to continue managing life in Alexandria without my husband. That was not always easy because it was not only often a bumpy road with the language, but was also otherwise difficult to interact with the Egyptians.

In 1979 we had finally saved enough, and the time had come: Fawzi came back to Egypt for good. We opened a practice in Mansura, which was where his parents lived. The family was very well-known there, and we hoped that would turn out to be an advantage. Originally that was my idea and I was quite proud that it actually turned out that way. The practice got off to a good start, and at last we had a solid financial basis for our life.

I still continued to stay with the children in Alexandria; after all the boys went to school there. Fawzi always came home to us on weekends, and so we had quite a pleasant life.

The apartment in which we still live today had to be renovated several times over the years because of water damage. The main problem in Egyptian multi-family dwellings is the sewer pipes. In our building there was only one common line for wastewater disposal for all the apartments, and when it was clogged, the whole mess immediately landed in our apartment. After that happened several times, we had to have our own line laid, and now at least that cannot happen again. But occasionally it happens that my wash on the line gets all black, because dirty water is poured out from above. Those are a few of the difficulties you have to struggle with here. You can't let yourself get too upset; that doesn't help at all.

I had kept in touch with my parents all these years, and we went regularly to Germany to visit them. My stepfather died quite early on, but my mother lived to be over 90 years old. Since her death in 1991, I have not been to Germany any more. I have grown fearful; so much has changed there. In December of this year (2006) though, I will fly to Germany with one of my sons. My brother lives in Hamburg and my half-sister in Lemberg; I really would like to visit both of them. I will stay with a friend though. Over the years I had only sporadic contact with my siblings. The longer one is away from Germany, the less frequent the visits back and forth become.

What else do I miss from Germany? Actually little; I am not homesick. A few minor things like German bread and herring, maybe. When I arrive in Germany, the first thing I will do is definitely buy a jar of pickled herring. Here I usually cook Egyptian food, although my husband likes German cuisine very much. But I like molokhia and bamia and actually all kinds of vegetables very much. Bamia is prepared with okra pods. Molokhia is a green, leafy vegetable, something like spinach. One eats it as a soup or with rice. Many people maintain that to like it, you have to grow up with it, but I like it anyway. My sons prefer Egyptian cuisine. They both agree that after a German meal they get hungry again much sooner.

My sons speak good German, but they consider themselves Egyptian. I still feel like a German; that will never change.

In 1980 I converted to Islam. Mainly for practical reasons, but I made the decision voluntarily. As a non-Muslim in Egypt, one must accept huge legal limitations: one cannot inherit, has no right to custody of the children and is otherwise at a greater disadvantage. Fawzi has never demanded that I wear a headscarf, and is otherwise very tolerant of my ways. Of course, my sons were brought up as Muslims, but they are tolerant of other religions as well.

Our sons finished school in Alexandria. Afterwards the older one studied business administration at the University of Alexandria. Today he works for a German company in Alexandria. He married and from this marriage has two children: Sandra is six and Nadim eight years old. Unfortunately the relationship fell apart after eleven years. He lives with us again; the children are with their mother in Alexandria. Fortunately, I have a good relationship with my daughter-in-law and see my grandchildren often. Our younger son studied at the Swiss Academy for Tourism in Cairo and now works as a travel tour organizer in Hurghada. He is married, but so far has no children. By the way, both my sons chose their wives themselves; there was no influence exerted from our side. In Egypt arranged marriages are still quite common. The strict morality does not allow young couples to date. And how are they supposed to get to know each other if they are not allowed to date? It is no wonder that they need the parents to make arrangements. Of course, it is strictly forbidden that unmarried couples spend the night together. If something like that becomes known, the police could come and quickly make things very uncomfortable. Hotels, too, carefully check Egyptian couples to be certain that they are actually married to each other.

We have been living in the same rented apartment in Alexandria since 1966 and feel very comfortable here.

Fawzi continues to run his practice successfully in Mansura. He still works there three days a week. He is 68 years old now, and currently we are trying to sell the practice.

Two years ago I started to run regularly at the Sporting Club. When my husband is in Alexandria, he runs with me. Recently my little granddaughter ran with me, and she was very proud that she was dressed just like me: sport pants (no shorts), T-shirt and baseball cap. By the way, people thought I was her mother. I was a little bit proud of that.

Although my Arabic has improved over the years, unfortunately I have not gone any further than "kitchen Arabic". I manage quite well, can go shopping and communicate with simple folk. But I can't really hold longer conversations of any depth. I always speak German with Fawzi, and have very little contact with other Egyptians. That is not only because of the language. They are very different from us; they are interested in other things than we are. There are hardly any topics that I could talk about with them. And then there are a lot of topics one does not even mention, never mind discuss. For example, religion or the family. So conversations remain very superficial, and interesting conversations never even get started. They promise a lot, too, but do not follow through; only very few actually keep appointments to meet up. That has been my experience anyway. Fawzi did have some friends, but there are no Egyptians among my women friends.

Would I move to Egypt again? I think so. One can live very well here in spite of everything. For sure I would not feel comfortable in Germany anymore. The weather alone would be very unpleasant for me. I am used to having the sun shine almost every day here. You get used to a mild climate very quickly anyway. In Alexandria it is still bearable even in midsummer, as there is usually a breeze. After almost 40 years I really feel at home here and cannot imagine another country as my homeland.

Through our move to Alexandria, my life has taken on an entirely different direction. As a young girl, I could not have imagined it. My life has become richer and more colorful. People who have lived in only one country can probably hardly comprehend what it means to live in two worlds with very different points of view and cultures. New impressions leave their mark, and one looks at things differently than before. For that alone, I am thankful that everything turned out the way it did. I never had a doubt about where I wanted to live. My life is with my husband.

Chapter Four
Margarete H. Egypt is My Second Homeland

Margarete was the first who volunteered on her own initiative to tell her story. Although petite, she has plenty of self-confidence. She talks fluently, without hesitation. Here is her story:

My story begins in a small town in Austria, where I met my future husband. In 1962 I was 23 years old and worked as a secretary at a wholesale distributor for paper and printing supplies. I had many hobbies: I went ice-skating regularly, and I sang in a choir. Actually, music was an essential part of my life, and I loved going to concerts and to the opera.

One of my friends had a boyfriend from Egypt. When they went out, they often invited me to join them, and one evening we went together to a party. The party itself was a disaster; the other guests were awful. At one point a man was lying drunk in the bathtub. It was weird instead of fun. I took off to the balcony, and there stood a man all alone just smoking by himself. He must have found the party rather stupid, too, because we had a long conversation. That was my future husband, Mohammed.

Since everybody else was drunk and the party could only get worse, we left. Neither of us had a car, so we walked to the last stop of the tram line. On the way we talked and talked. Even back then I was fascinated by the geography and history of Egypt, and so there was plenty to talk about.

For the next few days we met in a café and continued our stimulating conversation seamlessly. From that day on we met regularly. I had never met anyone else with whom I could have such long conversations. I found this wonderful and enjoyed it to the fullest extent. It went on for weeks.

Here I have to say that my parents had already passed away. I lived with my grandmother in a large apartment and it goes without saying that she was the undisputed head of the family. Soon I wanted to introduce my new boyfriend to her. That went rather oddly: I brought Mohammed home for coffee. After he had left my grandmother said: "For heaven's sake, a heathen; I believe he snatched an apple." The next day she thought she was missing a pound of sugar and later on she even missed some of her underpants. At this point my wise grandmother was already a little senile, and she had some prejudices, too. It quickly became clear to me that it was impossible to bring these two together. But that did not keep me from continuing to meet Mohammed on a regular basis.

Now I have to tell about my husband's family. Even before we got married, we traveled to Egypt several times. It was very important to Mohammed that I should be able to get an impression of his country for myself. I should get to know everything, including his relatives. Only then could I finally make a decision whether or not to marry him. I found this very decent of him, and in the end it made my decision even easier.

At that time his parents were still both living. Mohammed asked me to greet his father with a kiss on the hand: that was the tradition and would be considered respectful behavior. He thought with such a good start everything would be very easy. „For God's sake, Your Majesty," I thought. Kissing his father's hand was going to be a problem for me; I felt uncomfortable about it. Nevertheless, I brought myself to do it--- the kiss itself landed more or less in the air. But anyway - I was accepted very warmheartedly.

My husband's father had served under King Farouk, first as head of the province, then as governor of Qena in Upper Egypt, and much later as governor of Zagazig in the Nile delta. Then he was appointed Director of the Military Academy in Cairo. This career path meant moving many times, and as a child Mohammed often had to change schools. The family was well off financially; they had a large house in Zaitun near Cairo, with servants and housekeepers. My husband had a total of six siblings; the girls attended French schools, the boys went to English schools. The preparatory schools, of course, were separated by gender, which is still the rule today for most schools in Egypt.

After our first joint visit to Egypt, we returned to Austria. Two years later we decided to get married. My grandmother had died in the meantime and therefore could not raise objections any more. But there were some obstacles on the way to our marriage. The registrar in the marriage bureau showed me some documents that implied I would become unhappy eventually and that my husband could quite legally marry three more women in Egypt. He suggested I go to a lawyer and get advice. So I did, but neither one succeeded in talking me out of my marriage plans. In spite of all these obstacles, we had a normal wedding like any other couple. It was a civil ceremony. I was dressed in my black suit (the one I wore to the opera) and Mohammed wore a dark suit. We picked December 28, 1965 as the wedding date. An earlier date was not possible because I had to wait till the Christmas sales season was over – only then did I get time off.

It was not a big celebration, only some of my friends and some of Mohammed's colleagues from the university were there. Afterwards we went out together to eat and then returned to our apartment, where we continued to celebrate for a little while. That was our wedding.

The next day we went with some friends to Vienna and danced at a big New Year's Eve party. We watched an ice show and then went to the opera. On January 7 we came back from our little honeymoon trip.

Shortly thereafter I changed jobs. Now I was working at a new travel agency, which was for me the best job in the world! I had to organize all kinds of different trips, trips by plane and by cruise ship all over the world. That meant I had to do a lot of traveling myself, since you cannot sell what you are not familiar with. From October till February I was traveling more or less constantly: the Caribbean, South Africa, Spain, the Canary Islands, etc. I visited hotels and wrote reports about my experiences. Those were good times for me.

Meanwhile Mohammed had completed his degree and had started working as a mechanical engineer in the Steiermark, about 150 km (90 miles) from our town. My apartment, which had been my grandmother's and my parents' before me, became our joint residence. Mohammed had to commute to work during the week but every Friday he came home; then on Sunday he went back again. My job kept me very busy and I did a lot of traveling. Apart from that we lived like any other young couple. We went out together, met with friends, and drank wine, too. Though, while traveling, I always consumed very little alcohol, for which my colleagues nicknamed me „Mother Superior".

Religion played a rather secondary role in our lives. I myself was brought up as a Christian; my husband is a Muslim (in Egypt 90% of the population is Muslim, about 10% are Copts, that is, Christian). But this difference was not a problem for us. However eventually, as my income rose, I was moved into a higher church tax bracket and was asked to make a substantial additional payment. I went to the church tax office and asked that the tax increase be cancelled. This was sternly declined. I discussed the matter for a while, but then decided to leave the church. I would never set foot in that church tax office again anyway. Shortly thereafter I went to the nearest registry office and officially left the church.

Although so far religion had not been an issue with us, Mohammed was very glad. For me it was not so easy: I was confused and full of doubt. Soon I realized that spiritually it was indeed important to me to belong to a religious denomination. After some discussions with my husband, he asked me whether or not I believed that Mohammed was a prophet. „ Yes, of course", I answered. „There have always been prophets, such as Moses or Akhenaton, who believed in one God. So Mohammed was a prophet as well." „So, you believe that there is only one God and that Mohammed was his prophet? Then you are already a Muslim. There is nothing more, everything else is just rules." Later on we drove to the Egyptian Embassy in Vienna where my conversion was officially documented and thus became official. I had to repeat after Mohammed a statement of faith and then sign a document. Besides that I was supposed to choose an Arabic first name. Actually that was not mandatory, but I liked the ritual, and I happily agreed to it. I chose Azza; that is the name of one of my sisters-in-law, and I always found her especially likeable.

Soon thereafter Mohammed got a job as an engineer in our town and did not have to commute any more. In his spare time, together with other foreigners, he founded an Islamic Center. Soon this center became a favorite meeting place for all Muslims and their families. Mohammed also acquired Austrian citizenship.

Up to then we had not had any children, but now we were ready. In 1973 our daughter Nadia came into the world. Unfortunately I could not go on the last trip for my job: the destination was Kenya. Because I was pregnant, my doctor refused to give me the necessary vaccinations. Regrettably, I had to stay home for medical reasons. I worked at the travel agency up until six weeks before giving birth. Then my rest period began; in America one would call it „maternity leave".

After Nadia was born, my life changed drastically. While I stayed home with the baby, Mohammed continued to work. Since my grandmother had already died and no other relatives lived nearby, I was completely on my own. Given the fact that I had to manage without the generous support of grandmothers or neighbors, everything went quite well. Most of all I missed my work, my colleagues and the extensive traveling. When Nadia was two years old, my boss from the travel agency called and desperately asked me to help out. By the hour, by the day, no matter how. He was in great need of help and was pulling his hair out looking for assistance. I had luck and found a toddler room in a daycare center where I could leave my child. I was thrilled to go back to work, but unfortunately I could not enjoy it for long. Nadia kept coming home from daycare with every illness that was going around there. So it would be three days at daycare, two days sick at home, then daycare again, two days at home, always back and forth. Soon I had to admit to myself that this simply did not work. With a heavy heart I gave up my job.

So I thought, now that I have one child already and am unable to work anyway, I might as well have a second child. The plan worked, and in 1976 our daughter Jasmin was born. Now I was really very busy. Soon everything else was added, the usual pre-school education, piano lessons, ballet, figure skating. We were a very happy family. We would never have dreamed of moving to Egypt. Our life went on like this until 1983.

For some time my husband's company had been having problems. The company oversaw projects in Iraq and in Czechoslovakia. Suddenly there were problems everywhere; bills were paid late or not at all. More and more people were being laid off. In the beginning only the very young employees who did not yet have families were affected. Then experienced employees were let go, too, and suddenly, at age fifty, Mohammed was without a job.

Naturally, we pulled out all the stops; all of our friends and acquaintances tried to help us. I even asked the mayor for assistance. Mohammed could have got a job, but only at the salary of a young engineer fresh out of university. For us that was unacceptable, for economic reasons alone this would not have worked. The situation seemed hopeless and we were at our wits' end, when Mohammed's family in Egypt wrote us: „Come here, there are plenty of jobs, and we can help you find an apartment." One of my husband's brothers had an apartment available; he himself was on business in Saudi Arabia. The labor market in Austria would not recover anytime soon, so Mohammed gave up looking for work in Austria. He decided he would rather return to his old homeland. The preparations took some time, but then somehow we were ready. We sublet part of our nice apartment; that way I kept myself a door open in case I wanted to return. I was anything but certain that we would really be able to manage in Egypt.

At that time our Nadia had just finished the fourth grade, and I had already looked into the German School in Alexandria as a possibility for schooling. I was told to stop by in August. Unfortunately, both children barely spoke any Arabic. Six months before we moved, my husband tried using a card game similar to Memory to make it fun for the children to learn Arabic. Actually only nouns. It was very difficult and the results were not promising.

Then in the summer of 1984 we traveled, with some suitcases and lots of excess luggage, to Egypt.

My husband's parents had died a few years ago, and his siblings had sold the beautiful villa in Zaitun. So we arrived in Alexandria and at first lived with one of Mohammed's sisters. But how could my children feel comfortable there? They were used to playing outside. Here they sat in the guest room or the living room and were terribly bored. On top of that, my husband had great difficulties managing in his homeland again after more than 25 years in Austria. In Egypt time does not stand still either, and much had changed. When one has been away for a long time, looking back one paints a lot of things too positively. In any case everything was entirely different from the way Mohammed had remembered it.

Once I wanted to go swimming, and of course Mohammed was the first one I asked where I had to go. He did not know, so I asked my sister-in-law. She recommended that I go by tram to San Stefano to the beach where I could swim. First I got on the wrong tram, but then some very nice people pointed me in the right direction and I actually did arrive. By then it was clear to me that I was on my own; Mohammed knew as little as I did about where we were.

In the meantime the place we were to stay in the brother's little apartment had been renovated. Mohammed had already warned me that the nice view that looked out onto a garden that I remembered from our previous visits was no longer there. But when we arrived, I was really shocked anyway; I had not imagined it to be so bad. Directly outside the window was a wall about five feet away. One could see a little piece of the sky from only one window. Our apartment was on the second floor and below us was the worst stereotype of crowded apartment house living: chickens, noise, the TV across the way blaring all night. I was used to going to bed with the children at half past nine. Here that was completely hopeless.

My husband did not find a position in Egypt; it was just as difficult here as in Austria. True, he could have taken a job, but he would have earned just about 200 Egyptian pounds; not enough to live on. It was just as bad for many other Egyptians. The salaries were very low, much too little to feed a family. So Mohammed went with his brother to Dhahran in Saudi Arabia. There he had better luck and found a job with a British company. He came back for a few weeks to get his work visa. Then he left again, and we stayed alone in Alexandria. His family thought that was impossible; we could not stay alone without a husband in the house, especially since I was a foreigner. But we had no choice; it simply had to work. After we got settled, we did not find it so difficult at all. I had already always coped very well alone with the daily routine in Austria, and in Egypt it should be no different. The children and I could live just fine with this arrangement.

In the meantime I had registered the children at the German school. Nadia was eleven, Jasmin eight years old. Of course the principal, Sister Carola, threw up her hands because neither child spoke Arabic. At the German school all of the children have to complete the Arabic final and interim examinations. In spite of that my daughters were accepted. The older one went into the fifth grade and my little one into second grade. They quickly caught up on their missing Arabic with the help of a private teacher. I wanted to learn Arabic, too, at that time. It seemed important to me to at least master everyday expressions. In the beginning I participated in my daughters' lessons, but then they had to learn mainly classical Arabic and grammar and on that I quickly gave up. It would have been a lot of work and not really useful to me because in everyday life not a soul speaks classical Arabic. It is used exclusively as a written language in the Koran, in literature, in the newspaper and of course in all the schoolbooks. Classical Arabic is the same in all Arab countries and all the educated people, for example, in Morocco, Saudi Arabia or Syria, speak it and can communicate with each other that way. Egyptian Arabic is a dialect that is also understood in most other Arab countries. I continued to take private lessons, but more the everyday language, and today I can communicate very well.

School clothes were a big problem. I could buy skirts and blouses but black shoes and white stockings? My big daughter already needed a size 7 shoe. In a men's store we found low cut black shoes. I could not find the white stockings, only ones of very poor quality at Bata's, a shoe store. I saw other children wearing white stockings and I asked them immediately: „Where did you buy those?" „Min El Yunaen". „OK. Please tell me where that is?" It turned out that it was Greece; they also had socks from America or Saudi Arabia. In any case there was no such thing in Egypt. I wrote my husband that he should please bring us those kinds of things from Saudi Arabia. It became a very long list of all that we needed, and in December he needed an extra suitcase for all of the things. Every three months he got a few weeks of vacation and then he lived with us, of course, in Alexandria.

Groceries were another problem at the time, in 1984. It is hard to imagine now, but lots of things were still rationed: sugar, flour, oil, clarified butter and other things. For those things you had to have stamps; there was a food stamp book for the stamps distributed to each family. As my husband was in Saudi Arabia and we were not registered in Alexandria, we, of course, did not have a food stamp book. We were always dependent on the generous help of our family, who really took such good care of us during that time it was touching.

The children adjusted quickly and found friends; children often go about things more easily than adults. Most of the other children in their school (the Egyptian ones, too) already knew enough German so that right from the beginning communication was not a problem. A nine-year-old girl who also went to the German school lived in our building. My daughters learned Arabic from her and gradually became accustomed to this new world. As for me, I felt at the time virtually like a "drop-out". I had left everything behind and had to start anew. When one grows up in Austria, certain behaviors and customs go without saying; one does not question the rhyme or reason. What one cannot change, one accepts as it is. But in Egypt I found other ways different from home that were a matter of course to everyone else here. When does one learn that in Egypt it is dirty outside the apartment and that no one has thought to change this? Even after so many years, this behavior bothers me. All the garbage just ends up on the ground and no one cares. When does one learn that here no one keeps appointments, least of all the tradesmen? To this day I wait sometimes at the exact given time for a repairman and get upset, of course, when no one comes. My children, on the other hand, noticed very different things that they had to get used to. One comment from them was: „How strange, what a funny country; the cars park on the sidewalk and the people walk on the road." But that is how it is here, and everyone thinks it is normal. For a pedestrian it takes some getting used to, at first, to walk in between the cars in the traffic. There are neither crosswalks nor pedestrian walk signals; no one pays much attention to traffic lights anyway. Amazingly it nevertheless all works out somehow anyway; there are actually few accidents.

My husband's family was really loving and took very good care of us. They helped me and the children wherever they could. At first, communication with them was not always easy because they spoke only English or French and with my Arabic things moved forward only slowly. I missed speaking German and making friends with other people outside of the family. Then a coincidence helped me. I was in the process of bargaining for two pounds of tomatoes with a vegetable seller, when two older English women approached me. We started talking, and they told me about the „American Group" and gave me the address and the time of the next meeting. In addition, they said there were women in their group who spoke German. At first I was not at all sure whether that would be the right thing for me; after all, the women were all complete strangers. After some consideration, I went anyway and was received with open arms. They figured out right away who lived near me and brought us together. So I got to know Sophia, an older American lady, who had lived in Vienna for a long time. Not only did she speak some German, but also knew what Griesnockerln (semolina gnocchi or dumplings) and Leberknödelsuppe (liver dumpling soup) were. Soon she became a kind of substitute grandmother for my girls.

Through this group I met some German women and other German-speaking women, and that helped me very much. Finally I had people I could talk with, just like home. Only after some time in a foreign country does one notice how much one misses the mother tongue. Finally I had people who could answer all my questions, and I soon managed much better. We exchanged tips, where you could get certain things. Meat was available only on certain days; the same with poultry. Sometimes there was nothing at all. In spite of that I managed reasonably well with the children. Perhaps my childhood during and after the war in Austria did me some good, I often thought. At that time, too, we had to make do with very little and necessity, as we know, is the mother of invention.

Sugar was often hard to find. Once around that time our sugar bowl was almost entirely empty. We took a trip with the children to Cairo to see the pyramids and other sights. After several hours walking around, we at down in a café to catch our breath, and there -- I could hardly believe my eyes -- everywhere on the tables little packages of sugar had been put out, simply a dream! In the end I could not help myself and sent my daughters around to collect all the sugar they could. At home we tore open the packets and shook the precious powder into our sugar bowl. We felt really rich. But of course at some point this sugar ran short, too. An acquaintance from the club owned a piece of land with her husband; farmers cultivated it for them. She promised me she would look for sugar on the land. She actually turned up something, and what she brought me was none other than a real Zuckerhut (sugar loaf or cone of sugar)! I had never seen anything like it except in the German movie „die Feuerzangenbowle" ("The Punch Bowl"). My daughters and I sat at the table, put newspapers underneath, took a hammer and chisel and joyfully chopped the sugar loaf to bits. That was really fun! After our work was done, we filled the sugar bowl and had a nice supply again. Even at that time I was amazed at how much such little things could mean and how long one remembers them.

Every year during summer vacation my daughters and I went to Austria. We visited some friends, but most of all we went shopping. Everything we could not get in Egypt, we brought with us from Austria: shoes, socks, clothes, etc. After some years provisions fortunately got better, and with time almost everything was available in Egypt.

My husband continued to work in Saudi Arabia; every three months he came home for two weeks. It was not perfect, but we had come to terms with the arrangement. In Egypt many families live like that because well-paid jobs are still in short supply in this country.

After two years we had saved some money and could move out of the small apartment. The apartment still belonged to my brother-in-law, and it was actually only meant to be used by us for the transition period. Our new place was quite a bit bigger and was located in Smouha. We still live in this apartment today.

My children continued at the German school; gradually they learned Arabic, too. By the end of sixth grade my older daughter, Nadia, had to pass an exam. We had been in the country only two years. That was a very big challenge for her, even though only 50% was necessary in Arabic. She passed at the first try, and we were very happy and proud of her. She passed the exam after the 9th grade, too, and at the end she passed her German university entrance exams. Afterwards she wanted to study electrical engineering with computer science as a major. My second daughter, Jasmin, passed the exams well, too. She switched after 9th grade to the business school but after that she was able to complete a university degree in business administration whilst working. In Egypt it is extremely important to get a college degree, so Mohammed and I emphasized its importance to the girls.

Today Nadia is married and has two children herself. She lives very close to me in Alexandria, so I see my grandchildren often and can help my daughter now and then. After a short marriage, Jasmin was divorced and she now lives in Hurghada. Just like her mother, she works in tourism. She speaks four languages (German, English, French and of course, Arabic) – an invaluable advantage in that business. She comes to Alexandria only very infrequently; she finds it too noisy and crowded here.

Mohammed and I still live in our apartment in Smouha. I have a lot of contact with German-speaking women through the International Club and with English and French-speaking women as well. Unfortunately I don't have many friends among Egyptians; it just happened that way somehow. Although everyone is very nice and helpful, it is difficult to develop real friendships with Egyptians. Usually it stays at the level of superficial small talk, and after „How are you? And what are the children doing?" they cannot think of anything else to talk about that would be of common interest.

Looking back, we had some tough times financially. Since Mohammed never worked here in Egypt, he does not get any pension here. When he turned 65, he received a small pension from Austria. I have a pension, as well, from the time I was employed there. On that money we can live very well here. In Egypt it is the same as in many other places in the world: one can live well if one has an honest husband.

In 1984 we had no other choice but to go to Egypt. At the time I did not have a realistic picture of what that would mean for us. But now I see that move was a real new start and has made my life more colorful and more interesting. Would I make the same decision today? Probably, yes.

Chapter Five

Renate H. Egypt was My Destiny!

Renate is a pretty woman of medium height in her late fifties. She has blond hair, brown eyes and high cheekbones. She comes across as very energetic and self-confident. She wrote down her story herself for me; I added only a little to it, based on my questions to her. Here is her story:

It all began around 1930 in Upper Egypt when my parents-in-law sold their camels and moved to Alexandria with their savings. They bought a big piece of land and planted it with orange trees. The harvest was very good. Later on they opened a wholesale fruit business and a smaller fruit shop. At that time King Farouk still ruled in Egypt, and looking back they often said those were the best years in Egypt.

Both my in-laws dressed in the traditional way: they wore long black robes and covered their hair with cloths. In addition, the women had a black cloak; the men a white turban. My future husband, Ahmed, was their eldest. After him, my in-laws had two boys and a girl. Originally my father-in-law had planned to have Ahmed take over the orange groves, but Ahmed's mother had other plans for him. She wanted him to get his high school diploma and go to Germany to study medicine. A medical degree is still considered the absolute best in Egypt until today and doctors enjoy a high standing in society. They sent Ahmed to college preparatory school and with patience and persistence my mother-in-law got her wish -- Ahmed actually went to Germany. His younger brother Sayed went along, too, and this brother played a big role throughout my future husband's whole life.

In 1952 King Farouk was deposed and exiled to Italy. Gamal Abdel Nasser came to power and with that Egypt's good years were over for a time.

In 1957, after passing his university entrance exams, Ahmed booked passage on a Greek passenger ship from Alexandria and traveled to Naples. From there he took the train up north: first to Hamburg and from there to Kiel. At 20 he began studying medicine at the Christian-Albrecht University in Kiel. In the beginning he didn't know any German, so his life was not easy. Besides, he had great difficulty getting used to the different educational methods in Germany. In Egypt he had learned almost completely by memorization; one's own ideas or logic were rarely asked for. It is the same today; even at Egyptian universities much is learned by rote. So his preparation was anything but good and at first he progressed only very slowly in his studies.

At the same time I was growing up in Kiel in a sheltered household with my parents in a house with a garden. I had just turned ten years old and led a happy life. In my free time I took ballet lessons and went horse-riding. Both my older sisters also still lived at home. My father was a teacher and my mother was a housewife. My mother did not go back to work in an office until I was twelve years old. I rarely thought about my future; my father would always take care of us. On my thirteenth birthday, my sisters invited me on a shopping trip to the city. At the jewelry counter in Karstadt (a popular department shop, like JC Penney) I was fascinated by a little gold pendant in the shape of the head of Nefertiti. Dagmar really wanted to give me something for my birthday so she bought me the pendant.

Even then the country of Egypt fascinated me with its rich and mysterious history. At home we had many books, and the book "Gods, Graves and Scholars" was naturally a must for me. For my paper in geography I chose Egypt as my topic and handed in my project with photos and reports; it was the best in the class. I was especially taken with the pyramids of Giza.

My sister Dagmar was three years older than I was and loved to go dancing, like most teenagers. One day she had a date with the German shot-putter Uwe Bayer (he later played the role of Siegfried in a movie). But Dagmar was not allowed to go alone, so my mother and I went along as chaperones to the Florida Bar. I was sixteen by then and quite proud that I was already allowed to wear a close-fitting pink mini-dress. There on the dance floor of the Florida Bar, I saw Ahmed for the first time. He was already dancing and surrounded by girls. No wonder—he was very handsome. Nevertheless, he asked me to dance, and I did not wait to be asked twice. His exotic looks fascinated me right away and on top of that he came from Egypt, too! We made a date to meet in front of the movie theater the very next day. But it was pouring with rain so I did not go. But Ahmed did not give up easily. He called, and my mother made arrangements for a movie date. Of course, I never would have been allowed to go alone. But my mother understood how important it was to me, and so again like the three musketeers, Mother, Dagmar and I went to the movies with Ahmed. After the show, in my excitement, I slipped in my high heels and almost fell in a puddle. Ahmed just managed to catch me.

But there were no further rendezvous for a while because I really considered Ahmed too old for me. Like my mother, I wanted to work in an office later, and to do that I first had to finish my education at the business school in Kiel. Occasionally I would run into Ahmed in the city, but we did not go out any more and would have probably lost track of each other, if Ahmed had not been so persistent.

By the time I finished school, working in an office did not seem so attractive to me any more. Instead I wanted to become a nurse. Together with my girlfriend Anita, I enrolled in nursing school in Rendsburg. My professional goal lay clearly before me: I really wanted to help the sick.

After one and a half years in school—I was not anywhere near done—my mother called me and told me that Ahmed, who was in Hamburg, wanted very much to see me again. I had nothing against that, so I took the train to Hamburg on my day off. This time everything was clear from the first moment: we fell into each other's arms and both knew that we were meant for each other. Right after our reunion, I went back to Rendsburg and broke the news to the head nurse that I wanted to get married and intended to drop out of school. She was appalled, but she wrote me a good recommendation and said at the end: "I hope you won't change for the worse in Egypt."

It did not take very long to get all the papers together that we needed to get married. I also needed permission from my parents because I would not be 18 years old until July 27, 1966. But our wedding was supposed to take place on July 13, 1966. Of all things the 13th! But Ahmed and I believed in our good luck. I was in seventh heaven and bought myself a pink suit from a boutique in Kiel for the big day. Ahmed got the wedding rings and a beautiful bridal bouquet of pink carnations and blue iris. With his last money he also bought me a gold necklace. My mother took care of the guest list and organized the wedding celebration. My father's comment was rather dry: „I hope you have really thought this through!" But my parents supported me nonetheless, and I even asked my father, as a dowry so to speak, to buy us an old Mercedes, a refrigerator, a washing machine and an electric stove. Ahmed thought we could really use all these things starting out in Egypt. Additional clothes would not be necessary, because there was enough of that sort of thing in Alexandria. Ahmed also had bought a Mercedes that we wanted to take with us. On my wedding night I wept terribly. I hardly knew what I had let myself in for. Or maybe that was just the wine?

I was so in love that I failed to notice one small thing: Ahmed's brother Sayed was always there. They had studied together, and he traveled as a matter of course with us to Egypt.

So off we went with the two cars, the washing machine, the refrigerator and the electric stove. My sister had taken some vacation days and wanted to accompany us as far as Genoa. We traveled through Switzerland and Mount St. Gotthard to Genoa. On Mount St. Gotthard it suddenly looked as if we would not arrive at all: in the middle of the mountain, the brakes failed, and the car rolled backwards. I screamed. With the help of the emergency brake, we were fortunately able to come to a stop.

After some delay we got the car running again and drove on.

In Genoa we spent a night in the youth hostel. Dagmar and I really wanted to go swimming, and as chance would have it, we were soon being followed by some Italians. They tried more or less aggressively to talk us into going with them. Ahmed had noticed we were missing and was already looking for us. When he found us and we could finally go back, Ahmed decided it would be better if I dyed my blond hair black. But I would not even consider it.

Dagmar went back to Kiel, and Ahmed, Sayed, our cars and I got on board an old Egyptian passenger ship in Genoa heading for Egypt. We had hardly any money and therefore chose the cheapest kind of ticket. We slept in hammocks and had to provide our own food. Our meal plan consisted of bread we had brought with us, and water. We looked enviously at the other passengers who had booked with meals provided. After three days we finally reached Greece at the port of Piraeus, and we could eat a real meal. For the rest of the trip, we bought a watermelon and a big loaf of bread that had to last us until Alexandria.

After two more days we arrived in the harbor of Alexandria. There were so many people there; it was total confusion and deafening noise. I was tired and hungry from the passage and the noise grated on my nerves. Everything was entirely different from how it was at home; I was speechless at first and just amazed. A horse and carriage picked us up and took us to Ahmed's parents' house because the cars had to go through customs before we could use them. Sayed followed on foot with the suitcases. The carriage stopped in front of an old house with several floors. Ahmed's parents lived in a large apartment with six rooms in that old building. We were led in; I sat on a wooden bed and was at a loss as to what to do next. Then the door opened and a large woman dressed in black came in. She embraced me and slipped three gold bracelets over my hand. We could not speak to each other; I did not yet know any Arabic. My new father-in-law shook hands with me coldly. Ahmed's youngest brother was there, too. Their sister was already married to a cousin and had taken over the father's fruit shop. Of course, the family had had other plans for the eldest son; Ahmed was supposed to marry an Egyptian. And now he comes home with a German woman! They did not receive me very warmly. They probably thought that a marriage with a foreigner would definitely not last long. There they were greatly mistaken!

From the beginning I had resolved to continue with my swimming. We went to Montazah where I could swim in the sea while Ahmed just splashed around near the shore. He had never really learned to swim. At that time one still saw Egyptian women in bathing suits; today that practically does not exist any more. I wanted to visit the orange groves and help with the harvest. But my father-in-law was very much against that because it was not appropriate. So we drove home again. I had a whole lot to learn: what was appropriate and what not, how one behaved and what one simply did not do! In the beginning it was very difficult.

We shared our apartment in Alexandria with Sayed; sometimes the youngest brother lived there, too. Their parents lived in another part of the city. Later on I did not often see them. My laundry was picked up and brought back clean by little Egyptian children. But something was always missing. My mother-in-law sent me a roasted duck or a chicken now and then. I do not remember any more how else the household was run. I was in a state of shock that lasted almost a year. Then I got pregnant.

My sister Gudrun came with her husband and some friends to visit. They drove in their VW from Berlin through Tunisia and Libya to us in Alexandria. They stayed a few days and then drove on to the Red Sea. They were appalled at the living conditions and in all seriousness asked me how I could live here. Evenings the mice ran around; the cockroaches were permanent guests at our place. The bathroom and the kitchen were not at all up to our standard; we lived at the simplest level. But in the meantime I had gotten used to the conditions and did not let it upset me any more. My sister Dagmar visited me, too. She arrived on a Greek luxury ship and surely had a more pleasant passage than I had. She could hardly believe that I could live like that. Nevertheless she stayed with me in Alexandria until May of 1967 when my daughter Jasmin was born. She helped me wash the diapers in a big iron bowl on the propane gas stove because I could not hook up the modern washing machine that I had brought from Germany with such forethought. Thank God my mother constantly sent me packages because otherwise I would not even have had anything for the baby to wear. Besides cloth diapers and little dresses there was nothing else available to buy. There was only one kind of laundry detergent and one kind of bath soap.

But I did discover a little Greek shop where one could even get sauerkraut from the barrel. There was one kind of butter and only one kind of sheep's milk cheese and olives. That combination was often our meal. However, we did not starve. There were always plenty of fruits and vegetables available.

Nasser cultivated friendly relations with the Russian government; so many Russians visited the city. Now I was no longer the only blond in a miniskirt. As a matter of fact, I had never changed my style of clothing.

Eventually Dagmar went back to Kiel, and Ahmed and I looked for an apartment in Cairo (Dokki) on the Nile. He wanted to complete his studies in Cairo. We hoped that it would be easier for him there. First he had to get himself exempted from military service. With a few tricks and gifts he succeeded. Of course Sayed came with us to Cairo, always tagging behind. Slowly but surely that was getting on my nerves.

In Cairo there was a Protestant congregation where I was warmly accepted. There at Sister Liselotte's I got to know other German women. That really helped me a great deal. I felt less alone when I could visit friends regularly, and Ahmed quickly grew accustomed to it. By that time the thirst for adventure had taken hold of Dagmar, too; she came to us in Cairo and wanted to work as a physical therapist here. She actually found a position in a clinic and ended up staying three years. At that time we became acquainted with Ilana, who was Russian and married to an Egyptian professor. As she was already forty and therefore had more life experience in this strange land, we gladly let her give us advice, especially on how to handle our husbands. After a short time, Dagmar, in fact, married Sayed, so we were two sisters married to two brothers.

As the men were still studying, we were always short of funds. Our husbands were constantly going to their parents in Alexandria to get money, so we could live. The cars were sold.

In 1967 I became pregnant again. To have more support, I really wanted to have this baby in Germany. At the beginning of my ninth month, Ahmed, little Jasmin and I went by ship to Venice and afterwards directly to Kiel by train. It was quite an ordeal to make such a long trip in the middle of summer and in my ninth month! But the time in Kiel was nevertheless very special for us. In August of 1968 my daughter Mona was born there. We stayed until January 1969, and I enjoyed the conveniences of my old homeland. Then once again we bought a new Mercedes and made our long way back to Egypt.

We stayed five more years in Cairo, but Ahmed did not succeed in completing his studies. So it was packing the suitcases again and back to Alexandria. Now he and Sayed wanted to open a restaurant together. Of course they needed start capital for it, and as there were hardly any opportunities in Egypt to earn money quickly, we went again to my parents in Kiel. But it was not so easy there either to find well-paid jobs, especially without specific training. We tried out different things, but after only three months we had had enough of the cold and snow. Besides I was pregnant for the third time. But we had managed to set aside some money and once again we could take a Mercedes with us into Egypt. We went first through Venice to Alexandria and then to Cairo. There I had my son Karim in our Russian friend's clinic. During my hospital stay Ilana took care of both my daughters; they lived with her. Ahmed was already living in Alexandria again, but he was soon able to come to Cairo and take all four of us home.

Leaving Ilana was not easy for me; she had become a very good friend, who always stood by me in word and deed. We also really missed the pyramids of Giza; we had often gone there on our Sunday excursions with the children. In our absence our apartment in Cairo had been taken from us along with all the furniture and everything else that was in there. Ahmed had not paid the rent for three months, and the landlord had simply taken action. When we arrived there, strange people had moved in, the locks had been changed, and we could not do anything at all about it.

At first my three children and I lived in a single room in my parents-in-law's apartment in Alexandria. Ahmed's youngest brother still lived there, too. Dagmar had it somewhat better; she lived with Sayed by the sea in Camp Chesar. Our husbands completed their plans and opened their restaurant. Now they were in the restaurant practically day and night. I hardly set eyes on Ahmed any more; in fact, he came home only at night to sleep. And at some point I was of course fed up with living with the whole family in only one room. At Christmas I even squeezed in a small fir tree. All the Egyptian relatives thought I was crazy but they got used to it. The youngest brother, Saber, got on my nerves. He constantly hid the sugar and tea from me and begrudged us everything. The maid stole my underwear. We were always short of money. I decided to move to my sister's by the sea. She did not want me at all, but I did not let that stop me. I packed our things and together with my husband and children simply moved in with her.

Then Ahmed decided to turn the restaurant into the first pizzeria in Alexandria. So we had to put up with renovating and redecorating. That was a lot of work, but it was worth it because the Alexandrians were thrilled and finally the restaurant was doing really well. But success hardly changed our daily lives at all, because my father-in-law always collected the entire proceeds. What he paid out to us was just about enough to live on.

Dagmar was having problems as well. She could not get a work permit. In spite of that, she of course wanted to work and found a position with an Egyptian doctor. But because she had no proper papers, she was paid very poorly and was really taken advantage of. Soon she was fed up with life in Egypt and wanted only to get out. We took a vacation and flew together to Berlin. Dagmar just stayed in Berlin then; life in Egypt was simply too trying for her. At some point Sayed got a divorce and Dagmar remarried in Germany. Dagmar did not even have to go to Egypt for the divorce, because in Egypt it is enough if the husband files for divorce; the wife's consent or presence is not necessary. I, of course, left Dagmar in Berlin and returned to Ahmed, just as I had always done. Despite the many adverse circumstances in our life we belonged together always. We could not part from each other!

Upon my return, however, I did finally insist that I wanted to live with Ahmed and the children alone. Up until then my brother-in-law Sayed had always been with us and now I had really had enough. I stood firm and actually prevailed. At last, we had our own apartment just for us! We were still short of money, but we found a reasonable apartment in an old building in Saad Zaghloul. Even though the old furniture from the former tenants was still in the apartment, we moved right in. I did not want any delay; otherwise, Ahmed could have changed his mind again. My children went to the German school, and for the first time I set up house the way I would have at home in Germany. We were not able to shake off Sayed entirely; he still came every day for lunch. But we had made a start.

My mother-in-law died very early at only 55, and a few years later my father-in-law died, too. Now we saw more of Sayed again. I got him together with the neighbor's daughter, and soon thereafter they married. I was already looking forward to not having to feed him any more. I rejoiced too soon, as it turned out. In fact the girl continued to live with her mother in spite of her marriage, and Sayed showed up every day for meals again. In

Egypt it is just different, and it is not that uncommon for married people to live separately. Ahmed was very attached to his brother Sayed and did hardly anything without him. Sayed knew that very well and took advantage of it wherever he could. Every time we went to Germany on vacation, Sayed counted on it that my children and I would surely stay there. That would have been alright with him. But I never gave him the satisfaction. Instead I always fought for my family, my marriage and my children. I returned every time. Besides I had many visitors from Germany; my parents and siblings came on a pretty regular basis. My parents supported us financially more than once. My family helped me to stand it.

An older German friend took me along for the first time to the yacht club. She was married to a „Pasha", which is about the equivalent of an English lord. I liked it so much the very first time at the yacht club that I soon became a member. At last I could go swimming again and had balance in my life. To this day I swim there regularly. There is a large protected ocean-water pool and you can swim in a bathing suit without being stared at. At the public beaches here women go in the water completely clothed. They cannot really swim of course; the clothes get soaked with water and are way too heavy.

Since I first came to Egypt in 1966, a lot has changed. Most women dress in high-necked clothes with long sleeves and a headscarf. Occasionally you see some of them entirely in black with a face veil that leaves only the eyes uncovered. But Ahmed has never demanded that I wear a headscarf.

I frequently went to the sailors' home. It was a kind of club for German seamen who had shore leave in Alexandria. There were lodgings, a German pastor, a restaurant, and leisure activities, too. I quickly became acquainted with other German women there. In a foreign country it is very important to get together with like-minded people for mutual support. It makes life much easier and helps ward off homesickness.

I still find it very difficult to be friends with Egyptians. In all these years I have unfortunately found this to be true, as have many of my friends. The Egyptians are always looking for an advantage and only want to take. They are not capable of giving. It does not have to do with money all the time at all. They do a favor only when they think they will get something out of it in return. I am happy to be friendly to them, but I keep my distance.

After my father-in-law died, we wanted to try another business venture. We decided to make a fashion shop out of our pizzeria. By then, Sadat was president and goods were much more available; you could now import clothes from Italy and England. Although Sayed had always caused us a lot of trouble, we decided to forget our differences and work together with him on the remodeling and interior decoration of the shop. For six months we worked every free minute on setting up the shop and on the interior design. Finally, our lovely fashion shop was finished. We really had simply wonderful things, and of course the word got around. Soon customers were streaming in; even actors came to our shop. And very gradually we noticed for the first time that enough money was coming in. It could have all been so nice if it had not been for the dear relatives. The families of Saber and Sayed downright stole from our shop. They thought they could have everything for free, because after all they were family. There was a lot of envy in this family. I was almost always in the shop and that brought in many customers. Everyone was talking about us. And the main topic was that the shop belonged to a German woman. The relatives did not like that at all. Of course they were all for it that I should do the lion's share of the work, but the whole clan should be the ones to profit from it, if you please.

Saber went to court and sued Ahmed and Sayed. The Egyptian justice system has remained unclear to me to this day. In principle one can always find a reason to sue if one knows the right judge or helps things along with the necessary bit of money. In the end it is always about money. The inheritance had not been divided fairly, and his share was now invested in our shop, or so Saber maintained. The whole lawsuit was extremely unpleasant and a great burden for everyone. In the end, we had to give up the shop, but at least we got land for it. Sayed discovered a rundown shop for rent nearby. We bought it and decided to try again and open a new shop. We sold part of the land and imported a really wonderful interior decor from Denmark. After much preparation, things looked very good for us again. I worked every day and supported my husband. After a while, Sayed found another ruin, and we rebuilt that one into a nice shop, too. Almost all of our money from the sale of the orange trees was invested now in the shops, but there was just enough for a nice condominium in Roushdy for Ahmed and me. Our daughters already attended university; Karim was still at Victoria College, a college preparatory school.

Now things should have continued peacefully like this, but of course we rejoiced too soon. Envy reared its head again -- this time from Sayed and his family. They kept destroying my décor, and on some days all the money was suddenly gone from the cash register. They also helped themselves to the clothes in the shop at will. In a fire - the cause was never determined - our shop was completely destroyed. With much luck we succeeded in getting some money from our insurance. Again we had to start from scratch. My patience was by now really at its end. I wanted finally to be independent from the family and have a shop for us alone. After long discussions, we came to an agreement: Ahmed and I could run one of the shops alone. Now at last the work was really fun for me. I shopped and decorated with the saleswomen. Of course I had to be very observant; stealing was common. During the lunch break one of us had to stay in the shop or we had to lock up securely.

My daughter Jasmin studied biology and married a nice man from Alexandria. Both of them wanted to build their life in Germany. Shortly thereafter, my son Karim moved to Germany, too. He began an apprenticeship as a cook. Mona finished studying architecture at the University of Alexandria and joined her sister in Germany. Since Sayed was making life difficult for me again, I persuaded my husband to try our luck there as well and to open a shop in Germany. All of a sudden I was sick and tired of life in Egypt, even though the living conditions had very much improved by then: in the 80s all of a sudden everything was available to buy. Nevertheless I wanted to leave. We sold all our belongings and flew to Germany with only a few suitcases and the money.

All my children were already in Germany, so we flew to Frankfurt and were joyfully received. We moved in with them in Pforzheim and distributed the money, as each of the young people was just beginning to build a life. What was left was just enough for a small boutique in Karlsruhe. We bought it from an Italian who had gone bankrupt. We had to pay rather high rent for it. It was not until a few months later that we realized the high-class realtor and the Italian had conned us. The owner of the building wanted to evict us, but we hung on for one and a half more years. I always went to Sindelfingen near Stuttgart to shop for merchandise. There were big fashion houses with several showrooms for retailers in that city. I ran myself ragged, running through the four buildings with five floors just to get hold of some reasonable clothes. The customers who came to our shop were all very frugal. I think their main reason for coming in was to chat. To run a business in Germany takes much more effort than in Egypt. Every three months I had to go to the tax accountant and all the paperwork was really bothersome. First we all lived together, but then my daughter Mona found a position in an architect's office in Hamburg. After she moved out, we had to pay the whole rent for our apartment by ourselves. The money from our shop was not enough for that, and I moonlighted at a shoe shop. I did not get along with the manager at all; she bossed me around all day and the whole arrangement was not at all fun. It is no wonder that I suddenly had a real longing for Egypt again.

My dear father died in Kiel. With all the work, I had neglected him. My mother whined that she could not handle the house and the garden. On my vacation I went to my mother's, but it was not at all the way it used to be. The house seemed strangely empty to me, and the garden was completely overgrown. My mother was quite confused and sometimes downright malicious. She numbed her grief with wine and champagne and perhaps that is what caused her depression; I do not know. I tried to get the house into some order, but it was difficult because my mother did not want to throw anything away. Over the many years a whole mountain of stuff had accumulated because my parents could not bear to give anything up.

It all was a big strain on my nerves, so I called my sister Gudrun. She invited me to Berlin. I was to come and relax a little at her place. I visited her and we traveled together to Amrum and Oldenburg. Afterwards we went to Denmark. Gudrun, my older sister, was always a role model for me and I felt very comfortable in her company. Nevertheless I had the feeling that she wanted to keep me away from my mother. She was always against my mother going to live with us in Egypt. But I did not realize that until much later.

Back in Pforzheim the decision was made; we closed our boutique and turned it over to the owner of the building. I quit my job. Then we scraped together the rest of our savings and packed our bags once again. Back to Alexandria! Sayed had rented a large six-room apartment in an old building for us right next to his. We gave him a largish sum of money, and he had the apartment freshly painted before our arrival. Of course half of the money went into his own pocket, but I was happy anyway that we had an apartment by the sea again. Sayed had even visited us with his wife and daughter in Pforzheim. He promised Ahmed that he could work in Sayed's shop again. After our arrival in Alexandria it did not take long before I realized that he only wanted to get us to part with our savings. Sure we were allowed to clean the rundown shop and stock it with clothes, but the money from the cash register landed with Sayed again.

A little later, my mother needed my help in Kiel. My siblings wanted to be paid out their share of the family home because they wanted to settle in Spain. So the house had to be cleaned out and sold. I went to Kiel and looked for buyers for the household things and furniture that had accumulated over fifty years of marriage. When everything was taken care of and the house sold, the inheritance was divided up, and my mother went into a nursing home. With my share I wanted to furnish my apartment in Alexandria, as it was still entirely empty. The money was enough for inexpensive but comfortable furnishings. When our finances improved somewhat, Ahmed bought a condominium in my name.

We tried this and that with work but nothing amounted to much in earnings. When my mother was 75 years old, we brought her to us in Alexandria. She liked coming to Egypt; she knew the country from her vacations here. She could live well here on her pension, and she always had enough entertainment, too.

Our daughter Mona came back to Alexandria; she married an Egyptian dentist. They have three children: two girls and a boy. Nevertheless Mona was soon drawn to Germany again. It took nine years before she could convince her husband. He was very attached to his mother. But they both thought the children would have better chances for the future in Germany. All of my children were torn between Germany and Egypt, just as I was.

After five years my mother just died in her sleep one day; she was buried here in the Catholic cemetery. So Egypt kept her forever.

Afterwards my children brought me to Pforzheim once again. But it was a different life without Kiel and without my parents. I did not get along especially well with my siblings any more. They never understood why I had taken our mother to Egypt. My daughter Jasmin wanted me to help her with her big house and garden, but after three months I was drawn again back to Alexandria. And to my yacht club. After 40 years in Egypt, I see that everything here has become much more modern. Today there are big supermarkets everywhere where you can buy everything you want.

I cannot complain; foreigners are always treated with courtesy and respect by the Egyptians. If you can speak Arabic with them, they are particularly happy and are much friendlier than usual.

Nowadays I go regularly to the Sporting Club. Every Tuesday the „International Women's Club" meets there. The women in the club speak English, French, German and Arabic, too. Very often it is the Arabic language that unites us because many can speak it at least well enough to hold a simple conversation. We often discuss Egypt; how much it has changed, what we like and what we do not like so much. Despite different points of view, we all get along well, and everything goes very smoothly.

All the German-speaking women meet at the Goethe-Institute; there is even a woman from Finland there who speaks very good German. These meetings are not just get-togethers; on the contrary, the club is involved with social causes in Egypt. Every year a Christmas bazaar is held and the money flows into selected charity projects.

Today almost all of us have satellite television, and we can receive all the international programs, all the German channels, too. So we can stay current and feel more closely connected to Germany.

In recent years, my husband had become very sick and I expected that I would end up alone. But things turned around and today Ahmed is reasonably healthy. Now I look after him and take the best care of him I can. I swim regularly again at the yacht club and sometimes I gather pottery shards from the time of Cleopatra on the beach. Last year a group of archeologists from France and Egypt were here. They pulled out quite a few finds from the Mediterranean. There seems to be an inexhaustible supply of antiquities; it is a never-ending story. I am 58 years old now and continue to live with Ahmed in Egypt. We have been married for forty years and I hope that we will go on for a long time.

I have received the following poem from Renate. The author is unknown. It depicts very well the mixed feelings that run through Renate's whole life.

It's me. I can't explain it any other way

I can be happy only for some time.

If I'm up North, I want to be down South next day

And there is nothing that can keep me from that clime.

Once I accomplished what my longing is

The beach, in front of me the rushing sea

It is just after a few days of this

That soon I think how nice the snow would be.

If people are there, I need solitude

If I'm alone, I want more friends with me,

And being in the city, I just would

Go to the country with villages to see.

Tell me why I was often so beholden

To think it better on the other side?

Why my contentment always has been stolen?

And do you feel the same way, too, sometimes?

Chapter Six
Susan S. From America to Egypt

Susan is an American I met at an event held by the International Ladies Club of Alexandria. She doesn't speak German, so we wrote her story for the book in English together. I found her to be a very optimistic, positive person, well liked by everyone. She is outgoing and easy to talk to, and she was willing to share her interesting story:

I was born and raised in New York City. My father died when I was 15 years old. A year later, when our mother married a widower with three sons approximately the same age as we were, my younger sister and I accepted the new situation. The five of us did not consider the new marriage a problem. We were all on the verge of leaving home for college or the army - we just wanted our parents to be happy again.

In 1964 I graduated from a junior college. I was 20 years old, living at home, and working as a medical secretary. On weekends, I traveled to Princeton University in New Jersey to meet my boyfriend there. Unfortunately the relationship did not work out, but in February 1965 I again visited the university library to borrow a science book for my middle stepbrother. As I was walking up the stairs of the library, I happened to pass a young student with a huge load of books under his arm and a bright smile. I asked for directions to the science section, and he accompanied me to the shelf and found the book for me. Afterwards I joined him for a cup of coffee in the cafeteria. We felt an immediate mutual attraction. I learned that his name was Hamdi and that he was an Egyptian graduate student working on his Ph.D. in architecture. We exchanged telephone numbers and agreed to meet again.

We had our first date the following weekend, when I was to join him at a lecture. I thought it might be interesting to do so and learn more about his field. Hoping to be inconspicuous, I sat in the back of the room in the last row. It was a meeting of the New Jersey Chapter of Architects, and the president introduced my date as the speaker for the meeting, on the topic, "Architectural Values in Luxor." I was shocked! He hadn't mentioned he was going to be the speaker. The lecture began and the president sat down next to me. I was deeply impressed with Hamdi´s presentation and his answers to questions at the end of it. The president asked me if I was an architect. I assured him I was not, but mentioned that the speaker was my date. He replied, "This guy is really something!"

We dated each weekend for several months; going to movies and football games, taking long walks together, and we discovered we had common life goals. One weekend Hamdi came to New York and met my mother and stepfather. He told them he wanted to marry me. Of course, they wanted to know what his plans for the future were and what kind of a life we would have in Egypt. Hamdi told them that he would have to return to Egypt for seven years to repay the Egyptian government for the academic scholarship he had been given. We envisioned staying only seven years and then returning to the United States. My mother, although she did not tell me until many years later, was deeply concerned about the success of this marriage, but no one said a word against him. In June 1965 we got engaged and two months later we were married in a Methodist church with an Islamic prayer.

Hamdi worked hard to complete his thesis and project, which were required for his degree. The following year he presented his work and was awarded his Ph.D. I was already pregnant at the time, so we decided to leave immediately for Egypt and not wait for his June graduation. It would be easier to travel through Europe at that point rather than carrying a baby around later.

I had never been out of the United States before, and this trip was my first by plane. How exciting it was! I had assumed that I would have no language difficulty in Scotland and England. What an eye-opener that was – their strong accents and dialects were impossible for me to understand. Later we toured Belgium, Holland and

France where we met Hamdi´s brother, Munir, who was studying for a Ph.D. in economics in Paris. The two men had not seen each other for six years, so the reunion was joyous.

In Germany we picked up our new Volkswagen in Wolfsburg and drove through Switzerland to Italy. In Naples we boarded the ship to Alexandria with our luggage and car. The doctor had a chat with me, since I was very noticeably huge. I was seven months pregnant, and he had not delivered an infant in more than 30 years - he feared the crossing and Mediterranean Sea storms. Well, the sea was stormy - most passengers were seasick and remained in their cabins - but not me. I was famished and the only person in the dining room. The storm continued, making the approach to the port of Alexandria very hazardous. The captain made the decision to go to Beirut, Lebanon and then return again to Alexandria.

Hamdi´s father, older brother and brother-in-law met us dockside in the port four days later. They had waited an entire day because no one knew when the ship would arrive. I made my first faux pas within three minutes of meeting them. I said "hello" American style and kissed all the men! My husband had not told me this was not done. (Men can kiss other men or close female relatives - women kiss other women and any children, but women never kiss men). However, as shocked as they were, they realized my innocence in the gesture - it was a warm welcome and I felt included.

We stayed two weeks in Alexandria until our luggage, shipping freight and car had passed customs. I met Hamdi's sister, Ameria, who had four young children. She has helped me over the years, and we became very good friends. My relationship with Hamdi´s parents was also very warm, although only his father spoke English. I recognize now that my lack of Arabic was an advantage - I had no quarrels with anyone - I couldn't talk. My other sisters-in-law had frequent problems, so I emerged as the "favorite." During those early years, Hamdi´s father helped us financially; without his help we could not have managed to have a reasonable lifestyle.

Upon our arrival in Cairo, Hamdi learned that his employment papers had been shuffled to the Ministry of Housing rather than to a university post, which he had wanted. His salary was very small and did not even cover the basic rent on our furnished apartment. We needed to buy food, and hospital expenses were coming up very soon. Cairo was huge, dusty, crowded and noisy. We both wanted to return to Alexandria, which was cleaner and quieter.

Our daughter was born on February 1st. As a new mother I was afraid my child would be switched; the infant had not been given an identification bracelet. The nurse laughed..... "Come into the nursery", she said....... My daughter was the only blond infant in the room. My sister-in-law also gave birth the same week. Her husband, who came to visit me, said his wife had done better – she had had a son!

I was getting used to life in Cairo. There were no luxuries, but once in a while we went to the movies, which was the epitome of social life and where dressing as if for the opera was de rigueur. The films were usually in English with Arabic sub-titles, so I could understand everything very well. Three months after the baby was born, an advertisement for an Assistant Professor at Alexandria University appeared in the newspaper, and Hamdi applied immediately. Several weeks later we moved again, back to Alexandria into the summer apartment of my parents-in-law.

The university salary was slightly better and somehow we managed. I learned to cook with basic ingredients using the directions in my cookbook. Ameria would invite us for lunch, and I would sit in the kitchen with the servants (another social faux pas) as they prepared the dishes. I watched and learned but would also modify things as I thought best.

I had one servant, a 15-year-old girl with no experience. It was difficult training her as she preferred doing things the Egyptian way. Cleaning was always done with lots of water – the more water used, the cleaner the floor. What a sight my bathroom was with an inch of water pooled in it! So I had a maid, but most of the time I cleaned up after her.

In 1967 we decided to return to America and spend one year there working to save some money. However this departure was delayed until the Six Day War ended and ships could leave the harbor. After arriving in New York, Hamdi got a job in New York City, and we lived in a small apartment near my mother. It was a happy year and our daughter thrived with grandma and great-grandma in attendance. In August 1968 we returned to Egypt.

Our arrival was happy but our apartment was a disaster. Winter rains had seeped into the ground floor apartment; the flooring, rugs and furniture were all ruined. We moved out and found a larger apartment (the same one we are still living in today). Two months later I was pregnant again. In August 1969 our son Tarek was born and the family was complete. The delivery went well, but he contracted a serious infection in the hospital. He was ill for several months and the doctors thought we might lose him. Huge amounts of antibiotics saved his life, and he is a strong, healthy man today.

Still we had no luxuries and food was a problem. There were enough fruits and vegetables, but meat, oil, butter, rice and sugar were in short supply. Each family had a ration book with the quantities dependent upon family size. When people could get anything extra, they bought it and hoarded it, something I had never witnessed before.

In 1971 we moved to Beirut, Lebanon and stayed for four years during Hamdi´s university sabbatical. The children went to Arabic schools -- their English was excellent but they had zero Arabic. It was a good decision; they got an excellent foundation in Arabic, although their accent was wrong (Lebanese).

During one winter, my father-in-law paid us a visit. He had not realized that it was Christmas time and was shocked and ashamed he did not have presents for the children. I had put up a tiny Christmas tree and all the presents were beneath it. Each person had two to three gifts, mostly clothing that they needed. I had wrapped a few small items for my father-in-law, too. He was surprised and enjoyed the children's reaction to Santa Claus. At the dinner table we joined hands for a blessing, but he refused. He did not want to participate in a Christian ceremony. I told him it was a family tradition - not a religious act, which would have been forbidden by Islam. I further explained that the circle of clasped hands represented the unity of the family. The following morning at breakfast he insisted that we clasp hands for a prayer in Arabic! From then on, we followed this tradition whenever he joined us for a meal. My father-in-law stayed for two weeks, spoke Arabic with the children and forged a lasting close relationship with them. When he died years later, my children were the only grandchildren who cried, and the only ones to receive a surprise monetary legacy.

My husband was promoted to professor of architecture and urban design. Our life style had improved slowly over the years. He became dean of architecture at Beirut Arab University and came home only every six weeks. This mode of living (husband employed abroad and wife and children at home) is common in Egypt.

My private social life was also on an upswing. I had joined the American Women of Alexandria, (AWA) and I found many new friends and activities to enjoy. Within three years, women of other nationalities were invited to become members. For twenty years I was always busy on Monday mornings with friends, mostly German-speaking, rather than the Americans, who were there on more temporary employment contracts and tended to leave after one or two years. With the AWA we enjoyed many social activities for the whole family. There were cookouts on the Fourth of July with hot dogs and hamburgers, and Thanksgiving dinners where everybody provided side dishes and we shared the turkey. For our children it was the chance to grow up not only with the Egyptian but also with the American traditions. Of course they learned both languages, English and Arabic, equally well. The US Navy frequently visited the port of Alexandria and our children were able to translate for the sailors.

Our son went as a translator on shopping trips with these young men. Consequently, at the age of 11, he realized for the first time that it was an advantage to be able to speak two languages. He made some money translating and was part of a cookout where he flipped hamburgers and could eat and drink as much as he wanted. He had a lot of fun.

When the children were in junior high school, I wanted to go back to work. In the states I had worked as a medical secretary. My husband didn't like this idea because it implied he was not able to support me. After several discussions, Hamdi understood it would be better for me if I worked and that it did not reflect poorly on him as a provider for the family. I had to wait three years for a position, but finally one opened up at the American Cultural Center, and I was employed by an American company. I loved my job, my paycheck, and the opportunity to get out of the house and be someone other than a wife and mother. I worked for ten years -- the best and most satisfying of my life in Egypt. I was the forerunner; after me several Egyptian friends also went to work. It was not the first time I started a new trend in our apartment building and neighborhood. (Passersby always notice what foreigners do and copy their manners and actions.) Insisting on hot water in the kitchen, screening the windows, and installing a tile separator at the front door to prevent flood water coming into the apartment were just a few of the things I did that others copied.

In 1988 I surprised my husband by asking to become an Egyptian citizen. Having a dual nationality was legal and gave me several advantages. Although it took many months of government office interrogations, I did receive the naturalization papers. Shortly thereafter, I also became a Muslim, doing all the paperwork myself with a friend. The last obstacle was the Ministry of the Interior. The officer had us wait for almost an hour before we were ushered into his office. While we stood before him, he questioned us extensively and finally asked who my references were. "Several people know me," I replied: "the dean of engineering at the university and the head of the department of architecture." He was not impressed. So I said, "Also the governor of Alexandria, the minister of higher education and the president of the Parliament." The officer paled, picked up the phone and spoke to the governor. "Yes," the governor replied, "Hamdi is in a meeting with me now." The phone was replaced in its cradle, the air conditioning was turned on, we were asked to sit down and lemonade miraculously appeared. He quietly asked when I would like to pick up the final papers.

Within a week a government envelope appeared near my husband's plate. He refused to open the envelope, thinking it had to do with taxes, and he didn't want it to disturb his lunch. However, when the meal was finished, he reluctantly slit open the envelope. Suddenly I saw his eyes widen, and he looked at me unbelievingly. I had converted to Islam without his help! He telephoned Tarek and told him the great news: "Your mother is a Muslim!" Today, I consider myself a Christian/Muslim, if such a term exists. I believe that God/Allah is common to all mankind and religions are different only in the rituals and ceremonies they have. I follow the principles of the Ten Commandments but recognize that Islamic Law governs my marriage, my rights and the inheritance rules of my country.

My Arabic has improved over the years, although I am still not as proficient as I should be. Nevertheless, I do all the shopping myself and feel I cope pretty well. Although my preference would be to live in America, it is not possible financially. In Egypt we can live more comfortably and enjoy the good weather. I have adjusted to the climate -- the winter cold lasts only ten weeks with no snow; the summer is hot and humid; generally uncomfortable but bearable. As a family we have traveled extensively in Egypt, visiting all the tourist sights and museums. Egypt has such a rich heritage, culture and history. It has been rewarding and enjoyable to live here.

My mother and my stepfather came to visit us in Egypt after our daughter was born. My mother was very concerned about me. She saw that life in Egypt at that time was not easy. Many years later my mother came again for a visit shortly before my birthday. I had a party with all my friends because they all wanted to meet her. After everyone left, my mother told me:" All your friends are delightful, but I did not understand their accents!" I realized that all of my friends here speak English with different accents. They come from Hungary, Great Britain, Finland, Austria, Switzerland and several regions of Germany. But we understand each other easily. My own accent has also changed; now I speak more slowly. As a matter of fact, my own mother did not recognize me one time when I called her in the United States. I had to introduce myself as her daughter before she would talk to me.

Our children graduated from high school and later the university. Nadia received her master's degree in dentistry and then participated in the German Academic Scholarship Program (DAAD). Before she went, she had to learn German; she studied three months in Alexandria and then three months in Germany. We were very proud that she had learned another language and was able to study in Germany. In Germany she did two years of research for her Ph.D. When she came back, she finished her thesis and presented it to get her degree at the University of Alexandria. My mother flew to Egypt for this occasion. Nadia is her only grandchild with a Ph.D., and we were all very proud of her. Soon thereafter she was made an assistant professor in her department. Later she found the love of her life and married Erich, an American. They now live in California and have a daughter. I visited them there after the baby was born.

Tarek studied economics and business administration and was employed in Dubai. He remained with this company and eventually became a regional manager. All seemed to be going well for him – until the company went bankrupt. He then became a banker and got a master's degree. Today he is married to a woman from Lebanon and has two children.

I have mentioned my children's accomplishments but have said nothing until now of my husband's career. I have been very proud of his achievements. He was appointed executive director of an extremely important project and fulfilled his responsibilities with persistence and diligence until its completion. Unfortunately, he did not receive the expected government recognition and he fell into a deep depression. I stood by his side and together we rose out of that dark valley. Our marriage today is strong; we both know we can depend upon one another. Retirement has given us time to reflect and to pursue the activities we had postponed until now. We expect to continue to enjoy life unless health problems limit our activities.

Because I elected to marry a foreigner and live abroad, I have changed in many ways. I have adopted some Egyptian mannerisms, but only to a point. My American viewpoint still exists and many aspects of my life are still Western. If I were to give advice to a young woman contemplating marrying an Egyptian or any man of a non-Western nationality, I would tell her this:

1. You should visit the country, not as a tourist, but remaining long enough to understand the habits, living conditions, and rules that will govern your life if you stay. Your partner must explain in depth the various social and religious taboos, as well as promise you he will accept any independent activities you wish to pursue.

2. If you get married in your home country and your husband has been in that country for several years, he will have adopted the mores of living there. However, when he returns to Egypt, he will return to his original mode of life and behavior and you must be prepared for a new personality, which you may or may not like. After a period of time, you may not recognize him as the man you married!

3. If you intend to work in Egypt, you must have a firm agreement that you may do that prior to your arrival in Egypt. This was a big issue for me but is not necessarily such a difficult decision today. Times have changed and many wives work outside the home. Also the cost of living has skyrocketed and that frequently makes it imperative for a wife to work outside the home.

4. You must fight daily for your way of life and your ways of doing things and raising the children. It is always a battle. You should adapt when possible, but also insist on celebrations that are meaningful to you. You should proceed in small ways until you have reached your goal. Don't demand or divorce. Big changes mean big problems. Life has many blessings.... you may receive blessings you never thought of and your original goals might not be worthwhile in the end.

5. You should have your own bank account separate from your husband's account. It must be your responsibility to know how to use the bank's services. Do not give power-of-attorney to your husband allowing him access to this personal financial account. It could be too tempting for him to empty the account for social reasons without your permission. However, after over 20 years, this is no longer a worry. Husband and wife will know each other well enough.

6. As a young wife, you will find friends in your husband's relatives and his friends' wives. You will also form a sisterhood with women of other foreign nationalities for advice, support and laughter. They will become your relatives. It is surprising how much we are all alike in our life's goals.

If you can follow this advice, you will lead a happy, fulfilling life with your family in Egypt, as I have done.

Chapter Seven
Jutta S. A Little Box with Scarabs

Jutta is quite different from most of the women I came to know in Alexandria. She had received her degree from a German university, and when she met her future husband, she was already an independent and successful pharmacist. Before she went to Egypt with her husband, she had thoroughly researched the living conditions there. Before making a final decision, she visited Egypt to learn more about the country and the people. Unlike other women, she did not leap into the unknown. She has been very happy here and has adapted very well. At the same time she managed to keep her independence; for example, she is a very good driver, which is not so easy here in Egypt. Her husband, who allows her more freedom than normally granted by Egyptian husbands, deserves some credit for this. Most men are very jealous here and do not like it at all when their wives move around unaccompanied and self-confidently in public. Jutta tells me her story very freely. Here it is:

When I first met my husband, I was 28 years old. I had completed my pharmaceutical studies and was working in Düsseldorf as a pharmacist. I was financially independent and lived in my own apartment. I had a large circle of friends and many hobbies. I was young, in good health and enjoyed my life. Among other things I was a member of the „Jingling Wind Rose", a singing and dance group of the „German Youth in Europe". That organization fostered performances of international dances and songs, especially those from the former German provinces: Pomerania, Eastern Prussia and Silesia. The group originated as a folk dancing group from the east. My parents came from Eastern Prussia, and I really enjoyed the folkloric dances and songs. We often traveled abroad to perform. We went to Denmark, France, Norway, Brazil, the United States and Japan. Through those trips I had many international contacts, which surely influenced me very much. I was very open-minded towards other people and cultures. I studied at the university in Münster, and I still remember that in the beginning I felt very lonely. I had been brought up in a little town in the Münsterland region. At that time my mother was still alive although my father had already passed away. I am the youngest of five siblings, but only one of my sisters lived nearby with her husband.

I met my husband in 1975 in the pharmacy. He just walked in as a customer. He was always friendly and courteous, and I liked him very much. Since he lived nearby, he often stopped in, and at some point we started to talk. He told me that he was an artist and was planning an exhibition in Gent (Belgium). He asked me whether I would be interested in a catalogue. I thought that might be quite interesting. By that time I already knew that he was Egyptian and I was curious about his paintings.

After that I did not hear from him for a longer period of time. But somewhere down the road he actually showed up and gave me his catalogue. Furthermore, he brought me something else. It was a pretty little box containing pieces of costume jewelry in the shape of scarabs. There were a chain, earrings and a ring. I liked it very much, but I was not sure whether or not I was allowed to accept a present like this. I decided to ask the manager, and he said it was okay.

The little box also contained his card with his phone number on it. I later called him to thank him for his gift. He obviously was very happy that I had called and rather quickly asked me whether we could meet. I said yes and we arranged to meet on one of the following days in a café. But I did not dare to go alone, so I asked a friend of mine to go with me. At first Farouk assumed that my friend was my fiancé. „What a shame! She is engaged", he thought. I learned that, of course, only much later.

Later, after he had realized that this was not the case, that indeed I was not engaged, we met often, and he told me a lot about Egypt. I learned that he was employed by the University of Alexandria and that he would return to Alexandria after he acquired his Ph.D. - no matter what. Since 1974 he had been working on his doctorate. Before that he had been a lecturer at the art academy. But when the art academy was merged with the university, all of a sudden all lecturers were required to get a doctorate. However, there was nowhere in Egypt where one could receive a doctorate in his field, so many of the lecturers were sent abroad with a scholarship to acquire their Ph.D.s. Farouk had several options -- he could have gone to the United States, for example. But he decided to go to Germany because the subject of his thesis was the works of Käthe Kollwitz, whose art he greatly admired. So he came to Düsseldorf, even though he did not know any German. His own artistic style, too, was influenced by expressionism; his graphics at that time were only in black and white. Shortly after we met, Farouk began to work in color (lithographs, silk-screen prints, etchings). Even at the time, I thought that this must have a special meaning. Had his world become more colorful through me?

My mother was still living in Coesfeld-Lette in the Münsterland region, where I had been brought up. She visited me in Düsseldorf on a regular basis, and of course I introduced Farouk to her. She liked him right away. I should mention that my family was Catholic and Farouk is Muslim. In spite of this my mother did not object to our relationship; for her the only thing that mattered was my happiness.

Then Farouk fell seriously ill. Originally he only needed gallbladder surgery, a purely routine operation. But after the operation he spent three months in the hospital, including four weeks in intensive care. As we learned later, his pancreas had been damaged during the operation. That was very dangerous, and in those days nothing could be done about it at all. The doctor told Farouk that he would probably die. But Farouk did not die; on the contrary, he got well again, although the damage made him diabetic, and this experience brought us even closer to each other. Now I knew for sure that we belonged together. Shortly thereafter, in 1977, we became engaged.

Farouk described Egypt and the living conditions there to me. It was very important to him that I get my own picture of the whole way of life first. He believed I ought to look at everything myself before making a final decision. So I began systematically to inform myself. I borrowed books about Egypt. I read everything that I could find about Islam. I went to lectures. Little by little I began to understand. At the end of my efforts, I came to the conclusion that one is born into a religion. The religion is in oneself and every religion has its good points. Although I would not give up my Catholic faith, I could very well imagine living with a Muslim.

The next thing I did was to begin to learn Arabic. In Düsseldorf I learned classical Arabic at the adult education center. But my husband (and later, other Egyptians) laughed at my classical Arabic. Fortunately, Düsseldorf offered a course in Egyptian Arabic, too. There for the first time I met other German women who were married to Egyptians. There was always plenty to talk about. I met some of these women again later in Alexandria.

Then, in January of 1977, Farouk and I traveled together to Alexandria. It was my first visit. I still remember that it was very cold, much colder than I had imagined. When I started packing, I thought of course that it would be very warm and therefore I would only need summer clothes. Farouk very patiently explained to me that in January it could be quite cool in Egypt, and I should take sweaters and boots, warm clothes and a coat with me. I was surprised and could not really believe it, but to please him I packed some warm clothes as well, just to make sure. Nevertheless, during this first visit I was almost always freezing. In fact, the apartments in Egypt did not have heat. Instead one sat in the living room dressed in a coat. None of these apartments had a coat closet -- why bother! You could not take anything off; it was simply too cold for that. It often felt warmer outside than inside the house, since at least one moved around outside.

Farouk's parents were no longer living, so I had even more time to get to know his other relatives and friends. Of course they were all very curious about me. Farouk had had many opportunities to get married, but he could never make up his mind. He had rejected all suggestions, and now he shows up here with a woman from Germany. Who was she, and why did Farouk want to marry her, of all people? Everybody wanted to get to know me and accordingly asked me lots of questions. Obviously everybody agreed with his choice, because they were always very nice and courteous to me.

After this extensive round of meeting people in Egypt, we returned to Germany and got engaged the very same year. Farouk kept working on his dissertation, and as long as he was on a scholarship, we were unable to get married anyway. Around this time my husband began to make some very good contacts at the Egyptian embassy in Bonn. Both the attaché for cultural affairs and the press attaché became his close friends. But even those connections did not help him with the regulations and the embassy's fear that Farouk would simply stay in Germany once he got married to a German woman. As long as Farouk worked on his dissertation while receiving a scholarship, we just had to postpone the wedding. But even the longest waiting period comes to an end, and after Farouk finished his dissertation in 1980, we finally could get married at the marriage bureau in Düsseldorf. We intended to move to Alexandria soon thereafter.

But first Farouk traveled alone to Egypt. I would have loved to go with him right away, but Farouk wanted to find a suitable apartment first. I found that very considerate of him, since the housing conditions in Egypt are quite different from the conditions in Germany, and he wanted me to have a nice apartment right from the beginning. But to find something appropriate turned out to be more difficult than he expected. So for several years we shuttled back and forth between our home countries. Farouk lived in Egypt where he was now an art professor at the university in Alexandria, and besides that he was painting, of course. I continued to live in Germany and work at the pharmacy in Düsseldorf. We spent our vacations together, mostly in Egypt, but Farouk always liked to come to Germany as well. During the time we spent in Alexandria, we looked at countless apartments, but Farouk always thought they were not good enough for me. I would have been happy a long time ago and would have accepted some inconveniences, but Farouk remained choosy and wanted to keep looking.

This went on for several years. In 1983, our son Tarek was born in Germany. Only four months later I was working again at a pharmacy in Duisburg, although with a reduced schedule: in the morning from nine until two o'clock in the afternoon, four days a week. I brought my son to a family in the morning and picked him up again in the afternoon. Everything went quite well; I felt very comfortable with this arrangement. But of course my greatest wish was to finally move to Egypt and be together with my husband.

In all likelihood our situation would not have changed for a long time, if a crazy coincidence had not come to our aid. Farouk had painted a portrait; President Sadat's. At a reception at the university, the portrait was ceremoniously presented to the president, who wanted to meet the artist in person, of course. He liked the portrait exceptionally well, and so Sadat spared no praise for Farouk. Then the president wanted to know if Farouk had a wish -- if the president could do something for him that would make him happy. At first Farouk could not think of anything. But one of the other people at the gathering said: „This gentleman has been looking for a nice apartment for years."

Now all at once all the stops were pulled out, and only two days later we had in fact a very nice apartment in Fleming, a district of Alexandria. It is the exact same apartment where we still live today.

Naturally the apartment had to be renovated, which took some time. But then, finally, everything was done and in 1988 I moved to Egypt with our son Tarek.

Initially everything was new and unfamiliar to me. Having to find my way in a foreign country was only part of it. For the first time in years, I did not go to work but was exclusively a mother and homemaker. This adjustment was not that easy for me. Soon I even received a job offer from a pharmaceutical company and seriously thought about trying to work here in Alexandria. But the work hours were not convenient for me, and on top of that the commute would have been very long. Besides I wanted to spend time with my son for a while. After all, for him Egypt was entirely new as well; he needed time to adjust, too. Soon Tarek began to go to an English pre-school, and later on he attended an English school.

Right from the beginning my husband's family accepted me wholeheartedly. Nobody tried to influence me to convert to Islam. It was more important to them that I adjusted to Alexandria and felt comfortable. They even told me about a church nearby, and would I like to go there sometime? Farouk, as well, let things be as they were: he, a Muslim, I, a Christian. In our family, religion was never a point of contention. Since my husband was Muslim, my son also became a Muslim. I myself am a Christian. We celebrate the high holidays and traditional festivals of both religions; for us this is very natural. Farouk tolerates my faith and I his, and he has never ever tried to convert me to Islam.

It is sad that I did not get a chance to meet my husband's parents; they had passed away before we got married. But we are in regular contact with Farouk's siblings.

I have kept my German citizenship to this day. Since my certification as a pharmacist depends on my citizenship, I quite logically did not like the idea of giving it up. Up to now here in Egypt I have never experienced any sort of disadvantage just because I am a German national. My resident visa has always been extended for another five years without a problem.

In 1990 we went to Vienna for four years, where my husband worked at the Egyptian embassy as the attaché for cultural affairs. He supported doctoral candidates at the University of Vienna and organized projects for cultural exchanges between the two countries. His work at the embassy included a whole array of social obligations; for me, too, as his wife. In Vienna Tarek went to an international school where English was the language of instruction so that the adjustment was easy for him. When President Mubarak came to Vienna in 1992, I was one of a group of women who showed Mrs. Mubarak Vienna.

That was quite interesting; one met very different people from those one would have met in the usual course of life. We had a lot of official visitors; ministers of state, presidents of various Egyptian art academies, the director of the opera in Cairo, and musicians and movie actors, too.

All in all we liked Vienna very much; those were wonderful years. Directly below our apartment was a pharmacy. I was interested in it, of course, and soon an opportunity arose to talk to the owners. I have always been interested in new developments in my field; new methods and new drugs. But during that time in Vienna I did not work at all; I was fully occupied with all the social obligations. In spite of that we quickly grew very fond of the owners of the pharmacy, and we are still friends today.

During those four years I always worked in the summer as a substitute in „my" pharmacy in Duisburg. My boss was glad to have such reliable help at hand, and I still knew the ropes from my time there before Egypt. That way I kept myself sort of up-to-date, and moreover, I had some money of my own at my disposal. To this day I find it difficult to spend my husband's money. Somehow I always had certain inhibitions about that. I always asked Farouk for permission before I bought something for myself. Even though he had complete confidence in me and always told me that this was not necessary and I should buy anything I considered appropriate, it was a real effort for me to do so.

In 1994 we returned to Alexandria and shortly thereafter I got an offer to teach chemistry and biology at the German school. Although I had never imagined becoming a teacher before, I accepted the offer. Thank goodness, because I still work there today and really enjoy my work.

Only girls attend the German School of the Borromeoan Sisters (a Catholic order); boys are a rare exception and find themselves very lonely. Most of the children are Egyptian and only a few are German. Unfortunately, as a result, the children speak very little German. In the past it was probably different, but today the children speak a lot of Arabic among themselves.

In my classes I speak only German. I make an effort to speak in simple sentences as much as possible and to design my teaching materials accordingly. Today I create most of my materials on the computer, but of course in the beginning I had to work with a typewriter. That was rather tedious, especially since I never had any office training and can type only passably. I enjoy it much more on the computer where I can change everything very quickly and have access to all the previous information at any time.

I never worked in a pharmacy in Egypt. For one thing, the language would probably have been an obstacle. A pharmacist often has to give very detailed advice to the customers, who sometimes do not know themselves what they are actually looking for, and then the conversation with the pharmacist is all the more important. Even today my Arabic is not good enough for this kind of consultation. Besides that, the pharmacies in Egypt function quite differently from those in Germany. In 1977, when I first came here, the choice of drugs was very limited. Today almost all drugs are available under license and practically everything can be purchased without a prescription. Although that practice is actually illegal, here nobody abides by the rules.

Financially we were well off; we always had everything we needed. Farouk earned enough money to make a comfortable lifestyle possible for us, although the lion's share of our earnings came from the sale of his paintings and not from his salary as a professor. Even at the university the salaries are so low that for many it is not enough to make ends meet. However, Farouk had become very well known very early due to lucky contacts; his artwork sold well. So the image of the „starving artist" did not apply to us at all in Egypt. On the contrary, without his art we would have been more or less penniless.

Farouk still works as a professor of graphics at the University of Alexandria. Since in addition to that he is trained in classical painting, he has over the years painted a whole series of portraits. First he painted a portrait of my mother, whom he liked very much. Then Farouk made several portraits of President Sadat, whom he also admired. He also immortalized Mrs. Sadat and the former Egyptian ambassadress in Bonn, as well as several Egyptian ministers. After the Sadat years, his portraits were given away through the Egyptian embassy, and it would certainly be interesting to know where all the walls are that his portraits now decorate. He painted Walter Scheel, Mildred Scheel, and Helmut and Loki Schmidt of Germany. He received very nice thank-you notes from many of them, which he saved, of course. He has letters from Ronald Reagan, Franz-Josef Strauss and Kurt Waldheim, to name just a few.

Farouk paints landscapes and portraits in oil. He himself considers it to be a craft actually, not an art. When he fell so ill in Germany, he looked at his own blood cells under the microscope. The bizarre shapes fascinated him and inspired him in his landscape paintings. Over the years he developed his very own style, which became more and more abstract. Today, this kind of painting is what he calls his art, in which he becomes fully absorbed. He has shown his paintings at many exhibitions both in Egypt and internationally, and today he and his works are quite well known.

Our son finished school, studied business administration in Alexandria and now works for a company in Alexandria. He considers himself more Egyptian than German, and most of his friends are Egyptians. He speaks Arabic, English and German equally well. From his time in Vienna, he still has a few friends there with whom he corresponds mostly in English.

As far as food is concerned, I manage very well. Farouk often does the daily shopping, although he prefers to leave the cooking to me. Mostly I prepare German dishes. Although I like to eat Egyptian cuisine, I do not make it myself; others are better at it anyway. Many Egyptian dishes are very time-consuming to prepare, and I often lack the patience. Since I am still working today, I do not have that much time to cook, although I actually like to cooking and baking very much.

We have many Egyptian friends, and I can converse

now in Arabic with many of them, although most of them speak English, too. I have a very dear friend called Nadia. My husband knew her and her husband before we met. Even before I arrived with Tarek in Alexandria, they consulted together on how best to support me in the beginning. Often it is the very simple things that help you most in adjusting to a foreign culture. Nadia showed me all the stores; she helped me to bargain with the tradesmen. She helped me find a cleaning lady and translated at first for me. In general, she helped me when I did not know what to do; when in doubt she always took me to the right person or place. In the beginning I could not communicate with people at all, and here so much is entirely different from Germany. Since then my Arabic has improved, and I get along very well.

Only much later did I meet the German women from the Goethe Institute. Since 1991 this group has met once a month to exchange experiences and to support each other. The group is still active, and in 1996 I was elected its president. Besides the monthly meetings, we go on trips and work on social projects. Every year we organize a large Christmas bazaar and that income is funneled into social projects as well. To this day there is a lot of poverty in Egypt and the government does very little to help. Sometimes it is very difficult for us to get the money to the really needy people. Normally we help with donations of food and clothes; that means we buy specific things that are needed at the moment. There is a simple reason for that: it is the only way to guarantee that the money actually benefits the people in need. When you donate cash, it can be spent on something entirely different because so many things are lacking. Again and again one hears that cash donations trickle away somewhere or simply disappear. We monitor our donations as best we can.

In recent years, Egyptian society has undergone tremendous changes, not necessarily for the better. People are less helpful. Everyone cares only for himself. The nouveau riche do not feel responsible for their workers anymore. In the past, for instance, the companies paid employees' medical bills; today almost everybody has to pay for himself. For most people, making a living is very difficult; the wages are too low. A fortunate few can afford more and more luxuries, while most people have less and less. Selfishness is on the rise. Everybody does what he wants. This is noticeable especially when driving: traffic lights are blithely ignored and traffic regulations violated, most of the time by very young people.

What do I particularly like in Egypt? For one thing, of course, there is the weather. The sun shines almost all the time; I am still glad of that every morning. In the winter there are sometimes severe storms in Alexandria, but normally soon afterwards the weather is beautiful again. There are no endless gray days like in Germany in November. That really contributes to a good mood. And the people here are very friendly. They visit each other just for the fun of it. They come by without notice to chat a little bit and drink some coffee or tea. It does not have to be long, but this way people stay in touch.

Today I travel only infrequently to Germany. In the past we visited Germany almost every year, but as time went by the visits became fewer and fewer. As you get older, you become lazier, too, and traveling gets to be more of a burden. We prefer to enjoy our home here. We used to travel a lot. We went to Luxor and of course visited the temples. We also had the opportunity to see an open-air performance of Verdi's Aida held among the temples of Luxor. That was a unique experience, and I was very impressed. We also traveled to Aswan and of course we often drive to Cairo. It takes only two to three hours by car, and there you are. Some of our friends live in Cairo, so there are frequent opportunities to pay a visit.

When I first came to Egypt, twenty years ago, I thought if something happens or if I do not like it here, I will just go back to Germany. Today I think differently; my home is here in Alexandria. Here I have my family and my friends -- my whole life. Egypt is my new homeland.

Chapter Eight
Brigitte H. One Twin in Egypt (and one in Switzerland)

Brigitte was born in Switzerland. She is seventy years old and comes across as athletic and energetic. You have the feeling that she always knows exactly what she wants. Her Arabic is excellent, unlike most other women from foreign countries. She feels at home in Egypt; she has become very well integrated over the years. Maybe that has to do with her husband? I would very much like to find out. She tells her story:

In 1955 my twin sister Juliane and I took a vacation in Italy with a whole group of other young people. Bella Italia - that was for us, at 19, a dream of the big wide world come true. We lived in a student dormitory and loved our new-found freedom, far from parental supervision. We went sightseeing and swimming enjoyed the beautiful weather and life in general. I saw Mohammed for the first time at the swimming pool.

With his 31 years he was actually a little bit too old for me and I didn't think much about him at our first meeting. But he was charming and funny, and without my really noticing it very much, we met almost every day for the whole vacation. Two weeks later, just before I was supposed to go home, he told me that he wanted to marry me. I was really surprised and it seemed a little too fast for me. But deep inside me had already made up my mind.

Nevertheless, I went home to Switzerland first. I lived in Chiasso in the Italian-speaking part of Switzerland and was a secretary. Juliane lived there as well. Originally we came from the northern part of Switzerland, but we liked the South better. In the North it is often gray and foggy for days, especially in the autumn. I had always been drawn to the South and to its warmth so I applied for a position in Italian-speaking Switzerland and I got it. When we finished school, both my sister and I went to business school. We did not have much of a choice; my father thought that girls would get married and have children and therefore did not need higher education. At that time those views were widespread, and as our father was rather authoritarian we complied quietly and did not try to give him a song and dance.

At sixteen we had already become half orphans; our mother had died of an embolism. Our younger sister Sabine was just seven years old at the time. But my father did marry again later. On the one hand we were, of course, happy for him that he was no longer alone. On the other hand, Juliane and I did not get along especially well with our stepmother. At least we still had an aunt, our mother's sister. She soon became like a surrogate mother for us; with her we talked over everything - important or trivial.

Naturally after our Italian vacation I told everyone at home about Mohammed, but at first no one really took it seriously. What kind of future could a vacation flirtation have? But Mohammed and I were not swayed by that and we wrote to each other regularly. Soon it was clear for both of us: we wanted to get married. The letters became more frequent. My father was against this marriage at first. He thought it was nonsense; a young girl's mood that with time would pass on its own. Many years later I found out that my father had gathered information through the Swiss Embassy on this young man whom his daughter was now certain she wanted to marry. Apparently the information was positive because at some point my father gave in and agreed to our marriage. Finally it seemed that nothing more stood in the way of our happiness.

Unfortunately, the Suez crisis developed just then, in 1956 in Egypt. The newspapers described Egypt as a powder keg. We had to postpone our plans whether we liked it or not.

Mohammed had studied chemistry in Egypt and had already completed his doctorate. Like me, he had only been on vacation in Italy. To be closer to me, he began trying to come to Germany, and finally succeeded. He got a research position at the universities of Heidelberg and Karlsruhe. In 1957 he came to Germany and I left Switzerland for Heidelberg to meet him there. Of course our meetings were rather short; the morals then were still rather strict, but we were glad that we could see each other at all.

In September of 1957 we got engaged. We celebrated our engagement at my father's house in my hometown in Switzerland. We wanted to get married in Italian-speaking Switzerland the following March. I had already gathered all my papers in Italian. We asked at the Egyptian Embassy which papers Mohammed would need. We were told that he could get everything in Frankfurt because he was registered in Germany. We took great pains and conscientiously followed all the instructions step by step. We wanted to make sure we did everything right for the Egyptian officials. Finally the time had come and we could set out for the marriage bureau in Heidelberg. We had no guests; we were all alone except for two strangers as witnesses. Even my father had no idea. I waited until it was all over to call him and surprise him with the news. Maybe I was not so sure after all how he would react! But then we traveled together to Switzerland and made up for it with a wedding celebration with all our friends and relatives.

Although I was married now, I hardly had any money of my own. My father helped me buy a gas stove, a household hot water tank, and several other things. I relied entirely on Mohammed to know what we would need in Egypt and to let me know. I had no clear idea of what Egypt was like. I think what attracted me at the time was mainly the prospect of living in a foreign country in the South. Egypt seemed to me to be a huge adventure on the horizon. Besides, we were both very much in love and in that state one does not analyze things so much anyway. Of course we did not have enough money for a car. But that seemed normal to me; after all I rode my bike everywhere in Switzerland, too.

We packed everything up and made our journey to Egypt in the summer of 1958. We went by train to Venice and from there by ship to Alexandria. I know that it was an Italian ship, but otherwise I have no particular memories of the passage. We must have been very much in love…

On the other hand I still remember the port of Alexandria very well: it was the middle of July and terribly hot. It seemed to me that a huge crowd of people waited for the ship, and all of them looked so different! In comparison to the Egyptians, I suddenly felt very European. All around us was turmoil; I was completely overwhelmed. Everything was foreign and strange; I suffered a real culture shock.

Luckily, some of Mohammed's brothers had come to pick us up, and so I felt a little bit less lost. First of all we went to Mohammed's mother's house (near Cleopatra, a section of Alexandria) and she greeted us very affectionately. From the first moment I found her likeable and we immediately got along very well, although we of course had a problem with the language. Ever since I had known Mohammed, I had tried to learn a little Arabic and now I made a great effort to master at least the simplest idioms. Mohammed's mother was a very loving woman and in later years we remained close. Family is very important to most people in Egypt, and many families are very large besides. At that time eight or nine siblings were not uncommon. Mohammed himself had a total of seven siblings, all brothers. He was the second youngest.

Shortly after our arrival in Egypt, I sat myself down and wrote to my father. Mohammed observed this and requested that I not send this first letter; it would be better to wait a bit. Although he had not read it, he assumed quite correctly that there was much that I had not yet digested, and the letter could contain a lot of negative opinions. He was really right about that. As a matter of fact, I never sent that letter but instead wrote a second letter later, after I had become somewhat more settled in. Telephoning was still very difficult in Egypt at that time; most people did not even have a telephone. Only much later, in the mid-80s, did most of the households in Egypt get telephone access, and today most people at least have a cell phone. In general it was much more difficult then than today to keep in touch with the homeland. But Juliane and I always wrote to each other regularly.

My father-in-law did not live with Mohammed's mother, by the way. He had married a second wife and from the second marriage there was a whole team of half siblings. My mother-in-law suffered greatly from this separation but could do little about it. They were not divorced because in Egypt to this day a man can legally marry up to four women. My father-in-law was a lawyer. Of course he took care of his first family financially, but nevertheless there was always a shortage of money with so many people. My husband had a good relationship with all of his siblings and with his half siblings, too.

My mother-in-law always had a maid for the household. Usually they were very young things, little girls younger than twelve years old. Only later did I understand why. There were only sons in the family and two of them still lived at home. With adult women there could easily have been problems with so many teenage boys. In any case, as soon as the maids reached puberty, they were always sent away.

All of Mohammed's brothers but two had already married. And of course I was the only foreigner in the family.

But soon we were able to move to our first apartment together in Ibrahimia. True, at first we had very little furniture, but in spite of that we felt very comfortable there.

Mohammed worked at the university; later he became a professor. After I had halfway settled in, I began to grow tired of a housewife's existence. Mohammed thought I should work again, too. We could certainly use the money; even a university professor earned very little. Coincidentally I heard of an opening at an international organization. I submitted my application and was invited to a job interview. In the end probably my language skills (English, French and German) got me the position. But of course I was supposed to be able to type and that was not my strength at all. At that time there were only mechanical typewriters; antiquated by today's standards. On top of that, they used an English keyboard, which I had to get used to as well.

Nevertheless I got the job and could have started right away. But I did not want to because we wanted to go to Cairo for a few days first. The director agreed, although the people in the personnel office grumbled. But we did not care; the main thing was that we could go.

In Cairo we stayed with one of my husband's brothers. For the first time I had the opportunity to see some of the diverse cultural treasures of Egypt. We toured the pyramids, the Egyptian Museum, some mosques and much more. I was overwhelmed by the rich cultural heritage of my new homeland. Over the years I have seen much more; my husband and I have traveled a lot, and we were often in Upper Egypt (the south), too.

When we returned from Cairo, working life began in earnest for me. During my first few weeks at the office, I had big problems with my school English. Although I could make myself halfway understood, I could hardly understand other people in the office, who came from different countries - England, the United States, and others. They all had different accents and they used expressions that I had never heard before. It was quite a while before I got used to it. And then, as I feared, I had difficulties with the typewriter. At first I could barely function; I had to make many carbon copies; there were no photocopiers then. It was very difficult to correct a mistake and I was anything but satisfied with my work.

Then, to my great relief, I was transferred to another department. Now I managed much better; I had to work more independently and did not have so much to type. I got along with my supervisor very well. She had others who were better at it do the work that required a lot of typing and gave me jobs that were more in line with my capabilities; for example, organizational tasks.

Mohammed was the „finance minister" at our house. I learned only gradually how to deal with Egyptian currency. But even then he managed the finances, and we never had any conflicts because of money. What belonged to him belonged to me and vice versa. In the beginning of course, we had little income, but somehow it was always enough, and we could live very well. I had quite a substantial salary, and that helped us a lot.

Then I became pregnant, and in September of 1959 our daughter Nadia was born. Mohammed and I agreed that I should keep working. My husband completely supported me in that wish, and at work they wanted very much to keep me, too. Two months after the birth I was back in the office again. My workday began at eight in the morning and ended at 2 in the afternoon. I nursed Nadia in the morning before work, during the day she got a bottle, and in the afternoon I could nurse her again. Of course I needed someone to help at home who could take care of our child. I had Saturdays and Sundays off and Friday was Mohammed's only day off. But he had more flexibility in arranging when he would work at the university. So he moved all of his lectures to Saturday and Sunday so that our child could be together with at least one of us as much as possible. It actually worked very well. When Nadia was a year old, Mohammed took her to his mother in the morning, and I picked her up again in the afternoon. That arrangement was good for all of us, and my mother-in-law was delighted that she could see her granddaughter on a regular basis. So the question of who would take care of the baby was solved for the time being. In her third year Nadia unfortunately developed asthma. The attacks were often very severe, and we went to different doctors with her. She had to endure all sorts of examinations, but in spite of all that, they never determined whether the cause of the asthma was dampness, dust or something else. We had her tonsils taken out, and after that her condition improved somewhat. Eating was another constant problem with Nadia. Our child ate very little; feeding usually lasted for hours and often I fell asleep at it. This phase was not easy for any of us.

Although I was very happy in Egypt, I became homesick for Switzerland anyway. In Nasser's era Egyptians were hardly allowed to leave the country. The government feared a real exodus of qualified people, a brain drain, and so it was practically impossible for Egyptians to get a travel visa. That meant Mohammed could not leave, but that restriction did not apply to me with my Swiss passport. I put in for vacation time and traveled alone with my daughter to Switzerland for one and a half months. We went by ship to Venice and from there we continued by train. Nadia was three years old at the time and quickly felt very comfortable in her „other homeland". In fact, she soon felt so much at home that she adopted the Swiss German dialect (schwyzerdütsch). Very much to the horror of my mother-in-law, who upon our return realized with amazement that she could hardly communicate with Nadia anymore. But with children something like that passes quickly, and it did not take long until she was speaking Arabic again.

We moved into a new apartment in Saba Pasha. At that time a new domestic, Aziza, came to us. We did not know it then, but she was to become an important part of the family and stayed almost thirty years. She took care of our daughter, did the housework and shopping, and even cooked. She did not live with us; instead she came in the morning and left in the evening. Nadia was very attached to her. She was like a second mother to her, and Mohammed and I liked her very much, too.

In addition to my work, I knitted and sewed a lot because in Egypt there was still very little to buy. My sister sent me packages from Switzerland regularly, and when we were there, we brought back whole suitcases full of new things.

First Nadia went to a French nursery school and then to an English convent school. The German school was too far away and besides Mohammed thought that an English education would be better for her. English was and is to this day the most important foreign language in Egypt. At home I always spoke German (to be exact Swiss German, schwyzerdütsch) with Nadia, and so she learned that very easily as well.

Because I got very little vacation, we needed someone good to look after Nadia during school vacations, too. When she was little, Aziza took care of her. Later on I sometimes sent her to Juliane in Switzerland. Through all the years we were always actively in touch—though it was not always easy. Today with the telephone, instant messaging and email there are so many different communication possibilities and everything is affordable. But in those days we had to resort to good old letter-writing and only little by little did it become easier. Juliane and I get along very well to this day despite our long separation. Perhaps a special connection exists between us because we are twins. Sometimes I am thinking of her and in that exact moment she sends me a message. Although we have been separated for so long and lead entirely different lives, the same closeness we felt as children is still always there. A few times Juliane visited us in Egypt together with her husband. In 2006 the four of us celebrated our 70th birthday in Upper Egypt.

I did not really get to know my younger sister, Sabine, until later. The age difference was simply too great: she is nine years younger than I am. When I left for Egypt, she was just eleven. Only during my later visits to Switzerland could we really get to know each other, and in the meantime she has become a really good friend.

In the sixties it looked as if everything would change for us. Mohammed was supposed to get a grant to spend a year in Hungary. I put in for vacation time, and we were already planning our departure, but then nothing came of it. At the last minute the plans fell apart and we stayed in Egypt.

Later Mohammed got a position at a company in addition to his work at the university and I was able to get a better job with the same employer as well. Although in Switzerland I had only gone to business school and did not have a college education, I was assigned to a demanding position with quite a bit of responsibility. Occasionally I could travel outside the country and attend conferences or conventions. My husband always encouraged me to undertake whatever would advance my career. Without his support I certainly would not have managed it. I always really enjoyed my work and I received a lot of recognition and support from all sides.

In order to better myself professionally, I began to

study Arabic intensively. I signed up for evening classes in Classical Arabic and studied diligently. Classical Arabic is really very difficult. But I was always very curious and wanted to know everything exactly. Today at least I can read letters well enough to understand what they are about, although other colleagues took care of Arabic correspondence. In my specific domain I needed only English and French.

In 1962 the first television sets became available in Egypt. We, too, were excited about this new form of entertainment and proudly purchased a little black and white TV set. Nevertheless we noticed the 1967 war only marginally (please see Egyptian history in the Appendix); we were much too busy with our own lives.

Despite the shortfall in supplies because of the war, I myself did not have any problems getting provisions. I never went shopping anyway; our Aziza or my husband did that. In that respect I was privileged: I had my work and my family and did not have to contend with all of life's daily problems the way other women did.

In 1973, Mohammed received a job offer from Libya. As it was well-paid, unlike his position in Egypt, he accepted and stayed there a total of two years. Nadia, 14 at the time, and I, spent a total of eight months there. It was the first time that we could all be together as a family on Fridays. After some time I began to work there as well, as a secretary. During our time there we were able to save so much money that upon our return I could buy myself a car. It came from Germany and was held in Trieste for three months until it could finally be shipped to Egypt. We already had a car in Egypt, but Mohammed usually drove it. I have very positive memories of our time in Libya. One could buy so much more there: clothes, electric appliances, imported goods—they had everything. Nadia went to an Arabic school in Libya; that was, of course, difficult at first. But she met this challenge very well.

In 1974 I became pregnant again. We had wanted a second child for a long time. The doctor thought I was a little too old at 38, but in spite of his opinion I was looking forward to a new baby. Unfortunately I had a miscarriage and we were very sad for a time. However in the end my positive approach to life won out and I was glad that I could continue to work.

In 1996 I retired, although they soon called me back and I worked for another five months.

I got in touch with other women from foreign countries very late in life. My work schedule left me little time for casual get-togethers. Besides, many foreigners spoke very negatively and critically about Egypt. I thought that would only put a strain on me, so I avoided contact with them. It has always been important to me above all to see the positive side of things. Now that I am not working, however, I enjoy contact with other Swiss women, Germans and women of other nationalities at the International Club. I have been a member of GWA (German Women of Alexandria) and the Swiss Club for a few years now.

Mohammed finally and definitively retired in 2006. Of course he is still drawn to the university sometimes, and especially around exam time his expertise is always in demand. For his entire professional career he was a professor and a good teacher. He is very good at explaining things and his enthusiasm carried over to his students.

Since I took my first baby steps in the Arabic language, I have made great progress over the years. I still remember exactly my first success: it was an advertisement poster for Coca Cola - naturally in Arabic writing. By then I no longer had any difficulties with street signs and names. Today I can watch Arabic films on television without a problem. In the beginning I learned many new words through television.

But it is still very difficult to read words I do not yet know. In Arabic the vowels are not written out; one has to figure out where they should go. If one has never heard the word spoken, one has to guess more or less how it would sound.

In 1969 we built a house in Agamy. It is a bit outside Alexandria by the sea. There are many beautiful villas in this area, but most of them are occupied only in the summer. Mohammed designed the house himself and built it—it has everything we need, even a swimming pool. We spend a lot of time there in the summer, and I enjoy swimming in the pool every day. Swimming in the sea is rather dangerous because of the strong currents. Once my sister almost drowned and since then we have become very careful and prefer to swim in the pool.

We used to go swimming sometimes at a public beach in Stanley. Unfortunately the customs have changed. Today women can no longer go swimming unselfconsciously in a bathing suit. It used to be very different. In the 60s many women wore bathing suits; it was perfectly normal.

Our daughter studied architecture but she works in a bank today. More than twenty years ago she married a colleague whom she had met at the university. Although to this day many marriages are arranged in Egypt, more and more young people are meeting without arrangements.

They have two sons, 22 and 18 years old, who are both currently living in Switzerland. The younger one is taking a German course and then wants to go to a university; the older one is studying electrical engineering. Both have Swiss passports.

My husband is Muslim. For some time now he has been praying regularly and going to the mosque. When one grows older, one sometimes changes one's perspective, and faith in God becomes more important. But Mohammed has never demanded that I wear a headscarf. He would not think of it. He is very tolerant.

I converted to Islam fairly quickly. When we got married, the Egyptian Embassy in Frankfurt had recommended this step to me. Otherwise a wife has no rights regarding the children and is not entitled to receive an inheritance from her husband.

I only learned about praying much later from one of my grandchildren. He explained it to me and showed me. In all my years before I had never been religious. Through my time here in Egypt, I have become much more tolerant towards others. My daughter wears a headscarf, voluntarily. When she turned eighteen and broke it to me that from then on she wanted to wear a headscarf, I was not at all enthusiastic about it. But one has to sometimes simply break out of one's old habits and show tolerance. When Nadia then married and had children, she decided definitively to wear a headscarf. I had no choice other than to accept her decision. She has always been very independent and knows best what is right for her. I am just the same; I always think too that I know everything better.

However I do think that women who wear headscarves should behave accordingly. Today one sometimes sees young girls who are dressed very provocatively and act that way, too. But they are wearing headscarves anyway. The two things do not go together. Those people are displaying their faith superficially but not in their actions. A headscarf alone does not make a good Muslim woman, does it? Nevertheless today women with headscarves are definitely in the majority. In the past, everything was possible: miniskirts and western-style low-cut dresses. Today the young girls wear tight jeans and with them a headscarf. That does not always look very nice, in my opinion, but it is still more decent than before.

In any case, religion was never a point of contention for us. And as for nationality, I decided to have both: I have an Egyptian and a Swiss passport.

After more than thirty years in our household, our Aziza died twelve years ago. She was like a beloved family member for all of us, and we grieved greatly for her. It was hard to adjust to life without her; I was not used to cooking. Luckily Nadia had learned how to cook in the meantime and so she cooked for us too and Mohammed picked up our meals at her place. Sometimes she came to us, too, and brought us our meals. Of course, that was rather inconvenient for her. And then we wanted to move out of our apartment soon anyway. We did not have an elevator and we wanted a little more convenience. Together with our son-in-law we bought two apartments next to each other in the same apartment house. We let the young ones decide who would get what. Originally we had thought of two separate apartments, but our son-in-law rebuilt the two spaces so that they resulted in one large apartment. We have a common entrance and a big common kitchen with a common sitting room and dining room. Then Mohammed and I have our own living quarters with bedroom and bathroom. The younger family has their own area as well. This arrangement is really wonderful for us. Mohammed and I always have a lot of contact with the young ones and yet we can be by ourselves any time we want to. When our grandchildren were still living at home, we saw them every day. They did their homework with us and we could participate in their lives and see them grow up. We spent a lot of time with them, although the main responsibility lay with their parents. Now that they live in Switzerland, we naturally miss them very much.

My daughter and her husband work a lot, so we often see each other only in the morning in the kitchen, when someone is making breakfast. Every day our cook comes and prepares the main meals for all of us. I myself still cook only rarely and when I do, it is only to prepare a salad to accompany the meal. Mohammed takes care of the shopping as he always has, and we eat a lot of fresh fruit and vegetables. All in all we live together very harmoniously. When one gets older, one sometimes develops odd habits. Through our constant contact with others we are forced to be considerate and flexible. I think that is good for us. Of course, we have to consider that at some point one of us could be left alone. Then one really likes to have family around and to be able to take care of each other.

My twin sister Juliane lives in Switzerland to this day. She has a son. She is very well off financially, but I am not the least bit envious. I am very content with my life here, with my husband and with my surroundings in general. I like the sunshine; although in summer of course it gets very hot. But then we are often at our summer house in Agamy and we can enjoy the pool. Between seasons the weather is usually very pleasant. In the winter there are sometimes severe storms, but it never gets as cold as in

Switzerland. I still enjoy that and have never missed winter in Europe.

I can live well here on my pension and occasionally I can help my daughter financially, too. Life is expensive everywhere for a family.

Manners in Egypt are very different from those in Switzerland. I had to get accustomed to that at first. People are much less direct than in Europe. Basically one never gets to the point of any discussion right away; instead there must be general conversation for quite a while. „How are you, how are the children, is everything OK?" Only then does one come to the actual point of the conversation. To bring up the main subject right away is considered very impolite. Over the years I have learned how to do this. I do not become impatient so quickly; instead I just smile and put on a friendly face. Then everyone is very nice, especially when one can speak the language. Egyptians are more hospitable than Europeans and they really like to chat. That has been my experience anyway.

The environment outside the home, for example, the street or the sidewalk, is not so important to Egyptians. I had to get used to that, too. The apartments are all very clean, but once out of their door they no longer feel responsible. After one has been in the country for a time, one notices it less and it does not bother one any more.

My husband made life in Egypt very pleasant for me. Most of my wishes were indeed fulfilled. Perhaps it has to do with the fact that I have learned to shape my life according to my possibilities. I know that not all men are so considerate of their wives. That goes for Europe as well as for Egypt. But I was lucky and am very content here in Egypt.

Chapter Nine
Johanna O. In Spite of Everything!

Johanna was the first of the foreign women married to Egyptians I met in Alexandria. Through her, I first began to understand many things in Egypt. She has lived in Alexandria for a long time and knows Egyptian customs and traditions from her everyday experiences. In spite of that, she has always remained a German at heart, making it easy for me to talk to her about anything. She is equally familiar with Egyptian and German culture. Her life was not always easy, but she knew how to make the best of any circumstance – in Egypt as well as in Germany or in Switzerland. Johanna is petite, but she comes across as strong and energetic, despite her 72 years. Here is her story:

My story begins in 1960 in Zurich. I was 25 years old and had been living in beautiful Switzerland for a year. One Sunday in late summer, after a walk by Lake Zurich, some friends and I stopped in at a café where young people gathered. Two Egyptians and some Swiss men were sitting at one of the tables; one of them was a journalist. Soon we were all casually sitting together. I had recently read a book about Egyptian culture in the time of the Pharaohs and was now incredibly interested in what modern Egypt was like. How did the people live, what kind of place did religion have in the society? The young Egyptian men proudly told us of their liberation from colonialism and their hope that now progress would come to them, too. The discussion was very lively. We asked countless questions and of course came to no conclusions. Kamal, one of the Egyptians, was interested in me and wanted to see me again.

Three weeks later, we met for our first rendezvous on the Limmat Bridge by the lake. The weather by then had turned autumnal. He wore a long coat and a hat he had pulled down at an angle over his face. He looked funny somehow, but I liked him anyway. He was very happy to see me and we went to a café. While we were talking, I noticed his fine hands and his beautiful eyes that looked at me so honestly and openly and studied my face. Again and again, he smiled in a mischievous way.

Kamal had grown up in Tanta, in the Nile Delta. He had four siblings: an older sister, an older brother and two younger brothers. His father had studied Islam at the Azhar University in Cairo and worked as principal of a college preparatory school in Tanta and later in Alexandria. Kamal and his brothers all studied at the university in Alexandria. Kamal studied chemistry and because of his academic achievements had received a scholarship to study in Vienna. He liked it there very much; he made some nice friends and was soon able to report successes in his research. Although he had been expected to return to Egypt after two years, he wanted to learn more. He applied for a place as a doctoral student at the E.T.H. Zürich (Swiss Federal Institute of Technology, Zurich) and was accepted - a huge challenge for him. That is how he came to Zurich.

I was born in 1934 in a small town in Westphalia. The first five years of my life, I was the only child of my parents in a sheltered and loving environment. Then the war broke out. My 32-year-old father was immediately drafted into the army. The new house my parents were building was still only a foundation. My brother was born, and when my sister was finally born, my father was already in Russia. At some point, my father's mother moved in with us. I started school. In the beginning the war seemed far away; we children barely noticed it in our everyday lives. Later the low-flying fighter planes came almost daily and shot at the trains and later still even at the people on the streets. Schoolchildren began to have many war duties. We looked for leftover heads of grain in the harvested fields, acorns, beechnuts, berries, common horsetail, blackberry leaves and especially pieces of coal from the train tracks - anything that could be used for food or warmth. In our free time, we took hot coffee (eventually it was only water) to the soldiers passing through on the trains.

Every night we heard the heavy bomb squadrons flying over us. At some point -I was in school at the time - our city was hit, too. There was rubble everywhere; many, many houses were destroyed, some as if they had been razed. It was a terrible time. For a very long time I had to sleep in the cellar because of the air raids. Groceries were in short supply. Like everyone else, we had to forage for food. Little by little, we even traded my mother's wedding gifts for food. That time left a deep impression on me. When the Americans rolled in with their heavy tanks, I felt only relief. Finally no more being afraid!

The next thing that followed was the billeting. Like everyone else at the time, we had to take in refugees. Nevertheless, we were lucky: our house was still standing and we could even continue living in it. Other houses were simply seized by the occupying forces for their own lodgings.

My father survived the war and returned from captivity two years after the war ended. He had witnessed the invasion of the allies in France and was captured there and taken as a prisoner of war to the United States. However, he had survived and we were so happy! Sadly, the war had changed him; his carefree manner was irrevocably gone. He worked diligently and took very good care of our family, but the future seemed bleak to him. He was very strict with us children and rarely praised us. At the time we did not understand it, of course; we thought he did not love us.

I completed school after the 10th grade (a high school diploma without eligibility for university entrance) and then trained in retail sales. I would really have liked to apply to work at a publishing house. But I needed my father's consent because I was not yet of age. Although he loved books, he thought there was no money in that business and it was not suitable for earning a good living. Therefore, I complied and for the time being stayed where I was. After a short time as a sales associate and some courses in management, I was given a branch to run. I was very successful and made good money but had little free time.

I always found it easy to talk to men, but at 25, I still had not found the right marriage partner. At home, I felt more and more restricted. I found it increasingly difficult to bend to my father's will in everything. Besides, I really wanted to improve my language skills in English and French. At that time, it was not so easy to find a job outside the country and the only possibility was a position comparable to an au pair today. That is how I came to Zurich. There I had to give the lady of the house a helping hand and look after her ten-year-old daughter. In my free time, I could attend language courses. For the first time I was away from home and on my own.

I was eager to become familiar with Swiss cuisine, and the woman I worked for knew a lot about it. Her husband was, in fact, very fussy when it came to food. So she taught me everything I needed to know. Christine, the daughter, was a spoiled only child and could be very demanding, but often we got along very well anyway. I also had to look after the family dog, a German boxer, who had to be walked regularly in a nearby little forest. When the couple went out for the evening, I had to stay with Christine, of course. In the beginning, they really included me in their lives, and I felt very comfortable with that. However, when I began to spend some time with people my own age, they became a little distant. At some point they told me that before my arrival, they had envisioned a strong farm girl, and they were quite surprised when such a petite person arrived. They were looking for more of a real maid and were not pleased when I suddenly started to develop something like a life of my own.

I met my next employer through friends of the family. They really wanted to give me a position in their company in Zurich's city center, but my knowledge of French was not yet good enough. I could not get a work permit without the corresponding language skills. Therefore, they got me a job in a private clinic in Lausanne where I was supposed to help out in the office and in my free time learn French. I agreed to it and intended to carry out that plan, too – but then I met Kamal.

Kamal worked at the E.T.H. Zürich directly under a

well-known professor of inorganic and analytical chemistry. He positively threw himself into basic research and on the side, he had to read mountains of literature in his specialty. The only free time for carrying on a budding romance was at the weekends. Usually we met out to eat or met in a café. In good weather, we took day trips in the area, sometimes with a group of friends. I had already told Kamal about my plans to leave Zurich and he understood my situation. I was definitely going to leave. We got along very well, but we left it as a friendship without any commitments.

In the spring of 1961, I went by train to Lausanne. The clinic was impressive and the clientele international. It was exactly what I needed. In my free time, I took private lessons in French and made good progress. But I often thought of Kamal and missed him. I realized I had fallen in love. I thought that possibly he might feel the same way, too. Only - was it right to get involved with and commit to a person from such a different culture? Even within Europe there were so many differences. In Zurich Kamal and I had already had lively discussions about different ideas of morality, customs and traditions. Because of that alone there was a certain distance that remained between us. I argued with myself back and forth and after three weeks, I still had not heard anything from Kamal. I gradually began to wonder, out of sight, out of mind? Finally, I called his apartment. His roommate answered the phone and told me, to my shock, that after a serious accident in the laboratory, Kamal lay in the intensive care unit of the canton hospital. They did not yet know whether he would go blind or not. I did not stop to think; I knew he needed me now. I got the number of the hospital and reached him right away. As could be expected he was very down. During an experiment with explosive material, steam had built up and then exploded. I was very worried and went to Zurich the next morning. Kamal's eyes were completely bandaged, his face, chest and hands cut up from glass fragments. They had to remove them one at a time with tweezers. He was in great pain. They cautiously told us that one eye could not be saved and the other one was not yet out of danger. He, and especially his eyes, needed absolute quiet now. But I was allowed to stay with him the whole day and hold his hand. He was very depressed. I stayed with Kamal until he was allowed to leave the intensive care unit and was transferred to the first class ward of the eye clinic - then I returned to Lausanne.

I went to Zurich to be with Kamal every weekend. In between, I knew he was in the good hands of excellent nurses. Soon he was allowed to listen to quiet classical music, which helped him bear his life in darkness. Weeks later the bandages were removed, and we finally could be sure that his other eye had not been too badly damaged. True, he had to wear dark glasses for quite a while, but his courage and ability to face life returned and soon he was able to go home again.

I still had almost a whole year ahead of me in Lausanne. During that time, we each lived our separate lives and did what we had to do. I enjoyed the pleasant international atmosphere in the clinic, I was able to apply my language skills, and in my free time, I continued to study French vocabulary and grammar. After three months, Kamal was able to resume his research. Occasionally we met, but our relationship went no further for the time being. In Lausanne I met nice friends and the time just flew by. I kept my distance from men; in the back of my mind, I was still always thinking of Kamal. In the summer of 1962, I returned to Zurich as planned and began my new job in the company. For the first time I really stood on my own two feet and had to find an apartment and do my own shopping. I enjoyed the work; it was varied and I had contact with customers from all over the world. I got along well with my employers outside of work, too.

Soon Kamal and I were meeting practically every weekend: dinner, walks in the city, seeing the sights. Occasionally we went on trips into the mountains to hike, often for the whole day. We especially loved the snow - hiking up the Urtli Mountain with hot chestnuts in a bag or going to the Flums mountains to ski when Zurich disappeared in fog — usually finding bright sunshine there. One day up there was like two weeks vacation. I felt so thoroughly aired out when I tore down the slopes on my skis. But skiing was a bit too dangerous for Kamal; after all, he had no practice at it. He loved the snow, but his lack of experience got him into the funniest situations, and often we could hardly control our laughter. Really skiing was not the sport for him. Perhaps with vision in only one eye he could not see enough or had lost his depth perception.

After the accident, Kamal had moved into his own little apartment and I visited him there at the weekends. We cooked together and relaxed. Now we were really a couple with plans to marry. However, as long as he was studying, we could not get married - it would have caused problems with his scholarship.

My father was against our relationship for a long time and thought I would surely change my mind. He thought a marriage that crossed such sharp cultural lines could never work. It was not until 1963 that he met Kamal for the first time, at my mother's funeral. My mother died very unexpectedly in just five days from an intestinal obstruction. She would have liked to meet Kamal, but unfortunately it never happened. But this tragedy did bring the two men together. They had long talks and finally the ice was broken. Now my father knew that I was in good hands with Kamal and he became proud of his future son-in-law.

In 1964 Kamal completed his doctorate with the designation cum laude. While his dissertation was still at the printer's, he accepted a position as a consultant with a Swiss company. He brought good ideas with him and the company soon wanted to hire him permanently. It would have been nice for me, too, to stay in Switzerland. But there was the family... In Egypt the family plays a very big role; I would soon find out about that. Kamal had written his parents that he had met a German woman and we wanted to get married. Therefore, Kamal's younger brother came to visit us. The brother was probably supposed to evaluate me and maybe also talk Kamal into returning to Egypt. Apparently the brother found me entirely OK, because there were no complaints from the family.

Returning to Egypt was a difficult undertaking. We found the decision very hard; Kamal would have liked to stay in Switzerland, too. For Christmas, he even proudly dragged our first fir tree into the house, and we celebrated a little bit with an Egyptian friend who was a Copt. However we finally decided in favor of Egypt and began to plan our trip back. Kamal bought lots of appliances for our new apartment. He knew just the way he wanted it, but at that time in Egypt, you couldn't buy any of those things.

In the summer of 1965, we packed our car right up to the roof and headed for Venice. The mood was melancholy. This was not a carefree vacation trip to the Riviera as in the past. This was an abrupt change into harsh reality. With bag and baggage Kamal was loaded onto the ship "Syria". For the time being, he continued alone; I wanted to come for a first visit in September.

I left from Venice on the "Ascona". It was a relaxing and interesting trip through the Adriatic, full of beautiful impressions of the many Ionian Islands, a tour of the Acropolis and a short shore visit on Crete. Then one morning the flat coast of Egypt lay before us in the morning haze: Alexandria, the pearl of the Mediterranean. We docked and I realized immediately: this is an entirely different world! The dock was crowded with a throng of people, at times moving in a specific direction, then inexplicably in confusion again, almost like swarming ants. The air was full of screaming and shouting, incomprehensible fragments of sentences. Strange smells and sounds. They let down the suitcases on a rope from the ship's hull; below strange men dressed in wide robes picked them up. Where was my baggage? I had already found Kamal and his brother. "Don't worry; everything is OK!" From then on, I was a guest and had only to follow. They took care of everything for me! In fact, my suitcases were really there, so I just let it happen and took in all the new impressions.

Kamal had never painted a rosy picture of Egypt; instead he had clearly described the conditions there to me. He did not want to fool me. Once when we were watching a documentary about an Egyptian village, he told me he thought it looked better in the film than in reality. He even mentioned the cockroaches in Egypt. Now that I had arrived in Alexandria, I suddenly remembered that conversation and I actually had a nightmare the first night.

Kamal's parents and siblings were just charming to me and I felt welcome. I was even allowed to sleep in the same apartment as Kamal in the family's house. That was really unorthodox for a religious studies scholar from Al Azhar like Kamal's father. But our engagement was planned and was supposed to be celebrated soon. The apartment was furnished in more of a European than Eastern style, just more simply. Everything was very clean and my fear of bugs proved to be unfounded -- at least in this apartment. The family tried to fulfill my every wish; it was almost too much for me. Because Kamal knew how important swimming was to me, we went with his mother, his sister and her four little children to one of the clubs in Roushdy (a district of Alexandria). There were only a few people on the beach. It seemed quite natural that his sister and I went into the water in bathing suits. His mother wore an airy summer dress and put only her feet in the water; she visibly enjoyed it. The city itself seemed rundown and bleak; fresh paint, flowers, cleanliness were all missing. But people looked optimistically into the future, seemed content and did not appear to worry about money. I think Kamal himself did not yet know, at the time, how he could live on his salary. The others managed, didn't they? His three brothers had all gone to university and were successful. Nothing could go wrong, right? I knew Kamal well and had complete confidence in his assessment that we could live like Europeans. Lies were despicable to him. Besides, he had a permanent position at the university. We would manage together, of that I was sure, despite everything.

So I returned bravely to Switzerland to prepare for

the move. I gave notice, left my apartment in Zurich, and went to my father and his new companion, who had three grown daughters. They all lived in my parents' house. Now it was no longer my home. Because I was to be married in Egypt, I could bring in any goods duty free. It was financially advantageous to bring a car and then to sell it in Egypt. I had found a well maintained used Mercedes, and packed my wedding gifts and many German books into a heavy steamer trunk, when suddenly I was told there was a new law. In the future all cars would be charged a 200% customs duty; I would have to come immediately. I said my goodbyes to family and friends. This time I traveled through Venice with my brother. With all my baggage I felt safe with him there. So in September of 1966 I went on the same ship to Alexandria, full of suspense about whether or not I could bring the car in without the 200% duty. The journey proceeded normally, except for my worries about the car. When I arrived in Alexandria, I was still no wiser. Usually a law did not go into effect until six months after it was passed, but everyone was probably anxious about this one. I could not very well leave the car at the dock, so Kamal's father paid the high duty for the time being. The mood in the house reflected everyone's anxiety about the expense. I sensed it without understanding a word, and it gnawed away at me and left me no peace.

In October, we got married with just the family there; that was how we wanted it. We had both brought our wedding clothes with us from Zurich and were quite elegant and everyone was very happy. Then I had to go to the German consulate to report my new family status. I told them the unfortunate story about customs and they knew for sure now that the law could not yet be applied. I was hopeful again. Kamal filled out an application and applied a lot of pressure in the right places until finally after two years we got all the money back. We were deeply relieved. Of course, I had to open my trunk at customs, too, and many people were watching. They wanted to see all my riches. How disappointed they were when so many books came into view; all we heard was the word "books?" I thought that was pretty funny.

After the wedding, we moved to our 80 m2 (860 sq. ft) four-room apartment in a neighborhood with many Greeks, Lebanese and Armenians. Kamal was able to take over the apartment, along with the furniture, from a young man whose bride had run away. The couch and armchairs reminded me of the post war style of the 50s. Otherwise, the apartment in this old building had been well maintained and had high windows and balconies with French doors that had been brightly and perfectly painted. Kamal had thought of everything and so we had a view of a big garden. I liked the apartment and above all that we were by ourselves -- that was one of my conditions for getting married. When I lived with my mother, I had seen how difficult it is when the mother-in-law is constantly in the same apartment.

After only a few nice days in our new apartment, we had to set out for Asyut, where Kamal was to teach as an assistant professor. The university in Asyut had helped finance his scholarship in Zurich, but the condition was that he had to teach there for at least a year. Otherwise, he would have had to pay back the entire amount, which on his salary was completely impossible. The winter semester was beginning soon so we went by train through Cairo to the South, along the Nile the whole way. Approximately 50% of the people in Asyut are Copts, as the Egyptian Christians are called. They are not subject to the mandates of the Pope in Rome but instead have their own Pope, whom they call Baba. Although it was already the end of October, it was still very hot, and the wind blew sand from the nearby mountains. I had serious difficulties with my circulation, and felt constantly exhausted and half-dazed. As we would not stay long, we had furnished our apartment in Asyut only with the necessities: a bed with a mosquito net, a plastic mothproof garment bag for our clothes, a camping table and camping stools, a little butane gas stove with one burner and - very important - a broom and hand brush. You were constantly sweeping sand because the windows did not close tightly enough. Luckily, one of Kamal's college friends lived nearby with his American wife. They were going to stay longer in Asyut and had therefore taken a more completely furnished apartment. Those two really helped us a lot to get through our time there. Later in the year, in December, January and February, the weather became more pleasant. To get out of the house a bit and to stretch our legs, Kamal and I went walking through the fields. Soon we noticed that the other people were looking at us in a strange way and were watching us. Going for walks is not exactly common in Egypt; people just don't do it much. But there was a little club at the university and the Baladi Club where we could spend time together informally. We met some Egyptian couples, too. We went on day-trips together to the nearby desert, or had a barbecue or picnicked among the hills. Once one of Kamal's colleagues invited us to his family's fields. They had built a large canopy for shade with tables and benches under it, and they served us exquisite regional dishes in earthenware vessels. Although women were a part of our group, the local women did not sit with us at the table; that was not customary there. However, after the meal we women did go to them to thank them in our limited Arabic. We were amazed at the simple shelters they lived in during the summertime and began slowly to understand what Egyptian hospitality means.

When the Six Day War began in 1967, Kamal insisted that I go to Alexandria immediately. He was concerned for my safety. Could one know how the Egyptians would react to a foreign woman in wartime, when emotions ran high? Therefore, I lived with Kamal's parents until his return from Asyut. During that time, I became better acquainted with his sister, who spoke good French. At some point in one of our conversations, we touched on the topic of retirement arrangements in one's old age. But there I had stepped into a hornet's nest! In Egypt, people simply do not talk about those things; money and everything that has to do with it is a big taboo. Kamal's sister relayed the whole story directly to Kamal's parents, and they were truly horrified. From then on they considered me money-hungry and on top of that, rude. At the time, I did not understand the problem at all. Not until years later was the misunderstanding cleared up by chance during a conversation with Kamal's brother. At the time, I only noticed the change in mood in the house. From that incident, I quickly learned to avoid all candid discussions. How I would have liked to be able to occasionally talk to another European woman who perhaps would have understood me. But contact with other Germans and women from other countries happened only much later.

Life in the time of Gamal Abdel Nasser's government was full of deprivation. Many things were not available at all; others were contaminated with dirt and stones and had to be sorted first, like rice and lentils.

In the summer of 1967, Kamal returned from Asyut to Alexandria. In the meantime, I had found my way to the Goethe Institute, got in touch with them and after some preparation began to teach German there. The interaction and the work gave my life a new impulse. In1968 the position of executive secretary opened up and I did not have to think about it long. Even though as a local employee I was not paid very well, I enjoyed my work immensely and met many new people. Besides, because of the job I had my own money again.

In 1970, Kamal was offered a position at the University of Tripoli in Libya. Until then we had just about broken even financially and now finally he was offered an opportunity to earn more. I gave notice at my job at the Goethe Institute, looked for someone to replace me, and followed Kamal by plane. We had a pretty four-room apartment in a modern building there. I found a job, too, almost immediately, as secretary at an oil company. However, after only three months in Libya - I was still in the trial period at my job - I became pregnant. All those months in Egypt, it had not happened, but in Libya I apparently felt so good that my body was simply ready to give the gift of life to a child. Anyway we looked forward to our baby with delight. Even at my job they took my announcement with amazing composure. I was already 36 years old and a mother-to-be for the first time. In Alexandria, I had already gone through quite a few health problems, and the doctors there knew my medical history. Therefore, I flew to Alexandria for the delivery and lived with my parents-in-law again. My daughter came into the world by Caesarean section, but we were both fine and everything went well. As long as we were in the hospital, my little one was a really calm baby. But at home with the family, we both became increasingly nervous. Everyone wanted to put in his or her two cents, and I grew more and more uncertain. Would she get enough nourishment from me? If not, that would be a real problem because baby food for infants under three months was difficult to get. So I was more than glad when we found a suitable nanny who was willing to live with us in Libya. We got passports for the child and nanny and I could finally return to our own little world.

In Libya Jasmin, our little daughter, was soon a rather uncomplicated baby. My husband was so happy to have a little girl. Our „dada" (nanny) was very clean and treated Jasmin very lovingly. Before I began to work again, we discussed exactly who was responsible for which tasks, so there were no misunderstandings and everyone was happy. One of Kamal's friends and his American wife lived in Tripoli as well. They had a little boy the same age as Jasmin. As we did not have any family obligations, we could visit each other on the weekends or do things together and get to know the country and its people. Kamal and I made up our honeymoon in Tunisia. We went with friends to ancient places like Sabratha and Leptis Magna. We picnicked in the willow groves in the spring or went swimming.

In spring when the almond, apricot and citrus trees were in bloom, it was always especially beautiful on the coast between Tripoli and the Tunisian border. The gardens are very well cared for; separated by pine-lined avenues and cactus hedges. For irrigation, the Libyans use a spray system that is supposed to save water. The culture there differs greatly from that of Egypt: language, food, and clothing are entirely different. At that time, you saw local women in public wrapped only in big natural-colored cloths and completely veiled except for just one eye. In their homes, however, I found the women to be very self-confident. Luckily, this strict dress code did not apply to me as a foreigner. The men dressed either in the European or in the traditional style, similar to the Tunisians, with trousers, a black bolero, a big sheep's -wool cloth and a round fez.

Once I had the opportunity, through my company, to fly over the desert in a Fokker 27. The vastness of that sea of sand, before which everything else turns to nothing, greatly impressed me.

At the end of 1972, we moved from our apartment to a villa with a small garden. Now we had more room and in the garden grew wonderful grapes, apricots and blackberries (real blackberries!). In the summer, we could picnic on the grass under the shade of one of the big trees. When Jasmin was one and a half, I became pregnant again. Like the first time the pregnancy proceeded without a problem, but this time I wanted to have the baby in Tripoli so that I could be with my family again as soon as possible.

In the spring of 1974 - it was a very hot day - my son came into the world. From the very first day, Karim was entirely different from Jasmin. My daughter was a serious, quiet child with big dark eyes. Karim practically came into the world grinning. He was active early: at eight months he was holding on to the furniture and walking along the walls; nothing and no one was safe from him. When he woke up early in the morning, we heard him calling right away, „Chico, Chico!" That was our dog and Karim would have liked best to rush into the garden still in his pajamas to play with him. There was naturally more to do with two children, but we did have help and everything worked out really well. Once a year we flew to Europe to visit my family and friends and almost always, we were able to spend a few days in Austria in the mountains. We always fondly remembered those restful days later during more stressful times.

In the summer of 1975, our time in Libya came to an end. In the meantime, the relations between Libya and Egypt had seriously worsened and direct flights to Egypt were cancelled. We had to either return by bus or fly via Paris to Egypt. Our Dada took on the strenuous 12-hour bus ride; we took the flight through Europe and visited my father, my brother and his family. Afterwards we went to Eastern Tyrol and visited my sister. I had the feeling that we would not see each other again for a long time. We would miss the green of Europe very much, especially the fresh, clean mountain air. However, Kamal wanted to be back in his homeland again. He firmly believed in a better future under the new President, Anwar El Sadat.

In fact, much had changed in Egypt during the five years we had spent abroad. The cityscape had grown more colorful. Many more goods were available than before because Sadat had succeeded in ending the country's political and economic isolation. All at once, people seemed to attach greater importance to nice clothes; they fulfilled many a long-cherished wish and began to renovate their apartments. At the same time, though, the prices rose drastically - without any corresponding rise in the salaries at the state institutions. It was true that there were more possibilities in the free market, but everything just needed time. The working conditions at the university had not improved - and the pay was still very paltry. More and more often Kamal came home from work completely frustrated and the mood in the house reflected that.

How we would have liked to live in a house with a garden again! But the prices were so high that we simply could not afford it, so we continued to live in our apartment; 860 square feet would have to be enough now for four people. I really wanted to work again at the Goethe Institute, but Kamal was against it, and actually it would have been too much for me. The children were four and one and a half, and although I had someone to help with cleaning and laundry, there was still enough left for me to do. Kamal was so busy with his work that he rarely found time to help me out. The extended family wanted to see us every Friday; we sat together a long time, ate together and exchanged news. To get out into the fresh air in this huge city was easier said than done. We did live near the sea, but to walk along the Corniche (the waterfront promenade) was practically impossible. Once I tried it out with the children and was harassed by men several times. "Well in that case, I guess not," I thought to myself and from then on stayed home.

Then at a reception at the Goethe Institute, I met some German women and we decided to stop sitting around doing nothing here. First of all, we women wanted to take private lessons in Arabic to make our everyday lives easier. Then a circle formed for the purpose of giving our children some early music education. I took on the teaching with a friend who had studied at a music college. I learned a great deal from her and finally had meaningful work again besides my household duties. In addition, the children needed German lessons because many of them attended international schools and had no instruction in their mother tongue. Through the German school, I made further contacts. I joined a book club and began to sing in a choir. Slowly I found more and more things in Alexandria that I enjoyed doing.

At that time there was not yet any German television anywhere in Egypt, only „Deutsche Welle" on the radio, and to hear it you needed a good shortwave receiver. Therefore, we had to rely on other sources of information. The German teachers were like a breath of fresh air for me, and to this day, I still maintain friendships with some of the families.

Unfortunately, we could not send our children to the German school. They would have taken Jasmin, but not Karim. The school was still strictly divided by gender although exceptions were already being made for the sons of teachers. But all our efforts amounted to nothing; they continued to accept only girls. However, we wanted both of the children to go to the same school. Therefore, we sent them to a private school with instruction in English. From nursery school on, they heard English exclusively. At home, I spoke German with the children, and Kamal and his family spoke Arabic with them. To this day, it amazes me, how both children accepted and learned all three languages effortlessly, as if it were the most natural thing in the world.

Pre-school, school, birthday party invitations, friends - all of that ran its course the way it probably does in every other family. Every year for Christmas Kamal brought home a Christmas tree, which we lovingly decorated. That he is an observant Muslim did not bother any of us, least of all him. The children ought to know all the religious customs and Kamal especially liked the tradition of the Christmas tree. Sometimes we even went to a service on Christmas Eve at one of the many churches in Alexandria.

In 1978, almost at the same time, my father died of his third heart attack and only a few weeks later Kamal's father died, too. He was a loving father-in-law to me, always tolerant. He always tried hard to understand me.

As I have mentioned, it was not so easy here in Alexandria to become physically active. A woman could neither go walking nor swim in the sea. So we were tremendously happy when we could become members of the local Sporting Club at the end of the 70s. That was by no means easy as one was accepted only though the recommendation of another member, and moreover it was rather expensive. But it was worth it. Here we could all relax and participate in sports. We were still expected to visit the family clan for lunch every Friday at the house of my parents-in-law. I often felt it was too much for me. We ate together and sat around for hours. There was not much to tell as we had just seen each other the week before.

In 1980, another opportunity arose for Kamal to work outside the country, at the university in Mecca in Saudi Arabia, where he would earn good money. Unfortunately, as Muslims, our children were not allowed to attend any of the international schools there. So we decided that I should stay with the children in Alexandria. I found this long separation from my husband very difficult; however, it was absolutely necessary for financial reasons if we wanted to continue to manage. Luckily I was able to stay in our apartment with Kamal s consent. That was not customary at all; normally I would have had to move with the children to my mother-in-law.

Kamal felt very comfortable at the university in Mecca; they appreciated his direct manner. During the summer vacation, we traveled there to stay with him, in spite of the indescribable heat there. Of course, my daughter and I had to adhere to the strict Saudi dress code. Hair and arms had to be covered, and trousers were not allowed either. In the afternoon, we often went to Jeddah where they are more lenient with foreigners. The climate in Jeddah was decidedly more humid than in Mecca, but we could easily escape into the big, air-conditioned department stores.

In 1983, the children and I were included in Kamal's plans to go on the Hajj, the pilgrimage. That came out of the blue for me; I did not consider myself anywhere near ready for it. It was true that I had already converted to Islam a long time ago, but more for practical reasons than religious ones. Otherwise as a woman in Egypt, I would not have had any rights: I could not have inherited and in the worst case scenario could not have had custody of my own children. Two Egyptian women friends helped me with preparations for the Hajj; otherwise I would have felt quite lost. First, we read together about the pilgrimage and slowly I began to understand what it was all about. First of all there were formal requirements. The Hajj had to be made at certain times of the year. If one goes earlier or later, it is called Umra (the lesser pilgrimage) and does not count as much. The exact point in time is determined by the lunar calendar, like Ramadan, so that in the course of time it moves through all the seasons.

Pilgrims must wear white clothes. Women wear a so-called Abeya, which is a long white garment. They are not allowed to wear any make-up or nail polish. Men must be covered in only two white cloths. They are not allowed to wear anything with seams, not even underwear. Women are allowed underwear and items with seams. I had my Abeya sewn, and of course, I wore a white scarf over my head. This clothing is basically the same as that in which one is buried. It symbolizes that during the pilgrimage all people are equal, just as they are after death.

Then everyone makes their way towards Arafat, a large valley among high mountains. We drove in a group with four buses. There is a mosque there and big open tents. Of course, everything is very basic: instead of flush toilets, there are only latrines. It is always full of people (over two million come together in Mecca during the time of the Hajj) in many different groups. The women are separated from the men, but the tents stand close to each other. We were in a big tent with many other women and children. It was scorching hot, almost unbearable. In spite of that, people prayed and meditated. When it got too bad, ice bags were available to cool our heads. During the entire Hajj, one must have only good thoughts; one is not allowed to argue or become angry. All the people try to direct their thoughts to God. Amazingly even the children cooperate with it all very well. The atmosphere among so many people impressed them very much and they stayed very quiet most of the time. At that time, my children were 12 and 9 years old.

Afterwards we were supposed to go by bus to Mena. But our buses did not come; instead of four buses, only one came. Our group was separated and the bus was completely overloaded. Nevertheless, everything went very peacefully because one is not allowed to have angry thoughts or to quarrel. Instead of fighting, everyone took the whole situation with good humor; everyone remained calm and no one complained. Even with our bus driver's more than adventurous maneuvers in turning around, no one got excited. Everyone trusted in Allah that nothing would happen to us. There was really a lot of traffic; so many people were traveling the same road as we were.

Because it was already growing dark, we stopped once again in Mustalifa to gather stones there. Later, in Mina, we would throw at least seven stones (or seven times seven) at a column to stone the devil symbolically.

We had to stay In Mina for three days, but in between, we were allowed to go home to our apartment. We could then drive by car up to one kilometer from the tunnels. You must go by foot through one of these tunnels;

otherwise you have not done it right. All in all there is a lot of walking involved in all these ritual actions.

Afterwards the men shave their heads or cut their hair; the women are supposed to cut off a strand of hair. A sheep is slaughtered and donated to the poor. Today a big meat industry organizes the whole thing -- processes the slaughtered animals into cuts of meat and sends them to the poor. The sacrifice of the sheep takes place on the same day in all Islamic countries on the big, traditional sacrificial festival.

At the end of the Hajj, one must circle the Ka'ba seven times; that is called Tawaf. Beforehand one performs the ritual washing just as one does before every prayer. The Ka'ba is a big building in the shape of a cube that is covered with a black cloth decorated with golden embellishments. In former times, the covering of the Ka'ba was always made with great ceremony in Cairo. Then the cloth was brought in a great caravan to Saudi Arabia as a gift from Egypt. During all these actions, no one speaks; everyone is concentrated entirely within himself or herself. The prayers and the whole sequence of events are exactly prescribed.

(Note: the Hajj is described here from Johanna's memory. It is possible that the details are not accurate. You can find a lot about the exact sequence of events on the Internet by doing a search on such terms as "Hajj rituals")

What I liked the most was that during the Hajj all people are equal; there are no differences and everyone tries to think only good thoughts. One feels part of a large community (the word "Omma", meaning community or congregation, is used). This sense of security in the community touched me greatly. One returns from the Hajj a changed person inside.

Our children are Muslims, too. However, I always taught them to beware of fanatics. My husband has never demanded that the children pray. My son started to pray only much later.

In the winter of 1984/85, we bought ourselves a new

apartment in one of the best districts of the city. But because of the extensive renovations, we could not move in until 1987. Alexandria has grown since my arrival in 1966 from 3 million to about 8 million inhabitants. More and more villas disappeared; Alexandria became more densely populated; the apartment buildings kept getting taller and the real estate prices rose accordingly.

Now that our children did not need me all the time anymore, I joined the International Women's Club in Alexandria, which meets once a week. Although at first glance it may seem surprising, many Egyptian women were members there, too. I wanted to develop contacts with Egyptian women outside my family and find out what possibilities Egyptian society offered them. I learned a lot from them and later in my day-to-day life; my contacts were often very useful. For some years, I was actively involved myself. In 1991, I started to form a German women's group that still exists today. It offers a haven for all women from the German speaking cultural circle. We exchange information and can learn a lot about the possibilities, customs and traditions of our host country. Our annual Christmas bazaar, which takes place in the Goethe Institute, is known citywide by now. We support Egyptian social organizations with donations of food and clothes.

In the summer of 1986, Kamal moved back to us in Alexandria again, and now we finally had enough money to finish our villa outside the city gates. Our building project demanded all of our free time. We had to supervise it carefully to make sure that everything was done the way we wanted. That was naturally very nerve-wracking, but in the end, it really was worth it. In the 70s, not a single house stood in the area, but today it is a green spot of land with many small and large villas with swimming pools. Kamal has been a professor for years now and in addition does consulting work for different companies. In the 90s, he taught from time to time as a guest professor at the University of Beirut. Although it was a troubled time in Lebanon and attacks kept being launched on different provision depots, I went with him for six months. We used the weekends for trips through Lebanon and to Damascus in Syria. We had already traveled throughout Egypt with its wealth of sights and continue to allow ourselves this luxury to this day. Because Kamal always had complete trust in me, I could even travel on my own with other women. For that, I am especially thankful because in this conservative society you cannot take that for granted. In February of this year Kamal suffered a stroke, but since then he has recovered. He is even working again already because his work is his life.

Although today more women wear the veil than before, many taboos have fallen by the wayside. Women can get divorced more easily and live alone with their children when their husbands are out of the country. Young single women move away from their parents to advance professionally. Almost all the girls and women from the lower social classes work. All of them go to school and after their schooling is done, they want to use their education and earn their own money. Often it is simply a necessity for financial reasons. Most parents spend their last penny to make a good education possible for their children. There are more and more coeducational schools. The people here live in very close proximity. Perhaps for that reason they need strict customs. With a scarf on her head a woman can quickly and without complications maintain the necessary distance and respect.

In our immediate family, no one wears a headscarf. Some of our relatives have accepted it very casually: they do not find it bothersome to wear. Earlier in the 60s and 70s, one saw far fewer women veiled on the street. Why that has changed over the years, no one really knows. There are different theories. Once lower class girls simply used to stay at home waiting to be married off. They rarely went out of the house. Today almost all of them work and if there is not enough money for the hairdresser, the headscarf is a simple and inexpensive solution. Besides, over the years, more and more Egyptian men have worked in Saudi Arabia where all the women are always veiled. Many of those men probably brought that custom back home with them to Egypt and demanded that their wives wear a headscarf. Today there are more and more women who dress completely in black and have only a slit free for the eyes. They wear long gloves and do not shake hands when greeting strangers. You never used to see such extreme dress. This "wahhabistic" (of the puritanical sect of Islam) orientation of the Islamic faith has become increasingly prevalent in Alexandria since the 90s.

To this day, many young couples enter into arranged marriages. However, some young people look for their partners themselves. Until the beginning of the 70s there was hardly any color in the cityscapes of Egypt; everything was bleak. Only under Sadat, when there were imports again from Europe and the United States, did it change. The general standard of living rose although today there are still very poor people. However, the Egyptians are very inventive. When they do not have work, they think of something, some new thing they can then sell. Almost everywhere, you see small traders who offer their wares on the street -- from underwear to combs to glasses, everything is available. Occasionally the police shoo them away, but after a few days, they are back again. You often see people in the city who offer the use of their cell phones to make a call for a few pounds. Whenever there is a traffic jam in Cairo, people are always around to wash the car windows. Of course, everyone gives them a little something for it. There is no social safety net from the state as there is in Germany. That forces people to earn their own livings themselves. In spite of everything, it seems to function somehow. There are still poor people, but no one has to starve.

My daughter Jasmin finished school here with a high school diploma with eligibility for university entrance and then studied English Literature. She taught at the university and at the academy, and got her master's at the American University of Cairo. For her doctorate, she went to the United States, where she is now working on her dissertation. She has been married to an American since 2005. Her husband, who was brought up Catholic, had to convert to Islam before they could be married. Otherwise, the marriage would not have been valid according to Islamic law.

After high school, Karim attended the Maritime Academy (originally only for the Navy) and studied mechanical engineering. He got a first class degree and has been working since then for an international fertilizer company in Cairo. He has been married to a young professional from Cairo since 2006.

Both children feel entirely like Muslims, but in their thinking, they are completely Western. Karim was recently in Germany professionally and he returned from his second homeland very proud and enthusiastic. We do not have grandchildren yet.

In conclusion, I would like to point out that there are far more big churches in Alexandria than big mosques. Actually, new churches are built. The countless Coptic churches are open daily and can easily be visited. The Coptic Church in Egypt is one of the oldest Christian churches in the world; the date of its founding is estimated at 50 AD. Although Egypt had already become Islamic in the seventh century, the peaceful coexistence of Christians and Muslims was a matter of course most of the time. It is estimated that Copts make up about 10% of the total population of Egypt today. From my own experience, I can report that also today things are very peaceful between the two religious communities, although there are hardly any mixed marriages.

In 2004, the opera in Alexandria was reopened after lengthy renovations, and now we regularly attend concerts there. The orchestra comes from Cairo. They usually play classical music, occasionally Arabian music. Sometimes there are guest performances with ensembles from other countries like Korea, China, the Ukraine or Spain.

Since my parents have both died, I rarely go to Germany any more. Every few years we visit my sister in Switzerland or friends in Germany. But all in all after so many years, Germany is not any more so important to me. I do not particularly like the attitude of the people there. They are very quickly dissatisfied and whine a lot. At least that is how I perceive it, anyway, during our visits.

That is why I am always happy to go back to Alexandria again. In Egypt, the people are much friendlier; maybe that has to do with the abundant sunshine we are so lucky to enjoy here. The few little things I do not like In Egypt I have learned to accept over the years. Today I feel very comfortable here. I miss my daughter of course, but we often talk on the phone and now over the Internet. Otherwise, I have everything I need here. My Arabic has improved to the point where I can watch Egyptian television as well as the German satellite programs.

For me Egypt was probably something like my destiny. I have never regretted that I married an Egyptian. Despite all the hurdles and hindrances, I have been happy here.

Chapter Ten
Hildegard S. Married to a Copt

Hildegard lives with her husband in Germany, but for many years she has been traveling to Egypt on a regular basis and she is very familiar with Egyptian customs and traditions. Her husband is a Copt. The Christians in Egypt are called Copts, but today Copts can be found elsewhere in the world, too. The word „Copt" stems from the Greek and originally referred to all Egyptians. But after Islamisation, the word remained in the language for the Christian population. Hildegard converted to the Copt religion, too. For me this is a new and interesting aspect of Egypt. I wonder how her story differs from those of the other women. Are the Copts different from Muslim Egyptians? Or is the difference not all that great? I met Hildegard through other Germans during one of her visits to Alexandria. Her story, too, begins in Germany:

I met my husband in 1954 in Düsseldorf. I was 20 years old and Boutros was 24. He was visiting a girlfriend of mine there whom he had met the year before in Salzburg (Austria). Here is what happened: Käthe and I had both joined the scouts. Our scouts' activities gave us many opportunities to meet scouts from other countries, which we of course found very exciting. Almost every year there were international meetings and rallies where we met other young people from all over the world and had a lot of fun. Today there are still scouts in Egypt, and at that time Boutros was one of them, too. Each year the scout organization sent him to scout meetings abroad. For many young people in those years being a member of the scouts offered the only opportunity to travel abroad and meet other people there. All three of us (Boutros, Käthe and I) participated in various activities with different friends. At that time Boutros still lived in Egypt. He had studied economics in Cairo and was working at the Department of Education. His goal, however, was to study the hotel business in Germany. He saw the opportunities that the development of modern tourism would offer his country and wanted to work in that field later on. After his visit to Germany he returned home, but we stayed in touch. The next year he came to Germany again, and this time he stayed with us.

I still lived with my mother then. My father had died in WW II. Although we had only a three-room apartment, our home was always open to guests. No matter who arrived at the door, be it a young man or a young girl, everybody was accommodated and fed. We young people were not particularly demanding, and through my activities with the scouts we had visitors quite often. People were always coming and going, and we were always happy to meet somebody from another country. So Boutros lived with us for a few weeks. Again we spent a lot of time together and got along well with each other. Then he went back to Egypt.

The following year - 1956 - Boutros, together with his friend Mansour, drove up on a scooter to attend another scout convention. They had traveled to Germany on the scooter and by ship. Boutros wanted to stay longer and begin the course of study he had planned. But he needed to earn the money for that so he applied for a job with a manufacturer of bathroom equipment and supplies. Then suddenly he developed health problems: he was constantly tired, and then blood was found in his urine. At first the doctors were at a loss. After several extensive examinations he was finally diagnosed with bilharzias (schistosomiasis). This disease used to be widespread in Egypt. It affected many people who bathed in the Nile or in its branches. In Germany bilharzias is practically nonexistent, and nowadays it can be treated effectively. At that time, however, many third-world diseases had not yet been researched, and both the university clinic and the Bayer Company were very much interested in his case. They financed his treatment and really did everything they could for him. After a few weeks Boutros was entirely healthy again and could return to work. By then it was1956, the year of the Suez crisis. I was worried about what was happening; I feared that Boutros could run into difficulties in Europe if a war started. I urgently advised him to return to Egypt, and indeed he caught the last ship home just before war broke out. By then we had realized that we liked each other very much. Being separated just then was very hard for us, but there was nothing we could do. A little later I received a reassuring telegram saying that he had arrived safely.

Even before Boutros's stay in Germany, I had planned a trip to Egypt with a group of girl scouts. We had visited a travel agency to map out a detailed tour and were really exited about it. Then the Suez war broke out. Although it lasted only a few days, most of the other girls did not want to go any more. Only one friend and I still wanted to go, but with just the two of us it would have been too dangerous, so we thought we would have to stay home. Then a nice colleague of mine offered to go with us. I knew him well and knew that he was very reliable. So in March 1957, only a few months after the Suez war had ended, the three of us hit the road.

Boutros was now living in Kuwait where he worked at his brothers' company as the business manager. His two brothers, an architect and a civil engineer, were managing a big project in Kuwait and were glad that Boutros could help them. Naturally I had told him about our upcoming trip; we had planned many different stopovers and in Cairo his family was expecting us. But it was still a long way to Cairo! We started our trip in Düsseldorf and traveled first to Belgrade by train. Then we continued on to Istanbul and Ankara and finally to Aleppo in Northern Syria on the Baghdad Express. At that point we had to change over to a rickety bus that took us to Damascus. From there we took a taxi to Beirut. Here our overland travel had come to an end, because one could not travel through Israel to Egypt. So for the last leg of the journey we went by plane to Cairo. Just getting there took us two full weeks! To get back we wanted to go by ship from Alexandria to Brindisi and from there via Naples to Rome and Milan. From Milan we would take the train again to Germany.

It was an exciting trip and a big adventure for all of

us. At that time there were only very few tourists in all of these countries. We were welcomed very warmheartedly everywhere, on the train as well as in the cities when we spent the night. We slept mostly in youth hostels and if there weren't any, in Aleppo for instance, we looked for an inexpensive hotel. Often we were invited to stay in someone's home, and through the scouts we had a few private addresses. In Beirut we stayed with the leader of the girl scouts. On many occasions we received small farewell presents, such as pieces of jewelry. We were very impressed with the genuineness of all the people we met.

We learned very quickly that it was a good idea to do a little research into the customs of the countries we traveled through. In Aleppo I was even arrested because I had taken photographs. It was the national holiday, which was celebrated with a big military parade. I only wanted to take photos of the other girl scouts, but because there were many military installations there everybody with an open camera was arrested. Fortunately, as a West German citizen I had an advantage, and everyone involved soon realized that I was harmless. I was released after only a few hours and I was even allowed to keep my film. Since our departure from Germany, I had not heard from Boutros. We had agreed that he would write to me in Aleppo per general delivery, but I waited in vain for his message. As I discovered later, Boutros was not in any position to write to me. He had injured himself at one of the construction sites and his arm had been hurt.

But Boutros knew our travel itinerary well and had thoroughly prepared his family for our arrival in Cairo. The flight from Beirut to Cairo was very exciting for us because it was our first airplane flight. At that time traveling by plane was still something very exclusive; air passengers received the royal treatment. It was rather expensive and the number of flights was limited. As always I had my camera ready and wanted to take a picture of the Suez Canal from above. But that was strictly forbidden, as the stewardess informed me. I must have put on a very sad face because a few moments later she returned and invited me to come into the cockpit. I was allowed to sit there and even pilot the airplane for a short time. Of course the plane was always under the pilot's control, but for me it was very exciting, regardless.

We landed in Cairo without any incident. The airport building was tiny, there was no comparison to the huge terminals of today. It reminded one more of a small garage. Right at the end of the gangway stood a tall, good-looking man. It was one of Boutros's brothers, Fawzi. Boutros's whole family was there; everybody awaited us with great suspense at the airport building. Only Boutros's mother had stayed at home. Boutros had arranged everything. Fawzi always took care of me later, too, when I was in Egypt by myself. He greeted me with a huge bouquet of flowers and took us to their home. Although Boutros was in Kuwait, he had carefully arranged everything else for our arrival and our stay in Cairo. Every day Boutros's friend Mansour and his brother Fawzi took us on excursions through Cairo. I have never seen so much of Cairo as I did in those weeks. Boutros had planned everything in great detail and had written down exactly what the two of them were to show us. We were on the go from dawn to dusk. It was during Ramadan and since Mansour was a Muslim he was fasting; that is, he did not eat or drink anything the entire day. It was not until sunset, at the traditional breaking of the fast, that he helped himself to any food or drink. But he handled it very well. Like all Egyptians, he was very proud of his country and he enjoyed showing us the sights. His English was very good and we could communicate easily. We stayed friends with him all our lives until unfortunately he passed away a few years ago.

So that was my first visit to Egypt. My colleague and I stayed with Boutros's family and my girlfriend stayed with Mansour's family. Of course all the relatives and friends stopped by to check me out, but I did not even realize it because at that point Boutros and I were not yet a couple at all. Boutros came from a large family; he had five brothers and three sisters. Boutros is the third youngest.

Then one day Boutros's eldest brother solemnly asked me into his office. "Now what?" I thought to myself. He asked me very frankly whether or not I loved Boutros. I was a bit stunned because we actually had never talked about this. Without giving it much thought, I spontaneously replied "Yes!" Boutros's brother suggested that I cook or bake something for Boutros. The next day he would fly to Kuwait and would take it with him for Boutros. I thought that was a good idea and decided to bake a cake. But all the ingredients were different from the ones at home, and the oven did not work the way I was used to, either. There was no real temperature gauge; it was rather a matter of intuition. Anyway, my cake turned out as hard as a rock, and Boutros threw it away immediately. Of course he told me that only later…

One of Boutros' brothers was to be married soon in Lebanon. The family of the bride lived in Cairo. However, Boutros and his brothers were living in Kuwait. Traveling from Kuwait to Egypt had always been very difficult, so they decided to have the wedding in Lebanon, where virtually everybody could travel easily. One of the brothers' business partners organized everything locally and the preparations were already in full swing. Although I had already been in Egypt for a few weeks, I had not seen Boutros himself at all. The last time we met had been months ago. Boutros wrote to me that I should travel along to Lebanon to meet him there. His family would even pay for the trip. I didn't have that much money, and at first I was too proud to accept such a generous gift. But Mansour persuaded me, and eventually my curiosity prevailed and also my natural yearning to see Boutros. So I went with them. We traveled by plane, and Boutros was waiting for me at the airport. Almost a full year had gone by since we had last met. We talked nonstop and, for the first time, about a possible future together, as well. We knew we belonged together and we began to make our first plans for the future. Boutros was earning good money in Kuwait, but he still wanted to come to Germany again soon. But another separation was inevitable; I had to return to Cairo even before his brother's wedding because my ship from Alexandria to Italy was leaving soon.

So I flew back to Cairo again, and only a few days later my friend Irene, my colleague Kurt, and I left Egypt by ship for Brindisi. From there we continued by train via Naples and Milan to Düsseldorf. Altogether we had been traveling for six weeks and we returned home full of new impressions.

More than a year later, in 1959, Boutros came back to Germany. This time he intended to finally begin his studies. At that time Egypt did not yet have an adequate training program in the fields of hospitality or tourism. Tourism was still in its infancy. To be admitted to his program, first of all Boutros had to learn German. During his three months at the Goethe Institute in Arolsen he lived at a boarding school. Of course, other Egyptians lived there, too; even one of his friends from Cairo was there at the same time. Unfortunately, in their free time they spoke a lot of Arabic, which did not really help their progress in the German language. His friend, by the way, later married a German woman, as well, and we remain friends with her to this day, although her husband has already passed away.

To earn some money, Boutros went looking for a job. But it was not easy to find work then -- the unemployment rate was high. I wrote over a hundred applications for him, but nobody hired him. He finally found temporary work with a Lebanese man. But the work was not regular and it was not meant to be permanent.

In September, 1959, we got engaged. My family was at first totally against it. What they knew about Egypt was next to nothing. The newspapers were full of horror stories about what had happened to girls who married into an Arab country. They ended up in a harem, had no rights whatsoever, and were absolutely miserable. Because my father had been killed in the war and could not protect me, all my aunts and uncles were extremely worried about me.

Luckily, my mother quickly grew very fond of Boutros. She was very open-minded about everything and saw how happy I was with him. So we got married in

January, 1960. I was brought up Catholic and because at that time there were no Coptic churches in Germany, the wedding took place in a Catholic church. Boutros is religious, and on our wedding day he was very quiet. I noticed, of course, and worried he had changed his mind about marrying me. Only later did I realize that he had missed his family very much, particularly on this special day.

I myself had an interesting job, which I enjoyed very much. Right after graduation from high school (with the Abitur) I started as a trainee in a large insurance company. I would have loved to study at a university, but my mother was not by any stretch of the imagination in a position to finance this. Nevertheless, I was very lucky and was hired permanently by the insurance company right after I had finished my training. I had good luck with my superiors, too. I was always given work that matched my capabilities and I advanced steadily. Later on I led a department with fifteen employees. At the time that was something special, because in that industry female employees worked only as secretaries or claims clerks. Today it is entirely different and women work in all positions. Through my work we had a steady, permanent income. I worked at this insurance company right through to my retirement.

Boutros's working life was more complicated because he had to apply for an extension of his German work permit on a regular basis. Each time it was issued only for the length of time his passport was valid. We never knew beforehand whether or not everything would work out okay, and this uncertainty often got to us. It was not until 1970 that Boutros was naturalized and received German citizenship.

In 1961 our first son, René, was born. Initially he received a foreigner's passport. According to the law at that time he would have received the citizenship of his father. However, according to Egyptian law our marriage was null and void. Therefore it was also a problem for us to travel to Egypt together. Although we very much wanted to present our little René to the family in Egypt, Boutros could not travel there, because he might not have been allowed to leave the country again. So I traveled to Egypt with my five-month old child by myself to show René to his grandparents and to the rest of the relatives.

In 1961 a new college of hotel management opened in Dortmund, and Boutros finally could start his training. In recent years various financially strong investors had again and again planned larger tourist projects in Egypt. New tourist complexes were supposed to go up by the Red Sea as well as by the Mediterranean Sea. Onassis envisioned something like a new Monaco in Egypt, but nothing came of it. Mr. Blatzheim (he was the stepfather of the German actress Romy Schneider) planned several hotels by the Red Sea and the Mediterranean Sea, and promised Boutros a management position at one of his new hotels. So while still attending the hotel management business school, Boutros started to work for Mr. Blatzheim in Cologne. In spite of his work, he managed to successfully finish his education. The planning stage of the hotels in Egypt was postponed again and again, and instead Boutros was put in charge of various restaurants in Cologne. He was a good organizer and because of his studies had a good grasp of the business end of things as well. He was earning a fine salary, but because of his inconvenient working hours we practically had no family life any more. Often Boutros worked at night, while I was at the office during the day. We hardly had any free time together.

In 1963 our second son, Markus, was born. We were still living in a three-room apartment together with my mother and the children. Without a certain amount of capital it was very difficult to get an apartment. Although my company had some apartments for employees, they were only given to men.

Finally, Boutros started looking for another job. He found a permanent position as a business director at the hotel Breidenbacher Hof - with regular working hours and a good salary. Later on he switched to the newly opened Hilton hotel in Düsseldorf. Now he earned even more money, but often the employees were pretty much taken advantage of. There were many large events and

Boutros always had to help out in the service area. Eventually Boutros found a job at the Dresdner Bank. There he managed the cafeteria, a job he kept for nineteen years. He liked this kind of work very much, because he had to interact with people a lot. All activities in and purchases for the cafeteria came across his desk. He worked there until he retired.

Every other year we traveled with the children to Egypt. But for me that was not always so enjoyable. When we were in Egypt together, Boutros focused only on his family. After all he had not seen them in a long time. Sometimes he hardly spoke a word to me for several days. He sat together with his relatives, they laughed and seemed to be having a great time. Sometimes they would all suddenly stand up and start moving - destination unknown. I did not understand a word of the conversation and often felt quite lost. I would get maybe a one-sentence explanation, but then the conversation continued seamlessly in yet another direction. We visited all sorts of people whom I often did not even know. Frequently those visits lasted well into the night. My Arabic was quite fragmentary and not sufficient by any means for a longer conversation. When was I supposed to have learned it, anyway? We lived far away in Düsseldorf; I had a full time job and two little children to take care of.

However, whenever I was in Egypt alone, it was an entirely different story. Then everything revolved only around me and my needs. It was only when Boutros and I were together in Egypt that everything was done only according to Boutros.

Those visits were not easy for the children either, because they also could not speak Arabic. In order for them to learn the language, Boutros should have spoken Arabic with them from their infancy. But he had never done that -- in the beginning because he was hardly at home anyway, with his terrible working hours, and then at some point it was simply too late to start. Not that I could ever complain about his qualities as a father. Whenever he was home, he shared in all the work: feeding, changing diapers and everything that goes with caring for children.

When neither of us was there, my mother took care of the children.

In 1968 we finally got lucky finding a new place and were able to move to a bigger apartment. My mother continued to live with us because she took care of the children during the day. Luckily Boutros got along well with her most of the time; he is generally a very affable fellow. As in every family, there was occasionally a blow-up between my mother and me, but we all depended on each other and were basically very happy with the arrangement.

Then at some point Boutros met other Copts in Düsseldorf. A Protestant pastor let them meet in the Protestant church. Soon a Coptic priest from Frankfurt happened along and began to come once a month to Düsseldorf. So slowly but surely a small Coptic church evolved in Düsseldorf. Boutros participated in the groundwork as he was good at organizing and enjoyed doing it. Eventually, he became the parish council leader. The Coptic priest had the clever idea of including the German wives in the organization. Sundays there was a Coptic mass in which many Egyptian families participated. The German women always took care of the following get-together: they prepared the food and cleaned everything up again after it was over. That was necessary because we were just there as guests with use of the Protestant church. The Egyptian women acted mostly the way they do sometimes in Egypt; when it came to helping, they just sat there and let themselves be served. The children always did whatever they wanted to and were never told to behave. I was considered an uncaring, mean mother, because I would not allow my children to do certain things; for example, make a lot of noise or damage things. Later on the Coptic congregation got its own facility. The Coptic Church bought a building and leased the property for 99 years.

I myself was brought up Catholic. After I married Boutros, we both always went to the Coptic Church service. I did not find the difference between the two religious persuasions to be that great. Everything that is said three times in the Catholic mass is heard at least ten times in the Coptic service. The creed differs in a few small details.

After a few years, a new priest came to our church. Boutros had been parish council leader up to then. The new priest found out that Boutros had not been married lawfully in a Coptic ceremony. And that I had never been a Copt! That meant Boutros would not be able to be council leader any more, because he was living in sin. I was supposed to be baptized Coptic and afterwards we were also supposed to get married in a Coptic ceremony. I found all of this unnecessary. But I said to Boutros: "If it's important to you, I will do it. " Although I was Catholic, this ritual would not change my religious practice much. But if it had to be, no problem. We decided that I should at least submit to the baptism. So I was baptized, and in 1991 Boutros and I got married once again - this time according to the Coptic ritual.

The church in Düsseldorf has grown a lot in the meantime. In addition there are whole lot of other Coptic churches in Germany. The Coptic Church is one of the oldest Christian churches, if not the oldest. It was probably founded by Markus in AD 61. There is lots of information about it on the Internet at: www.coptic.net

In 1992 I had the opportunity to meet the head of the Coptic Church, Patriarch Shenouda of Alexandria. The Patriarch had been awarded an honorary doctorate from the University of Bonn and afterwards visited all the Coptic churches in Germany. He was highly praised for his constant efforts towards the reconciliation and rapprochement among the leading religious communities, and he impressed us very much with his personality. Patriarch Shenouda is a very charismatic and extremely intelligent man, and he readily accepted German women in the church. At that time I, too, tried to study the differences among the various Christian persuasions. The main point of contention was originally the person of Jesus Christ. Some say he was God and man at the same time - in itself a tricky matter. Others maintain Christ manifested himself in two separate ways. This argument arose for the first time at the Council of Nicaea in AD 325. Personally, I do not really understand all the details and that is probably true for most Christians. Anyway, later at the Council of Chalcedon in AD 451, it came to a schism; both the Church of Alexandria as well as other Eastern Churches separated from the Catholic Church. Probably political reasons as well as questions of belief were behind the split. Since then the Copts have had their own church. Since 1988 there has been a convergence again between the Catholic Church and the Coptic Church. More can be found about it for English speakers on the Internet at www.coptic.net/EncyclopediaCoptica.

At the beginning of Islamisation the Copts were repeatedly victims of discrimination in Egypt. However the conversion to Islam usually proceeded peacefully. It was like this: the Muslims had to pay lower taxes than the Jews and Christians. Therefore many converted to the Muslim faith purely for financial reasons. Today the same rate of taxation is applied to everyone--independent of religious affiliation. About 10% of the Egyptian population are Copts, and they live mostly in Asyut and Alexandria. Many of them are more affluent than the average Egyptian populace and because the Copts attach great importance to education, their average level of education is somewhat higher, as well. In 1981, President Sadat sent our esteemed Patriarch Shenouda into exile at the Wadi Natrum monastery. Shenouda had expressed a negative opinion of Sadat during a trip to the United States. Bishop Samuel, with whom Sadat cultivated friendly relations, was supposed to become Patriarch. However this change was not accepted by the Coptic Church because with the Patriarch it is the same as with the Pope. One does not simply give up the papal office but rather remains Pope or Patriarch until death. When Sadat was assassinated in1981, Bishop Samuel was sitting next to him and was also killed. Patriarch Shenouda was reinstated by Mubarak in 1985.

Since then, the relations between the State and the Coptic Church have improved again. The two religions have lived side by side in Egypt for many centuries, along with Jewish congregations, as well. For the most part they all lived together peacefully, but in the course of history there were disturbances from time to time, and they continue to occur today. In spite of that, you cannot say that the people are deeply divided. There were and are many friendships between Muslims and Copts.

The foundation of the law in Egypt is the Koran. And although they are not exactly forbidden, mixed marriages between Copts and Muslims rarely occur. Occasionally a Copt converts to Islam, but one rarely hears of a Muslim becoming a Christian.

Family plays a very important role in both religions and you see that in everyday life. We take care of each other. Parents come first. Brothers must take care of their sisters, fathers of their children. That is a fundamental component of life in Egypt - independent of religious affiliation.

During my first visits in Cairo, I often went alone to the Catholic Church. I took the tram, which at the time was still open at the sides. Today the carriages are enclosed and hold many more people. I usually got a seat and was always treated with respect. Often in the church someone even thoroughly cleaned my place in the pew - just for me. I was always treated decently and courteously.

Once years ago (in 1976) I was with the children and friends in Mamura, Alexandria. We went swimming, in bathing suits of course. All of a sudden a couple of young men came over and wanted to speak with us. We thought at first they were just curious. But then, in a way that left no doubt about their intentions, they kept touching me and the young girls (13 und 14 years old), until we managed to chase them away. That was the first time that anyone had molested me. We did not tell the girls' father, though, because otherwise they would never have been allowed to go anywhere with us ever again. These days you can be jostled by young men and touched in a way that leaves no room for misunderstanding. They imagine that every woman who does not wear a headscarf is just waiting to be propositioned. The best thing for a woman alone in a crowd to do is not to make eye contact with any man.

Today many women are veiled. The headscarves come in many colors; they always match the clothing and sometimes look very beautiful. It is even convenient because you don't have to fuss so much with your hair. As soon as girls are grown up, they usually wear a headscarf. It used to be that women, especially those from the country, did not wear a headscarf. Their clothing was colorful and sometimes they wore a cloth with a small pompom fringe, too. Now many are dressed completely in black with a face veil that leaves only the eyes free.

In 1993, I retired. Boutros had already retired two years earlier. As a parting gift I received a tidy sum of money, and we wanted to buy an apartment in Alexandria with it. We found our apartment in Glym, on the Corniche. It was exactly what we were looking for. Unfortunately it was not completely finished, so we had to help organize its completion and above all supervise the work. Here in Egypt it is much more difficult to find reliable tradesmen than it is in Germany. Many simply do not keep appointments. In addition they don't work as neatly as in Europe. After every stage of work, after every visit from a craftsman, a thorough cleaning was necessary. With my own hands I cleaned off cement from the tiles in the bathroom. Plus everything always takes so long. We had to wait five whole days for our water meter. You cannot make any firm plans the way you would like to because - guaranteed - something or other will crop up to interfere. We quickly noticed that the Egypt of today had become very complicated. As a tourist one does not notice that so easily.

But at last in 1994 our apartment was finished, and we loved not having to stay with relatives when we visited here. It took a little while longer to completely furnish the apartment because much of the furniture in Egypt simply did not match our taste.

For years we went to Egypt regularly. Little by little I became ever better acquainted with the country and felt more and more comfortable here. We also traveled around a lot and toured all the temples and museums.

Unfortunately none of Boutros's siblings are still living. But there are many of nieces and nephews. If they are married, both husband and wife are usually working. For childcare they have a nanny -- servants are still available in Egypt for little money. Almost all the women from the upper classes go to college today, but to get a good job they have to fight for it, as they do everywhere. The education itself is free and almost all of the students live at home with their parents or in a dormitory.

Over the years much has changed in Egypt. On the one hand, working has become more difficult. One has to struggle to get a good job and for many the earnings are scarcely enough to live well. On the other hand, almost everything is available in the shops; groceries, electric appliances and luxury items. Anything that is imported is going to be expensive. But more and more is being produced domestically, and one can get those goods at affordable prices. For us Europeans, everything here is a bargain, but the Egyptians moan about inflation.

It has been a hardship for my husband not to be able to live in his home country. For Egyptians, the family is very important and we lived in Germany the majority of the time. When we bought the apartment in Alexandria, Boutros could devote more time to his family again. In that way he felt closer to his roots and enjoyed our stays here to the fullest. We met some of our German friends again here in Alexandria. As a matter of fact an amazing number of Egyptian men are married to German wives. We always have a lot to talk about.

I like Egyptian cuisine very much but I do not know how to prepare it myself. But when we are in Egypt, we eat everything that is customary here. Some things, for example Molokhia (see Appendix A), I do not like. But a lot of it tastes very good to a German palate.

The center of our life remains in Germany because our children live in Europe. One of our sons lives with his family in Paris. He is married and has twins. We visit him often and help out now and then with the children because both parents are very busy professionally. Neither of our sons wants to move to Egypt. They always liked to spend their vacations here, but their homeland is in Germany, and since their childhood, Egypt has not played a big role in their lives.

That's why in 2006 we sold our hard-won apartment. Our sons were not interested in it and for us it would probably eventually become too troublesome. I have found that health care in Egypt is not as good as it is in Germany, by far. I would not like to have to go to a hospital here if it can be avoided. The language alone would make things very problematic for me. Now we go to Egypt only for vacations. We still have relatives and friends here, and we like to go to the Red Sea. We have made many nice trips and there are still areas we would like to see. But we are spending most of our time in Germany again now.

My husband has settled in very well in Germany over the years. He too considers Germany as his home now. But his heart will probably always belong to Egypt. His roots are here in Egypt just as mine are in Germany. Like so many of our friends in multicultural families we had to overcome many differences. But with mutual tolerance and understanding we found happiness.

Chapter Eleven

Martha H. A Love Story in Germany

I met Martha in Germany. Her husband, Sami, is a physician, like my son, Achmed. They met by chance in the hospital where Achmed worked, and became friends, and the families get together now and then. On one of those occasions, Tarek, Sami and Martha's son, told Achmed he would be going to Alexandria to study Arabic. "You will meet my mother; she is there, too," said Achmed. I actually did meet Tarek in 2005 in Alexandria at the Faculty of Arts. Unlike mine, his Arabic was perfect by then. The acquisition of a new language is evidently considerably easier for the young. We met the rest of the family at Achmed's the next time we were in Germany. When Martha heard about my project, she announced immediately that she would very much like to take part in it. She told me her story while we took a walk together in a little village in Lower Saxony. We kept turning the recorder off as we talked in order to discuss things in more detail, and we laughed a lot as we talked. At 56, Martha is the youngest of the women who appear in this book. She lives with her Egyptian husband in Germany. Of average height and slender, with red, curly hair, which she usually wears in a braid or pinned up in a bun, she seems very self-confident and energetic. Here is Martha's story:

My husband Sami and I met at a party in 1979 in Bad Bevensen (a small town in the Lunenburg Heath). I was 27 at the time and worked as a medical technical assistant in a hospital. Sami was 28 and already a resident at another hospital. Even at our very first meeting we felt we belonged together - love at first sight. We arranged to meet again right away and in the following days and weeks we did a lot of things together. A little while later I introduced Sami to my parents, who accepted him with open arms. That was not necessarily something I could take for granted, when I think back on it. My parents were both staunch Protestants. I, too, was brought up in the Protestant faith. Sami on the other hand is a devout Muslim. Despite this obvious difference we got along very well right away, and it has remained that way to this day.

I spent my childhood in Saxony-Anhalt as the youngest of four daughters. My father, a mechanical engineer, had built up a small company manufacturing cranes. But in the former East Germany, they made it hard for him. There were always difficulties, and at some point he was even supposed to be dispossessed of his company. In 1961 my parents decided to turn their backs on the East and take a chance on a new beginning in West Germany. When we fled through Berlin to the West, I was just nine years old. At that time many people left the East that way until the wall was built in August of 1961. In Bad Bevensen (Lower Saxony) my father had to start all over again at the age of 49. First he found a job at Siemens. Later he built up a small company of his own again in the machine building industry. He employed fifteen workers, and my mother assisted him. She was responsible for all the bookkeeping and other administrative tasks. We girls went to school; I got my diploma for university entrance and then trained as a medical technical assistant in Hamburg. After graduation, I found employment at a hospital in Bad Bevensen. Like many young people in the 70's, I pursued a wide variety of hobbies in my free time, but my greatest passion was the theater. For a time I even acted in the Stadttheater Uelzen (city theater of Uelzen). Later when I was married and had a family, I had to give up that hobby because of lack of time.

Sami came into the world in 1950 in Alexandria, Egypt and grew up there, too. After high school, he studied medicine in Alexandria. He came to Germany to further advance his knowledge in medicine. Medical advancements were already much further ahead in Germany than in Egypt, and he hoped for better training and better career opportunities. He was soon able to work as a resident in internal medicine. Later he began to specialize in cardiology, as well. Since 1991 he has had a practice in cardiology in Gronau (Lower Saxony). When we met, he was a resident at a hospital in Bad Bevensen -- not the same hospital where I worked.

We fell in love, and both of us had no doubts whatsoever that we belonged together. Sami wanted to introduce me to his family, and naturally I also wanted to become acquainted with his homeland, Egypt. That very same year in 1979, we went to Egypt together for the first time and I met Sami's family. He is the third of five siblings: he has a sister and three brothers. Sami's father was a graphologist and handwriting expert for the Egyptian court. In addition, he was a calligrapher; he painted the Koran on large sheets of paper in decorative script. In the Arab world the art of calligraphy is highly esteemed, and in many apartments in Egypt and in other Arab countries, framed pieces of calligraphy hang on the walls. The works of Sami's father were shown in calligraphy exhibitions, as well. Sami's family accepted me very warmly. They were Muslims but not at all narrow-minded. On the contrary, my father-in-law was exceptionally tolerant. In my whole life I have never met a person more understanding and more tolerant of other points of view than he was. My mother-in-law, like all mothers-in-law, was of course somewhat skeptical about me at first. Is she good enough for my son? But it only took about ten minutes for her to grow fond of me, and we get along very well to this day. In preparation for our trip, I had already learned some Arabic in Germany, so we could at least communicate with each other a little bit and that made everything considerably easier. My father-in-law and the younger members of the family all spoke English. Over the years I continued to learn more and more Arabic with the help of my father-in-law. Eventually I could converse quite well in Arabic.

During this first visit to Alexandria, we saw some of what there was to see: the port and the Greek and Roman archeological excavations. But we spent most of the time with the family, because that seemed the most important to us at the time. Once we went to Cairo and visited the pyramids. That was the first time for Sami, too. During later trips, of course, we saw much more of Egypt.

The whole family was happy about our upcoming marriage. Luckily, no arrangements had been made for

Sami to marry a distant relative or a woman from the neighborhood. To this day, many marriages are still arranged by the families, although not as often as before. However, women from Europe were always very welcome as wives in Egypt. For one thing they do not require a morning gift; that is, a gift after the wedding night, nor do they expect jewelry, a complete apartment, or compensation for a divorce. In Egypt many women are very demanding before the marriage, and often many young men cannot afford it. That is why it takes years until the couples can marry. Sami's family had nothing of the kind in mind; they were just happy that he was so happy. Everyone was very nice to me and accepted me with open arms. Later on Sami's parents visited us several times in Germany.

After our vacation in Egypt, we returned to Germany content and happy. We were very much in love and had decided to get married as soon as possible. In 1980 we were married according to German law at the marriage bureau in Bad Bevensen. Beforehand the registrar „instructed" me in detail about the consequences of our marriage. Sami could marry three other women in his country, and moreover Islamic law applied to me there, too. Inheritance rights and everything that has to do with the children are entirely different and not exactly set up to the advantage of women. Even then there were many sham marriages between Egyptian men and German women, who were treated very badly once in Egypt. For the man it was usually a matter of getting as much money as possible from his wife and then of getting rid of her as quickly as possible. The German women were powerless; even the German government could not help them any further. I did not let that scare me off, and the marriage took place as planned. My parents were there, my sisters and my girlfriends. In addition, one of Sami's uncles who lived in Germany came.

In contrast to the young Egyptian couples, by the way, we owned nothing at all. Our only possessions consisted of a frying pan (from Sami) and a large glass bowl (from me). Little by little, we together furnished our entire household the way many young couples do in Germany. Money was, of course, not so plentiful, and when we moved into our first apartment together in Gronau, we could only afford used kitchen cabinets. Later on one of my sisters-in-law declared, during a visit in Germany, that she would never have accepted a used kitchen from her husband. She actually turned up her nose at my kitchen. But we liked it because it was handcrafted and unique, and we still have it today.

Right from the beginning we were certain that we would live in Germany. Sami did not want to return to Egypt; he saw his professional future in Germany. Moreover he appreciated the higher standard of living, the German culture and lifestyle. For me living in Egypt was not a consideration either. That had less to do with the mindset of the people, than with the living conditions there. In Egypt only farmers can live in the county -- everyone else has to live in an urban area. In the rural areas there is no infrastructure to support a „normal" life according to our standards. Cairo and Alexandria, however, are huge cities with all that goes along with that: noise, crowds, exhaust fumes and so forth. I do not especially like big cities in Germany either; I prefer to live in the country. Therefore it was our joint decision at the time to live in Germany.

Sami liked the German way of living; he still likes it here in Germany today. But I think that all Egyptians (or perhaps even all people from another country) who are far away from their homeland are somehow torn inside

In 1981 our daughter, Jasmin, was born; in 1985, our son, Tarek. Until the children came, I continued to work at the hospital as a medical technical assistant. Then I went on maternity leave, and when Tarek turned three, I began to work again. Sami always did a lot to support me. When I went back to work, I left the house before seven in the morning. Sami was responsible for breakfast for the children, and he saw to it that they got to school on time. Sami loves German punctuality; that is something that just does not exist in Egypt. The children's class schedule hung in the kitchen, and the children soon became very independent. Sami liked that. Sami witnessed in his own family that his father also took care of the children. So in that way he was just the same. In general, however, Egyptian men are more apt to let the women serve them.

As the children got older, of course, as in all families, there were vehement discussions - maybe a little more vehement because Sami is an Egyptian. Jasmin was sixteen and wanted to go to the movies alone, as all her girlfriends did. Sami was, of course, against it, because in Egypt that would have been unthinkable. Jasmin did not give up so easily, and at seventeen she was allowed to go alone. In Germany the whole society is just different, and after all we could not raise our children in complete contradiction to it. That would soon have become impossible. To a certain degree, one always has to conform to the society in which one lives.

During the first years of our marriage, we lived in an apartment. Twenty-three years ago we rented a house, and sixteen years ago we finally moved into our own house where we still live today. The kitchen, by the way, always moved with us. Our location is very idyllic, like Snow White's, behind seven mountains in Lower Saxony.

In 1991 Sami completed his exams for cardiology and opened his own practice in Gronau.

For a long time we went to Egypt almost every year. We visited the family and all the siblings and relatives. Of course, there was a lot to catch up on. There was a lot of talking, and my Arabic was rather limited. Those visits were often very stressful for me and not always what I would call a „vacation".

Sami was very happy when we traveled to Egypt. But he was also very happy to go home again to Germany. He had grown completely accustomed to the German way of life. I am glad of that because I could not have lived in Egypt. It is simply too loud and too crowded for me there in the big cities.

Sami would have liked very much to raise our children in his faith. I could not agree to that because I am Lutheran. Our children attended the Protestant religion classes in school (in Germany religion is taught in the public schools). In his free time Sami tried to make Islam accessible to them. He kept telling them about it, but as he did not have much time, their religious training in Islam was limited.

When Jasmin turned eighteen, she finally decided very deliberately against the faith of her father and also against the Egyptian customs. She prefers to live in Germany and feels Germany is her homeland. She is now a veterinary doctor with a Ph.D. and has a German boyfriend whom she will probably marry soon. For Sami this is all very difficult. For him it would be important that the young man convert to Islam, but that is out of the question for them. It causes a conflict in the family in which Sami suffers most of all.

Sami has begun to practice his religion more since the death of his father in 1987. He follows the rules of his faith; prays, fasts during Ramadan and does not drink alcohol. He has undertaken the Hajj to Mecca twice.

After high school, Tarek went to Alexandria for a year to learn Arabic at the university. He was able to live with his relatives and he spent a lot of time with his cousins. They took him along everywhere, and Tarek learned almost perfect Arabic during that time. During his year in Alexandria, he turned to Islam and became a devout Muslim. He is very consistent; prays, fasts and does not drink alcohol. Originally Tarek wanted to study medicine in Egypt. However in Germany he had dropped chemistry and physics before he took his high school exams (final, cumulative examinations that lead to a high school diploma with eligibility for college entrance) and was therefore not accepted at medical school in Egypt. In Germany that is no obstacle, so Tarek is studying medicine now in Halle. After college he wants to settle in Egypt for good. He feels more at home in Egypt than he does in Germany.

As a mother, I want my children to make their own decisions. I just want them to be happy. If Tarek should marry a Muslim woman, I will accept her into the family just as warmly as I have accepted my German son-in-law.

Of course Sami wanted both children to choose his faith. But with Jasmin it is an entirely different matter. Recently Sami explained to Jasmin's boyfriend: "If you do not become a Muslim, I will be friendly to you, but I will not become your friend."

I think that is a shame, but we have to accept it and live with it. Clearly Sami is the one suffering most in this situation.

Why is it that usually only the sons feel drawn to Islam? There is a simple answer to that, I think. The freedom and rights of women are very restricted in Islam, and choosing such a religion demands much greater sacrifice from them than from the men.

For example, according to Islamic law, the testimony of a man counts twice as much as that of a woman. Moreover, a woman is considered weaker and has to be taken care of by her father or brothers if she has no husband. Family in Egypt is very important, and helping within the family is taken for granted. My husband loves all of his siblings. He, of course, takes care of his sister, too; that responsibility is part of his faith. He does it without expecting anything in return. If the assistance is financial, no one ever talks about repayment. This solidarity greatly impressed me. In Germany such a strong sense of family bonds is more the exception than the rule.

When I first came to Egypt in 1980, the women dressed very differently from today. One saw miniskirts and low-cut dresses. Since then, society has changed greatly, and many women wear a veil today. Often they are the very same women who ran around in miniskirts twenty years ago! There are now posters hanging in the trams to illustrate how women must dress "correctly". The behavior of women in public has changed greatly, too. They are less self-confident, more introverted and afraid to look directly at other people. That behavior is in clear contradiction to the fact that many women in Egypt go to university and work in public positions.

These societal developments are one of the reasons why I do not like to go to Egypt so much any more. In 1980 I experienced Egypt as a fantastic, open-minded country with a wonderful, modern culture that was fun. Now everything has changed.

On their wedding day, the women still wear a low-cut dress and lots of make-up. Just one day later they are veiled and cover themselves from head to toe. Not a bit of skin or strand of hair is visible.

I know that many German women have converted to Islam for practical reasons. One can easily do so at a government agency by means of a simple declaration of faith. There is no requirement to study the faith in any way. In contrast, in Judaism one has to have instruction for at least three years, and with Christians, too, one has to study the foundations of faith at least two years before one is accepted into the Church. For me conversion to Islam was never a consideration. I have lived in Germany all these years content with my faith. Why should I change anything?

Unfortunately, my father-in-law died years ago. My own parents, as well, are no longer with us. My relationship with my mother-in-law is very good. In the beginning my Arabic was quite good, and I could carry on a good conversation. Unfortunately, it has grown worse over time because I do not travel to Egypt as often as I used to. If one uses a language only rarely, one forgets quite a lot.

When the children were a little older, we did a lot of traveling through Egypt. We visited Cairo and Upper (Southern) Egypt; we saw Aswan and Luxor. Of course we toured the temples and graves. Egyptian culture impressed all of us, and after such a trip we always felt much enriched. There is so much to see, and one brings back home many splendid impressions that continue to have an effect for a long time.

Personally, I really like Egyptian cuisine. Sami, of course, has his favorite dishes, too. If I want to give him a special treat, I make an eggplant casserole. The whole family loves this dish. By the way, I even like Molokhia (see Appendix A), a dish that people normally have to grow up with to like. It is a green, leafy vegetable that is cooked and served with rice and meat. Its consistency is a bit slimy, and most Europeans find it takes more than just getting used to in order to stand it. But all the Egyptians love it. For the holidays, we found a pretty simple compromise: we celebrate all the Muslim and all the Christian holidays. Usually this combination means a lot of time and effort with cooking and baking for family and friends.

More than ten years ago I inherited some money and began a new venture professionally. I had always dreamed of running my own bookshop. First I completed a six-month training program and learned all that was necessary: purchasing, accounting, management, taxes - everything important for a bookshop -- as well as business plans, sales, profit and loss. Since then, I know I would never have managed without these theoretical basics. In1996 I opened my little bookshop in Gronau and am now a proud independent bookseller. I have one woman helping me, but in spite of that I can never take a vacation for very long. That is another reason why I do not travel to Egypt so often any more. A further reason is that I cannot really rest in Egypt. I find the city of Alexandria very stressful with all its turmoil and traffic, and I cannot really relax during the visits to family either. Therefore, in the last few years Sami has been traveling more often alone to Egypt. He visits his mother, and sees his entire family and his friends. Nevertheless, he is always happy afterwards to come back to us in Germany - to come home.

While my father-in-law was still living, my parents-in-law came regularly to Germany to visit us. They came twice a year and stayed four to six weeks sometimes. They got along astonishingly well with my parents, although they could barely communicate with each other. Nevertheless they had a lot of fun, and on such occasions my father-in-law even drank a glass of wine sometimes. My parents never traveled to Egypt, though. I really do not know why. I suspect my father was always too busy with his company.

Sami and I have never regretted our decision to spend our lives in Germany. A marriage in our circumstances requires more tolerance from both partners than with couples who have grown up in the same cultural environment. But with mutual good will you can learn from each other, adjust to each other, and accept each other. Through his determination to live with me in Germany, Sami made the decision to marry him easy for me. Surely we had fewer problems to overcome than the mixed families in Egypt.

The center of our life is here in Germany. But Sami has his roots in Egypt. That will certainly not change. By „homeland“ Sami always means the country of Egypt. Probably all Egyptians see it that way. Our son Tarek is attracted to Egypt, too. In a discussion about both countries, Tarek said once: "Egypt has a soul!" I had to think about that for a long time.

Chapter Twelve
Beate S. My Life in Two Worlds

Beate and her husband spent most of their lives in Germany, where they met. I got to know her in Alexandria in a group of other Germans. I was immediately impressed by her open and spontaneous way of approaching people. She is of medium height, and has dark hair and a youthful air. Her Arabic is remarkably good – better than that of many people who have lived in Egypt for years. In spite of her accent, her Arabic sounds very natural - a fact that is confirmed even by Egyptians. In our preliminary conversations we talked extensively about her own story as well as about other stories. At one point she remarked, "When I think about the problems other people had, I got a really good bargain with my husband!" She seems to have a naturally positive attitude towards life. Beate tells me her story, which she has prepared with some of her own notes:

We met in April of 1971 in Aachen. Abdu was 36 years old; I myself was almost 24. I worked at the Technical University of Aachen, and Abdu, after having received his doctorate, had just started his first job. Both of us had been married before and were accordingly cautious about new commitments. That we started a new relationship at all was surprising.

But first our previous history: Abdu was born in 1935 in Alexandria as the third of eight siblings. His father was a businessman; the family was middle class. About his mother I know that she got married at a very young age. Not even her own children knew her real age. In Egypt many women keep their age a big secret. Abdu received his high school diploma (Abitur) in Alexandria, as did his younger brother. Both wanted to study in Europe; they considered the education there superior to the education in Egypt. But both were still undecided as to what field of study would be the right one for them. In 1955 they traveled first to Vienna and enrolled in the university there in pharmacy. Their parents financed their studies and the money was paid out to the students through the Study Mission of the Cultural Office of the Egyptian Embassy. In Vienna they shared a room that they rented from a very nice landlady. In spite of that, things were not easy for either of them. They were away from home for the first time, and everything was new to them. For instance, in the winter they had to fire up their coal stove themselves, and they were completely unused to cold weather. In Egypt they did not have to deal with this at all. Moreover, neither of them spoke German yet, and besides Arabic they knew only high school French. They acquired a French-German dictionary and tried to plow through their work somehow. In Alexandria both brothers had graduated from the language branch of their school and had read such demanding authors as Victor Hugo or Honoré de Balzac in the original French. In addition they learned a lot about Arab poets, which is very unusual today. However, they both had substantial deficits in mathematics and physics, which they had to catch up on as soon as possible. After a first year of only modest success, both brothers decided to change their field of study. Abdu's brother stayed in Vienna and later graduated as an engineer.

Abdu, however, left Austria, and with his friend Ahmad headed for Alexandria for a vacation, planning to return to Europe after that. For them, the oil industry seemed to offer more promising jobs for young engineers, and their studies were supposed to go in that direction. Their next destination was Sweden, because they believed life would be more interesting there than in Austria. On their way to Sweden, they stopped in Aachen, Germany. They liked the city right away, and the Technical University had a very good reputation. Although nothing was offered there that dealt with the oil industry, there was a branch of study for mining. They did not think twice about it, but simply enrolled and embarked on their studies.

During the semester breaks they had to do mandatory internships in the coalmines. One can imagine what that meant for these young men. So far they had spent their summers in Alexandria: three months with nothing to do but look at girls and have fun on the beach. All of a sudden they found themselves more than 3,000 feet below the surface of the earth, performing backbreaking work. It was very strenuous, but in spite of all the drudgery, they persevered. Since that time Abdu has suffered from asthma, which was most likely caused by the hard work in the coal dust.

Of course Abdu did not only pursue his studies, but also had a private life. In 1958 he met his first wife, a fashion designer. In 1962 they got married, and in the very same year their son Ahmad was born. Abdu continued his studies, his wife worked, and in 1965 he received his degree as a mining engineer.

In 1965 the small family traveled to Egypt. Abdu intended to look for work there and then move to Egypt permanently. At that time qualified workers for the construction of the Aswan Dam were in demand. Abdu could indeed have found a job there; however, his earnings would have been so low that he would not have been in a position to feed a family. Therefore, after six months, they returned to Germany. Abdu had talked to his father and decided that he wanted to earn his doctorate. His father would continue to support him financially. In Aachen Abdu started to work on his doctorate in civil engineering, and his wife went back to work again. But in 1968 their marriage was already falling apart. Both parents had a lot on their plate professionally and little time; therefore, their son Ahmad was sent to foster parents initially. The divorce and the related decision about custody of the child dragged on for some years. For Abdu it was very important that Ahmad grow up with him, but his wife wanted custody of the child, too.

Understandably after these complications Abdu was very guarded as far as women were concerned. One of his friends once mentioned he would need "a custom-made" wife; that is how cautious he had become.

I myself grew up near Aachen as the middle child of five siblings. After I graduated from high school (10th grade), I completed a bank traineeship and began to work at a savings bank. At the age of twenty, I got married, against the advice of my parents. Today I know that my first husband and I were far too young for such a decision, and moreover, we were not a good match at all. Anyway, the marriage was dissolved after only two years. We separated on good terms.

After the divorce I returned to Aachen. I was lucky enough to get my old job back at the savings bank. A few years later, I wanted to make a career change and saw an ad for a position at the Technical University in Aachen. I submitted my application, got the job, and from then on worked as an office assistant at the institute for process engineering. The job itself was not too exciting, but I liked the environment and the people there very much. Besides, I could exercise at the sports facilities of the university. That is where I came to Abdu's attention, in April of 1971. I had just turned 23.

We both had our first marriage already behind us. I had decided to think twice and scrutinize everything before entering into another relationship. But regardless, it clicked between us at the very first meeting. Abdu even felt certain right away; it took a little bit longer for me. I had been divorced only six months previously. For my family, the divorce was a disgrace, although today people have quite a different view. On top of that, Abdu was a foreigner, had not been legally divorced yet, had a nine-year-old son, and was in the middle of a custody battle. A tricky situation. But in spite of all this, I found Abdu very exciting right from the first moment. My parents, however, were not at all thrilled about this new development. Back then all kinds of rumors about "the Arabs" were afloat. Terrible things happened to women who went to such a country! But all that did not bother me; we were in love, and for me that was the most important thing.

In July 1971, when we had known each other for only three months, we traveled for the first time to Alexandria, Egypt, together with Ahmad. Before making any far-reaching decisions, I wanted to learn about the country and Abdu's family. We lived with Abdu's family during this time. I do not know what he had told them - whether or not he said we were married. I could not speak Arabic at all, so there was no way I could spill the beans, and there were no discussions. There was always something going on in his family, a continual coming and going; siblings, aunts, uncles, nieces and nephews, in and out daily, and I did not have the slightest idea who belonged to whom. I did not understand a word when they talked, and almost no one thought it necessary to translate or explain anything to me. And I found another thing very disturbing: Abdu had not told me anything about clothes for women. I had packed only miniskirts, and now I felt very improperly dressed. Even though at that time women in Egypt also wore summer dresses with short sleeves, their sleeves were not as short as in Europe. The whole time I felt uneasy, but I did not have anything more appropriate with me. It was midsummer and very hot. Many things were strange to me, but I wanted to make a good impression, of course, and under no circumstances wanted to make any major blunders. We had traveled from Germany to Egypt as a young couple in love, but unfortunately here in Alexandria I hardly felt the glow anymore. Abdu was busy with his family from dawn to dusk. We visited all kinds of people and then sat around for hours. I did not understand a word. Ahmad, too, was always with us, of course, and slowly but surely the first difficulties cropped up. Ahmad grew up with few rules, and in Egypt he did what he wanted to do. I myself was brought up very strictly. In Egypt attitudes toward children differ quite a bit from those in Germany. Children basically can do whatever they want; nobody corrects them when they are noisy, either. For me this situation was very complicated because I did not want to make any mistakes. In addition, the family watched my attitude towards Ahmad very closely.

Occasionally Abdu and I had communication problems, too. We had known each other only for a short time. So occasionally I took something that he said the wrong way.

Both the in-laws were very kind to me. They really

went out of their way to make me feel comfortable. Once, my father-in-law even came up with a bottle of wine. At that time the supply situation was very problematic, and he must have gone to a lot of trouble to get hold of this bottle. For many food supplies one still had to queue, and some things simply were not available at all. For example, there was no toilet paper and no soap. This situation was perhaps comparable to the situation in the early German Democratic Republic (the former East Germany). In spite of that, everybody was very friendly and simply beamed at us. There was a lot of laughter and joking.

We lived with the in-laws in their apartment directly by the seaside. I really wanted to go swimming, but under no circumstances could I be allowed to go alone. That was completely out of the question. A few times we drove with the family to Montazah to a private beach. Swimming was good there and nobody minded my bikini. The family, however, spent the whole day at the beach eating. A large picnic would be unpacked. Only the children would go into the water while the adults sat on the beach and chatted and ate....

I really would have liked to have spent a few days with Abdu alone, or at least take a walk with him in the evening now and then. But in Alexandria that was impossible. So after three weeks we returned to Germany having hardly spent five minutes alone together.

Before our vacation Abdu had already worked on a project in Hamburg. In December we moved to Hamburg altogether; we simply did not want to commute any longer. I had given up my secure position in Aachen, with some misgivings, and of course against all well-meant advice from my circle of acquaintances. But for both of us having a normal family life came first. Abdu was working; I stayed home at first. By now Abdu had obtained custody of Ahmad, and so Ahmad lived with us, as well. He attended school, and little by little we got used to each other. Naturally in the beginning he did not let me tell him very much. The age difference between us is not that great, and he was brought up far more liberally than considered appropriate. But bit by bit, we got along better and better with each other. As a family we really liked being in Hamburg, and Abdu and I were learning better how to deal with each other. But the cultural differences turned out to be far greater than we had initially thought. When, for example, I was nice to a man, Abdu immediately thought that I was trying to start something with him. Being from the Rhineland, where we approach people very openly, I was not used to anything like that. In Egypt, however, things are quite different, and most Egyptian men are very jealous. It took quite a while till we could settle on a compromise. I learned to adapt a little, and Abdu became more tolerant, as well. Most of the time, our disagreements were just little things, but they led to real debates on principles. Luckily, they could be easily resolved with a little bit of good will.

Actually, I would have liked to work again, although only part-time. But nothing came of that idea, because I became pregnant. I still remember exactly how I felt coming out of my gynecologist's office. I was so happy I could have embraced the whole world. I was 25 years old, just the right age, I thought. Although we were not yet married, that did not bother me in the least. My parents, though, were upset at first and were very worried about me.

Unfortunately, our time in Hamburg ended after less than a year. The project Abdu was working on was finished ahead of schedule, and Abdu returned to his employer in Cologne. Once again this meant looking for an apartment and moving. This time we rented a three-room apartment in a small town near Cologne. Although I now lived a little bit closer to my parents, I was pretty much cut off from the rest of the world. We did not have a telephone; the whole village did not have telephone lines yet. There were no cell phones then. I did not have a car, so I was stuck during the week. Ahmad attended school; he was picked up by the school bus. At least that was not a problem. But the village itself was boring to death; I did not have any friends and little to do.

In September, 1972, our daughter Samia was born. She was a very easy baby, and Ahmad, too, loved her immediately. Now I was pretty busy, of course, and soon met other mothers, too. Shortly after that Abdu accepted a job in Düsseldorf. We would have liked very much to move from the little village immediately, but we had a two-year lease and could not break the lease before it was up. So for the time being we stayed there. By then I had my own car and could do more things.

Later on in a suburb of Düsseldorf we found a nice townhouse, which we rented at first. After a few years we could buy the house, and we still live in it today. Here we have schools, day care centers, and a direct train connection to Düsseldorf. All of our children consider this house their home, including our son Monir, who was born in 1977.

Finally, in March of 1973, we got married. In the end everything had fallen into place according to our wishes. The registrar did not miss the opportunity to warn me about all the risks that might come with this marriage: Abdu could marry three more women in Egypt, my rights there would be very restricted, and so on. He then literally said: "You don't need that!" That almost triggered a brawl between him and Abdu. But after the ruffled feathers had been smoothed again, the marriage ceremony could eventually be carried out after all.

Now we were finally married and very happy. Even my parents did not object any more. In 1977, our son Monir was born. Now our family was complete, and I was very happy about it. I had to take care of the children, the house and the garden. In my spare time, I did all sorts of things; I made pottery and tried to learn Arabic. For that I took a course in Classical Arabic at the community college. But Classical Arabic is quite different from Egyptian Arabic, which always earned me lots of laughter from other Egyptians when I struggled with my few bits of Arabic. This was not really motivating and eventually I dropped it. But in that class I met some other German women who also were married to Egyptian men, which for me was almost as important as learning the language. One could compare notes, and I developed some friendships that way. Some of these women I later met in Alexandria. I was also able to improve my Arabic in Alexandria by listening and babbling away, so that now I can make myself understood quite well. For me this is very important; it gives me a feeling of security and independence when we are in Egypt.

Naturally, we went to Egypt on vacation during all those years. Most of the time, we stayed in my in-laws' apartment. Later on, we added our own large apartment in the same house. The in-laws owned the house, and over many years Abdu had renovated it and had made improvements. This is how things are done in Egypt: if more space is needed, one simply adds another floor to the top floor. This way the houses keep growing and growing over the years.

Naturally Abdu was brought up as a Muslim. I myself was Lutheran, but this did not cause a problem for us. As far as beliefs and religion are concerned, we actually had very similar views. Abdu is very tolerant and is not impressed at all by tight regulations. In 1972, I converted to Islam, because I thought that in a family all the members should belong to the same religion. According to Islamic law the children of a Muslim man are Muslims by birth as well, although that does not automatically mean that they abide by the religious rules.

In the meantime Abdu worked on and off on projects in the Arab region. He had specialized in project management and monitoring. To do that he had taken different courses in critical path analysis with computer-assisted programming and had gained further qualifications accordingly. At that time that was something entirely new, and initially many customers did not want to know anything about it. Only after they realized how efficiently one could monitor such large projects did they change their minds little by little.

At the beginning of the eighties, orders fell off in the German construction sector. Together with a fellow Egyptian, Abdu started up his own company, and they tried out project monitoring in the Arab region. But the economic situation there was not that good any more either, and the business did not take off.

So in 1986, we seriously considered relocating to Egypt with the whole family. The situation there was not a bit better, but Abdu believed that we could live a better life there with our savings. We would have to sell our house; in Alexandria we at least had an apartment. But I could not warm up to this idea at all. I thought that in Egypt without money one would be even poorer than in Germany. In general the standard of living is much lower, the infrastructure far less developed. In addition it surely would have been much more difficult for our children. Ahmad was already an adult; he was 24 years old and had left home. But Samia was 14 and Monir only 9 years old. Would they be able to cope with such a change? For nights on end I racked my brain about this. Then I realized I could look for a job myself. After all I had not even turned forty yet, had a good education and had several years of working experience. By chance I actually found a job at the Xerox Company, although initially it was only meant to be a temp job for three weeks. I had to sort files; it was a very simple task. Hardly a dream job, but I put in all my effort regardless and tried to accomplish everything as well as possible. By the way, when I decided to work, I did this on my own, without telling Abdu, because he happened to be in Egypt once again. After he returned we had fierce discussions about it. A wife who works - that absolutely does not fit in with the masculine ego of an Egyptian -- it looks as if he is unable to care for her. But Abdu more or less had to face a fait accompli. My working hours were only from eight to noon, leaving me more than enough time for the children and my household. Abdu realized quickly that in spite of my work everything was running smoothly at home, and he gave in. Then my position was extended again and again, apparently because I could adapt very well to any position. I got along with all the people and soon I was familiar with all the departments. I pitched in everywhere, when somebody had called in sick, or when extra help was needed at short notice. In the beginning I actually did not want a permanent position, so I could be more flexible. During the summer I could always take a long time off and I could stay home at short notice when one of the children became sick. I stayed with the Xerox Company for four years as a floater.

In 1990 Xerox merged with a second company to become XES, and now they wanted to hire me full time. I got a job as a sales assistant, working in a „job sharing" arrangement, meaning that a colleague and I were sharing a work area, and one of us always had to be present. We were free to schedule our work hours ourselves and got along with each other very well. Together we organized the appointments of the sales people and took care of the order processing. I really liked this job, and on top of that I earned more money than before. My steady income made it possible for us to continue with our former lifestyle without any major cutbacks. At the newly created XES Company employee motivation was especially important. There were many seminars and events; sometimes even including the families. Personally I learned a lot in these seminars. They helped me to structure my thoughts; I learned how to deal with conflicts better and how to make decisions. I could use these accomplishments not only in my profession, but also in my family life. At that time Samia was in a difficult phase, in the middle of puberty, with all the problems that usually come with it, and what I learned in the company helped me to deal with it better. As the daughter of an Egyptian father, she also had to fight her own unique battles: going to the movies or to the disco alone – entirely unimaginable in Egypt. In the end Abdu had to adjust his perceptions, but that time was not at all easy for everyone involved.

In all of Germany, ten women worked at XES in the same job in the different branches. We were a wonderful team; I never ever experienced afterwards such cooperation and acceptance. My friendships from those times still exist today. Besides that, I was sent to international trade shows and exhibitions, which I enjoyed very much. All in all I had a lot of fun at work, and my self-confidence was boosted. That in turn really helped my relationship with Abdu because my achievements commanded his respect.

He had more and more confidence in me, and therefore I enjoyed more and more freedom. What was once a drama in the beginning when I needed to go to an appointment with a colleague by car, had now even turned into my being able to travel alone to a seminar.

Abdu continued to work on projects in the Arab region and to do construction work and renovations at his family's house. So he was in Egypt often. When he returned home after a longer absence, it took a little while until we all got used to each other again. Just the fact that life goes on even without them is hard to take for many husbands. But that, incidentally - as far as I know -goes for German husbands as well as for Egyptian husbands. Here is how it works: in the absence of the husband the wife makes a decision about something herself – what else can she do? Once the husband is back again, the decision is reversed. That is unacceptable to the wife, of course. So there is always plenty of material for an explosive situation. But in spite of this Abdu and I were able to cope with these difficult times very well.

From the beginning of our marriage, we always had a joint account and discussed all our financial issues together. Abdu is very good at planning and organizing. That is a must in his profession, but also has its advantages in private life. That way we never had any real financial problems and were always able to make a good living. A few years later Abdu admitted that my work at that time was of great importance for our family.

In 1998 XES was restructured once again, and at first I stopped working. I received a nice severance pay and then took seven months off. During that time I spent a total of four months in Egypt. The children had already grown up, and I only needed to go to Germany every few weeks to take care of what was absolutely necessary. In those four months in Egypt, I really settled in. Little by little my Arabic improved, and I could finally go out on my own to do some shopping or to meet the women of the „International Women's Club" in the Sporting Club. To do that, I took the tram or a taxi.

Since then I have friends and contacts in Alexandria

outside the family, as well. Now I feel really comfortable there, and Egypt has become very familiar to me. As time went by, I got used to many things that I found annoying in the beginning: the dirt, the noise and the many people. At the same time I discovered many positive things that are missing in Germany. The people are much more helpful, and women from other countries enjoy preferential treatment everywhere. When somebody falls down in the street, everybody rushes to the scene to help. In Germany one can sometimes wait a long time before anyone helps; many look the other way, or just keep walking. When I go shopping, I often think about women's emancipation. Is it really progress to go shopping alone by car and then have to lug the beverages and shopping bags? In Egypt couples go shopping together. The wife walks very unhurriedly beside her husband and instructs him what to put into the shopping cart. Then the husband picks up everything and later has to carry whatever was purchased.

In these four months Abdu was in Alexandria, too, but most of the time he was busy with renovations. He, too, had to readjust himself to life in Egypt. His German methods did not always work there. The biggest problem during construction or renovation is to find reliable people who keep their appointments and do good work. Some leave so much dirt behind that after they are finished, a major cleanup is necessary. In the course of time, Abdu became quite experienced and now knows craftsmen here who do a very good job and clean up afterwards.

Back in Germany I started looking for work again. I still knew many people at Xerox, and through these connections I found another job in 1999. This time I worked directly in sales, visiting customers and negotiating with them. Up until then I had always imagined sales as something dreadful, like selling vacuum cleaners. But it turned out to be quite different. I sold a product -- paper and accessories to be exact -- that all customers absolutely needed. I always had to be well-informed to give them solid advice. And I was responsible for my own accounting and for reaching the pre-set sales goals. It was a very responsible position and sometimes very stressful. In sales, employees are motivated through awards and prizes. For good work there are incentives, and now and then I, too, was awarded some prizes. I worked 25 hours per week. For me the seven years at Xerox were a good time; I was appreciated and felt comfortable.

In 2005 this company, too, was restructured again. I was 58 years old and did not really want to work any more. Besides, I thought it was finally time that we should implement our plan to spend more time in Egypt. After all, how much longer should we wait? Abdu was already 70 years old. So I retired, and we rearranged our life once more. Now we spend two months at a time in the spring and the autumn in Egypt. The rest of the year we live in Germany. In 2006 I found another hobby for myself -- I completed some training to become a tour guide in Düsseldorf. Through that I learned a lot about the history and the architecture in Düsseldorf. Although I have not really started this job in earnest yet, I definitely want to do that pretty soon.

All our children live in Germany. Ahmad is married and already has children himself. We love our house in Germany, where we like to putter around in the garden. In Egypt hardly anybody has a garden and when there is one, it is taken care of by the servants. When we are in Germany, we do a lot of bicycling and often spend time in the country. As long as our health allows us to travel so much, we would like to keep switching between Egypt and Germany.

Abdu still has some school friends in Egypt, and over the years we have met some other intermarried couples who live in both countries as we do. We visit each other's homes or meet at the Sporting Club. We also travel together; for example, in 2007 we went on a cruise on Lake Nasser with a very nice group. I am a member of the German Women's' Club of Alexandria and of the Swiss Club. That way we have many contacts here and lead a pleasant life.

I like the Egyptian cuisine very much, too. I am always thrilled anew with the awesome choices of fruits and vegetables. They eat a lot of vegetarian dishes here like molokhia, ful and kosheri (see appendix A). In Egypt meat dishes are abundant as well, but we ourselves eat only a little meat. Since I came here for the first time in 1971, the supply situation has changed greatly. At that time many staple foods were in short supply but now almost everything is readily available and most of it is produced domestically. Many imported items are available, too. Even small electrical appliances of good quality are produced in Egypt now. With enough money to spend, one can live very comfortably here. The population has grown immensely. In 1950 there were 20 million people; today there are at least 80 million. In spite of this, the provisions are good. This sometimes seems incredible to me.

As far as religious fanaticism is concerned, I have the impression that regrettably it is increasing more and more. In the past only elderly women or women from the countryside wore a headscarf . Today there is hardly a girl without a headscarf. Sometimes, to me, this seems to be only a fashion thing, but the whole cityscape has been changed by it. The large crowds in the streets often lead to an unpleasant crush of people. Maybe that has caused the change in behavior of the Egyptian people, and one does not encounter as many cheerful people as before. When I first came here, I was impressed at how lighthearted and sunny the people seemed to be.

I have never ever regretted that I decided to marry Abdu. Through him I have had many new experiences, and my life has become much richer and more colorful. However, I now see Germany through very different eyes. I have become more critical, and for the first few days in Germany, I have to adjust myself the same way I had to in Egypt.

Because our children and grandchildren live in Germany, our home will always be there. But over all these years I have grown very fond of Egypt. In the beginning I had great difficulty adjusting to life here. But in the end I succeeded, and it was worth it. Now I consider this country my second homeland.

Chapter Thirteen
Anita W. A Plantation in Egypt

I became acquainted with Anita and her husband through friends from Alexandria. I had just started working on this book, and a friend thought I really should include Anita's story. Anita and Mohsen had bought a piece of land and through years of labor transformed it into a beautiful fruit farm. So far none of my acquaintances had done anything like that, so naturally we were curious. Soon we were invited to visit them in their little Garden of Eden. It was a fantastic idyll: a little paradise full of big trees, date palms, banana plants, orange trees, roses, and a multitude of other flowers. I had never seen such beautiful grounds anywhere else in Egypt. They live in a spacious house with several terraces. Stairs lead to the roof where one has an incredible view of the stars at night. An elaborate, colorful mosaic adorns the roof itself.

Anita is a vivacious woman with light blond hair and brown eyes. She speaks very quickly in a Rhineland dialect, so that it is not easy for me to understand her. Her husband, Mohsen, does not actually look Egyptian at all, more like a German. He has green eyes. During our short stay at their plantation in the fall of 2007, Anita told me her story:

I met my husband-to-be, Mohsen, on New Year's Eve in 1959. I was 20 at the time; Mohsen was 22. It was love at first sight. And it was only by coincidence that we met at all...My friend Karin and I actually wanted to go to a party at our friends' place. We had arranged to meet an acquaintance at the Cologne train station who would give us a lift. But she never came. It got later and later and we waited and waited. It was 10 o'clock, and we were still waiting. It was New Year's Eve and there was a lot going on at the train station, but eventually we grew impatient.

By chance my brother, Klaus, came by—still undecided as to how he should spend New Year's Eve. We discussed our options. Then suddenly Klaus decided: „I'll take you both out; we'll go to Aachen." I have forgotten why it had to be Aachen of all places, but anyway we went by train to the Aachen station. Then we took a taxi to the Congo Bar. That was really nonsense as we could easily have walked the short distance, but Klaus absolutely insisted on driving up in a taxi. The New Year's Eve party was already in full swing. There was a lot of action. We danced a lot and had a splendid time. Mohsen was also there, celebrating with his friends. He was dancing with a Dutch woman who danced so wildly that the two of them, along with the Christmas tree, fell over. After all the excitement, Mohsen did not dance with the Dutch woman anymore—only with me. We talked to each other as best we could with all the noise, and I decided in that moment: „I will marry him." Mohsen felt the same way—he told me later. Since that evening we have belonged together.

Mohsen was born and raised in Cairo. His parents were well-off land owners. His father was a civil engineer for waterways and for city planning. His mother was descended from the Egyptian royal family who originally came from the Ottoman Empire to Egypt. Mohsen was not a good student, but in spite of that, he got it into his head to study in Germany. Money was no problem, and his father promised to pay for his studies abroad if Mohsen succeeded in completing his university entrance diploma. That promise awakened his ambition. Mohsen definitely wanted to succeed. He came up with the strangest tricks to spur himself on to study. He shaved his eyebrows to prevent himself from going out socially, which meant he had fewer distractions. Day after day he sat at home and studied like one possessed. His diligence was rewarded: he completed his university entrance diploma, and his father kept his word and financed his studies. In 1957 Mohsen flew to Munich, and right away he liked it so much, he decided he would never leave this beautiful land. Even the fact that he now had to complete the German university entrance diploma did not scare him off. He went to a special school with an associated boarding school in Bad Aibling, improved his German at the Goethe Institute in Munich, completed his German university entrance diploma and then matriculated at the Rhineland-Westphalian Technical University in Aachen. After finishing the first level of study toward his degree, he transferred to Cologne where he completed his degree in electrical engineering.

As for me, I grew up in the Rhineland in Buir, a little place with a population of 1,000 souls. I am the fourth of five children—I had one sister and three brothers. My parents ran a big bakery in town. They were always very generous. We often had guests at our table, sometimes other children but often poorer people who were provided for. I was my father's favorite and a tomboy, always out and about with my brothers and--- to my mother's dismay—often coming home with dirty trousers or skinned knees. My older sister was entirely different—she always took great care with her appearance and never got dirty. My mother was just as blond as I was, but for reasons unknown she had dyed her hair chestnut brown. To this day I do not understand why she did so. My sister and my youngest brother had dark hair like my father; the rest of us were blond.

Well, now I had met Mohsen and we were in love. But how should I tell my Catholic mother? With my father there would be no problem; I would manage that somehow. He was Catholic, too, but very tolerant and always somewhat more lenient with me. I debated with myself how best to arrange things without making a scene. My parents often allowed us to celebrate at home and invite our friends. We used to call it a house fest, but today one would probably call it a party. They always thought it was better when we met friends at home rather than somewhere else. So I arranged with my brothers that they would invite Mohsen as an acquaintance of theirs to our house party. No sooner said than done. Mohsen came and was very charming. He talked with my parents, even danced with my mother, and everyone thought he was nice. Even my mother really liked him. She did not notice at all that we already knew each other. She thought until the end of the evening that we saw each other for the first time at that party. Of course, pretty soon the whole story came out. My brother, Klaus, could not resist and told my mother that Mohsen had come to the party only because of me. At first she was upset, but then luckily she calmed down again. No wonder with such a nice young man!

Mohsen became a part of our family. My father and he got along right from the beginning. Later Mohsen called my father „Pap", too, just as my siblings and I did. It quickly became clear that we wanted to get married, and my parents agreed to it, too. We were married in 1960 at the Civil Registry Office in Buir. Of course our entire family was well known in town, because everyone was a customer of our bakery. Now there was finally a topic of conversation of absorbing interest to the whole town: "Anita married an African," the people said. Sometimes our customers brought us newspaper articles that reported the horrible treatment of women who married in an Arabic-speaking country. That did not bother us.

At first Mohsen and I lived with my parents, and in 1960 our daughter, Mona, was born. When I walked through the village with the baby carriage, people tried to peek inconspicuously under the many blankets to see if the child was black or not. They had no more idea of Egypt than they did of Timbuktu.

Mohsen completed his studies and we moved to Düren into our first apartment. He got a job at Siemens and was often away on construction. When he traveled, I took Mona and stayed with my parents. Why should I sit around alone at home? When the people saw me in the village, it went around immediately: „Anita has moved back in with kid and caboodle to her parents." They could not imagine that our marriage would last. In that they were mightily deceived! We were just fine, and soon, I started working again too in an office, just as I had before my marriage. Mona went to day care and I also had a nanny for her. Financially things went very well for us, because until Mohsen started at Siemens, my father-in-law, as promised, provided for Mohsen's needs. We were a very normal young family, and in 1965 our son Ahmad was born.

In the first few years of our marriage we did not travel to Egypt at all. My father-in- law had retired by then, but as idleness did not agree with him at all, he had accepted a consulting position in Saudi Arabia. He was in a high position as a city planner in Riyadh. He liked to travel and visited us regularly in Germany. He usually stayed at the Hotel Excelsior in Cologne. Sometimes he brought a whole delegation of businessmen with him from Saudi Arabia. Once even a prince from the royal family came, and the hotel hoisted the Saudi Arabian flag. On such occasions Mohsen could often jump in as translator. According to protocol, he would be picked up with a stretch limousine. That caused a stir in our little village! "Now he has to translate again for the sheiks!" said the children on our street.

My father-in-law was a true linguistic genius; he spoke six languages. On one of his visits to Germany, he mentioned casually that he would now learn German. And he actually did. By his next visit his command of the German language was good enough that he could read the children their bedtime stories. Now I could talk with him in German, too. But even before, communication was not a problem for us. Although I did not speak Arabic at the time, we all managed very well in English. My mother-in-law continued to live in Egypt during those years. She did not want to move to Saudi Arabia because of the many restrictions on women there. But she, too, visited us in Germany, sometimes at the same time as my father-in-law. I remember in detail her first visit in 1965. Of course, I had on occasion seen Egyptian women at the airport or in films. They usually wore long dresses, sometimes with headscarves. We stood waiting at the airport in Frankfurt for Mohsen's mother. „There she is," called Mohsen, but I looked for her in vain until I could look no more. I could not see an Egyptian woman anywhere. When Mohsen then pointed her out to me, my jaw dropped. She was the epitome of fashion; very chic in a light blue suit and high-heeled shoes. From head to toe everything was color- coordinated. Her hair was Titian red; she had green eyes and wore a lot of jewelry. For heaven's sake, she looks as if she came directly from Paris! I thought. Suddenly I felt much underdressed. I was so stunned that I could not speak. The little Arabic that I knew was totally gone. But that did not matter. She embraced me very sincerely and kissed me several times. Then she sat down with me on the airport bench and immediately unpacked the jewelry she had brought me. There were rings, a beautiful bracelet, and pendants with rubies; necklaces and much more. I was overwhelmed. I could not speak a word—and that rarely happens to me!

We saw my parents-in law often, but not in Egypt. They preferred to visit us in Germany. On one of their visits, we picked them up at the airport with our old Opel. On the way to the airport, the muffler broke and the car made terrible noises. Mohsen's mother decided immediately that the „boy" needed a new car. No sooner said than done. A few days later we had a brand new car. Another time when we picked them up, our children were with us and Mona fussed and fussed; she gave us no peace. In a sinfully expensive boutique in the airport, she had seen a pair of red leather lederhosen that she just had to have. O f course they were way too expensive. I would never have spent so much money on something like that. My mother-in-law, however, insisted on fulfilling the child's wish. They were both very generous to us and to the children. But because they were not always around, things worked out very well. Our children grew up very normally; only Grandma and Grandpa spoiled them thoroughly. But that happens in most families anyway.

Religion did not play a big part in our daily life. Mohsen is Muslim, but he is very liberal. He and his family did not demand that I convert to Islam, and I did not see any reason to. Our children were not baptized. As they grew up and got bigger, we answered their questions as they were asked. They were not brought up in any particular religion. Instead they sorted out questions of faith later for themselves.

As soon as the children got older, I went back to work again in an office. But then I realized I would rather do something independently and be my own boss. However, I did not have the educational background for that. So far I had only a high school diploma and training as an office manager. I registered for a course and prepared evenings for the exam for retail salesperson. That was not easy, as I had to take care of the children and the household at the same time. But I kept at it and I passed the exam and got my certification. With the money we had saved in the meantime, I opened a baked goods shop in Düren. My brother, Günter, had taken over my father's bakery and was able to supply me with baked goods. After some beginner's difficulties, my business went very well. Word got around quickly that our breakfast rolls and other baked goods tasted very good. Occasionally Mohsen helped out in the shop. He was always very generous, though, and gave the customers lots of free samples. That was good advertising but bad for the profit.

We enjoyed a peaceful life for many years in Düren. The children went to school, Mohsen worked, and I had my shop. Later we built a house in Buir, which meant that I had to drive every day to my shop. We were very busy, but I liked our life and was very content and happy.

Then in 1975 I had a bad car accident, and on top of that I was at fault for not paying attention. It happened on the way to school, and both children, at that time 15 and 10 years old, were sitting in the back seat. The car was written off. I was badly hurt and unconscious—they flew me immediately by helicopter to the hospital in Cologne. The children were taken by ambulance to the hospital in Bergheim, but apart from a few scrapes they had no injuries. It was several days before I regained consciousness in the intensive care unit. I had various broken bones in my ribs and thoracic vertebra in addition to cuts and scrapes. „Where are my children? Is everything all right with them?" were my first questions. I was assured that both of them were fine. I could not believe it until I had seen them with my own eyes and was very worried. Every day I asked Mohsen about the children. Then I suddenly came down with a high fever and the doctors did not know what to do. Mohsen came up with the idea of bringing Ahmad und Mona to me in the hospital, although they did not want to let him in with the children at all. But he would not give in; he literally stuck his foot in the door and brought them to me. When I finally saw that the children were safe and sound, my condition improved right away and I recovered. Much later when I found out that I had been brought to the hospital in a helicopter, I was annoyed that I had not been conscious and able to experience it. But then again, if I had been conscious, they probably would not have needed to go by helicopter!

Soon after that, I gave up my shop and went to work part time in an office again. It had become just too much for me with the work and driving back and forth. Now at last I had more time for the family again. Mohsen changed employers and drove every day to the city clinics in Duisburg. It was not really far, but that stretch often had traffic jams.

In 1972, we went to Egypt together for the first time. Mohsen had not been there for many years. My parents-in-law and our other relatives had always visited us in Germany all those years, so Mohsen had not felt the need to travel to Egypt. But in the end, at the wish of my father-in-law, we did go. By then my mother-in-law had already died. We spent our vacation in the family summerhouse in Ras el Barr, which lies east of Alexandria. I was very surprised at the many stones on the sidewalks. Everything looked the worse for wear. Only much later did I realize that it always looked like that in Egypt. At first I thought: „Well, of course, there was a war here." But that had been several years ago. We went to a beach in Gerby to go swimming with the children. At that time one could go swimming in a bathing suit without causing a sensation. We also toured Cairo and visited Mohsen's sister there. Her husband worked as the director of a big hospital and she had a large household with different servants and an abundance of everything. At mealtimes, the table was set as if for a holiday with silver and valuable china.

But another Egypt stood in stark contrast to this wealth. I remember well a little incident at Ras el Barr. We had run out of cooking oil and Mohsen offered to get some. The „shop' was a tiny dilapidated building. What was being sold there was not completely clear to me. Besides, everything was covered in dirt. Someone wiped off a black bottle with a black rag. Then the bottle was filled with our oil from a metal barrel. At first I thought it was lamp oil and could not figure out exactly why we were there. In spite of the splendor and wealth of some very privileged families, when it came to supplies, things were still handled in a very primitive manner.

Two years later, in 1974, at the great age of 94, my father-in-law was hit by a car in a street in Saudi Arabia and died of his injuries. Until his death he had been physically fit and mentally sharp and had even continued to work.

In 1985 I found a very nice new hobby through sheer coincidence. My daughter, Mona, had signed up for a pottery course but then soon lost interest in going. I decided to take her place and was fascinated right away with this creative and sensual activity. I did not stay long with little pieces; on the contrary, I got going right away with a large vase and a lamp base. Without any sizeable setbacks I finished the pieces, fired them and discovered that my work was very well received. After the course was over, I continued with pottery on my own and soon had many nice pieces ready. By chance I heard of a planned exhibition in Kerpen. I got in touch with the organizers and was actually invited to exhibit my work there. It was a great success for me. Although I was just a beginner, I won the second prize. Besides I was able to sell some of my pieces and with that money I was able to buy my own kiln. I really worked hard for the next exhibition the following year and was rewarded with first prize this time. Later, when I no longer had room for the kiln, I began to paint. Our life had changed; the children were out of the house, and we spent part of the year in Egypt. Painting has remained my hobby, and still brings me much joy.

For several years a lifelong dream had haunted Mohsen: a plantation with fruit and vegetables, flowers and large trees. I was interested in the idea too, and could imagine our developing it together. Originally we looked at Spain as the spot for our orchard. We regularly spent our vacation with the children on the Costa Brava, in Sitges, and had diligently learned Spanish at Adult Evening Classes. Mohsen knew that he would inherit something in Egypt from his mother and we wanted to buy the land with it. Mohsen really did inherit a piece of land that after a time we were able to sell at a good price. Unfortunately we were unable to transfer this money out of Egypt. The Egyptian requirements and laws are very complicated, and we quickly met with insurmountable obstacles. After some back and forth, we decided to realize our dream of a plantation in Egypt.

In 1987 it was finally time to get started. Land west of the Nile was available. American Peace Corps workers had had canals built that drew water from the Nile, making agriculture possible in that part of the desert. They constructed paved streets and laid electric power lines. Mohsen took a leave of absence for two years from the clinic in Duisburg and went with Ahmad to Egypt. He bought 20 Fadan (approx. 8,4 hectares or 20.75 acres) in the area of Nubreya in the Western Desert, about 150 km (93 miles) from Cairo and 100 km (62 miles) from Alexandria.

When Mohsen and Ahmad arrived, there was literally nothing there, only fallow land. First Mohsen had a wooden shack built so that they at least had a roof over their heads if they needed it. Foremen and workers were hired to divide the land into parcels and build smaller canals. Then the plants were bought and put in. At the same time Mohsen planned a house out of stone that was actually framed in only three months. When I first arrived, we still lived in the wooden house. But at least we had electricity and water. The shower and toilet were in an outbuilding in an extra house, but everything worked. In spite of that, the climate took its toll on me. It was unbelievably hot, and I became ill at first. I developed rashes and was constantly bitten by mosquitoes. I lost weight. It was a very difficult time for both of us. After seven months when we could move into the big house, my condition slowly began to improve. In our new house it was not nearly so hot, and from the first day on I felt very comfortable there.

Slowly but surely our plantation progressed, although not everything went as we had planned. We had to overcome some failures. For example, the almond trees, from which we had expected a good harvest, did not really grow and remained puny. In the end we had to pull them all out by the roots.

For protection from the strong winds out here, we planted little gasualin trees (they are also called pioneer trees). Those trees still stand today on the plantation. They grow very fast to 30 m (100 feet) high and provide a lot of shade. When they grow too tall, we have them felled and sell the wood for a good profit.

One can walk everywhere on our plantation. Groomed paths invite one to go for a walk. This is by no means the case everywhere. On many plantations, the fields are overgrown with knee-high weeds and one cannot get through in regular shoes. Unlike most plantation farmers we have cultivated quite a variety of plants instead of a monoculture. That means more work, but it is much more beautiful than with only one type of plant. We have date palms, banana plants, figs, quite a variety of roses and other flowers. Oranges, limes, grapefruit and mango produce the best yields. All of those fruits are loaded at harvest directly onto trucks that can drive right up into the fields. The trucks take the fruit to Cairo where the wholesalers buy them from us and sell them at the large indoor wholesale market. We use organic fertilizers for the most part. All the plant waste, for example from the banana plants, is cut up and spread out on the fields again. In addition, we irrigate by gradually flooding the entire area through the little canals. For that purpose an entire system of these canals has been laid and they can be opened one after the other. The ancient pharaohs irrigated their fields with the help of this technique. The land was flooded every few days with water from the Nile from the big canal. Much less water evaporates than with the usual drip irrigation. We get our drinking water from the 22-meter (72 foot) deep well that we had dug. A pump sends the water to the water tank on our roof. Of course we sent a water sample for chemical analysis to Germany and it was perfect. And it tastes excellent.

2007 was our first really good year, in which we made a profit from our plantation. We are, of course, very proud that we succeeded in building everything up.

Sometime during 1989 Mohsen's unpaid leave came to an end, and we had to go back to Germany. We contracted with a foreman who would run the plantation in our absence. During the two years on our plantation we had put all our energy into the farm and had not taken a single day of vacation. So first we enjoyed our homeland when we returned. Mohsen worked again in the clinics. The children were no longer at home and the daily drive from Buir to Duisburg was taking its toll on him. So we sold our house in 1995 and moved to an apartment in Duisburg. At the time Mohsen had heart problems, too. After his operation we were glad he did not have to drive so much. Mohsen worked in Duisburg until 2002; then at 65 he retired.

Since 1989 we have gone to Egypt every year in spring and fall for a few weeks to check on our plantation. That was our "vacation". Unfortunately it did not always turn out the way we imagined. We had different foremen who were sometimes good and sometimes not so good. At present we have a very good man who has everything under control. Since Mohsen's retirement, we live half the time in Egypt. Mohsen is now 70 years old; I am 68. Recently we have both had problems with our health so we travel more frequently to Germany. Medical care in Egypt is not anywhere near the standard of that in Germany. We gave up our apartment in Duisburg in 2007 and moved once again to Düren. We have a nice apartment there that provides everything we need. It is near our children, who are both married, and we now have four grandchildren.

Mohsen was able to make his dream come true. In the beginning we had to struggle and experienced disappointments and failures. But in the end it did become our little paradise. It will be very difficult for both of us when we have to give it up some day. This plantation is our work, our baby. We thought it all out ourselves, planned it and transformed it. It is a piece of Egypt but perhaps more a piece of us. I hope we can live here for a very long time and enjoy the fruit of our labor.

Chapter Fourteen
Ilse T. All My Gardens

Ilse converted to Islam after her wedding and is now a devout Muslim, although she has retained her tolerance towards other religions. She is of medium height, very slender, and usually wears long dresses or trousers. Of all the women in this book, Ilse is the only one who wears a headscarf. What else distinguishes her from the others? When she told me her story, she came across as very candid and sometimes even emotional. Much that happened a long time ago still moves her very much today. Her story impressed me, too. Above all what happened in her Southern German village after she got engaged to her future husband is hard for me to believe and most of all sad. Here is her story:

I met my husband in 1962 in our village, where my mother was born and I was brought up. Throughout my youth I was deeply rooted there and had many relatives: great-aunts, aunts, uncles and cousins. People stuck together and supported each other. My favorite aunt taught me all kinds of things: we did handicrafts and often pottered around together. As a child, I developed a penchant for all sorts of handicrafts. Unfortunately this favorite aunt died when I was only twelve years old. My mother could only knit, and always the same two items, a little jacket and a little hat. Year after year she knitted the same articles for all the children in the family and for acquaintances in the village. She always said about me: "That Ilse is a skillful little thing." And since I was so skillful, I had to do everything, too. My mother thought nothing of recruiting me for all kinds of housework and mending jobs; on top of that she sent me shopping every day. That usually meant running around a lot, to the grocery shop, to the baker, to the butcher, and so on. When I was older, I was allowed to ride my bike. I also had to mow the lawn – of course with a rotary mower without a motor; at that time there was nothing else available where we lived. The lawn mower had to be pushed with muscle power alone, which was quite strenuous. Anyway, my mother kept me quite busy, and I almost always went along with it.

Even as a child I had my own little garden. We only rented our apartment - our landlord lived with his family on the first floor, and we occupied the second floor above. But the landlord allotted my sister and me each a little piece of garden which we could work with as we liked. Once he gave my sister and me each a rose bush that he had grafted himself as a present. Together we planted the roses in our gardens, and my rose became quite gorgeous although unfortunately it did not have any fragrance. Our landlord also had a daughter named Sophie, who was already a teenager when I was born. I was there when she got married and had her own children, and we still see each other from time to time today.

One of my many great-aunts also had a wonderful garden, and in my spare time I helped her with great enthusiasm. I learned a lot about plants and flowers from her even then. The village gardener was right next to our garden, and naturally the people there knew me from my regular visits. When I had to go shopping for my mother, I often picked up little plants for myself. The gardener liked me very much, and every now and then she gave me a little flower or a little something for my garden.

My father was from Silesia (a former German province in the East) and had come to South Baden to study. After he passed his exams in dentistry, he settled down in our little village in 1936 and married my mother. Both my parents were Lutheran but not religious. My father loved nature and being outdoors, and I often went along with him. Sometimes we took our bikes and rode up to the Glotter Valley until the path became too steep. Then we had to push our bicycles and continue on foot. Somewhere on the way we always arrived at a farm where we could get fresh buttermilk with little lumps of butter in it. That tasted so great. As my father was the dentist, he knew everybody in the village and in the surrounding area.

Like everywhere else in Germany, religion was taught

in our school. Our teacher urged us to go to church on Sundays. At that time I was about eight years old. So I told my mother that I would attend church on Sundays. She was surprised but did not say much about it. So the next Sunday I went to church with a friend of mine. The following week I wanted to go again, although my mother did not think it necessary at all. But nevertheless I went a second time. After the third time, my mother started to tease me about it. That was way too much for me and I stopped going to church.

A few years later - I was about fourteen years old - a friend of the family invited me to Switzerland during the summer break. She was a native of Russia who had Swiss citizenship and was quite well off. She often visited our family, and one of my cousins was her godchild. This cousin then learned that I was supposed to visit Aunt Valerie. She made a few derisive remarks which I understood only much later. "I see our aunt has invited you. I hope you have lots of fun!" This aunt led quite a luxurious life in Switzerland. My cousin, her godchild, was always invited and was pretty much spoiled. At least that's what I thought. But after I arrived, I first had to help close down the winter residence. Then I was told that we would move into the summerhouse and there would be renovations. I had to slave away while my aunt just stood around and gave instructions. Once we ate plum preserves with whipped cream. I noticed some maggots in them and was really disgusted. In our house everything was very clean because my mother cared about hygiene. Nobody except me had noticed the maggots; everybody was eating it. My aunt saw that I hesitated. I protested that maggots were in there, but she forced me to finish the dessert, all the same. She said so far nobody had died from it. Now at least I knew that one can tolerate much more than one thinks.

Yunis (my future husband) was born and raised in Alexandria, Egypt. His father was a businessman and would have liked his son to study economics in Sudan. Initially Yunis obediently complied and went there, but he soon returned. He simply did not like it; that course of study was not his cup of tea. Even as a little boy he wanted to become a doctor. In his opinion the best education could be found in Germany. When his father died, he left his children some money, and with that money Yunis was able to travel to Germany and begin his studies. To finance his living expenses, he held a variety of different jobs. For instance, he worked as assistant to a painter and along the way became an excellent house painter himself. Yunis studied medicine in Freiburg and also lived there. In his spare time he tried to improve his German. Once he took the train to our little village to go on an excursion and look around. Right away he liked it so much that he looked for a room and from then on lived in our village.

I attended a public college preparatory school (Gymnasium) and actually would have liked to study art. But my mother talked me out of it - no money in it, she thought. Then I talked over the possibility of becoming a dental technician with my father. I would have liked to work with him, and I was always very good with my hands. So I left school and started my training.

Then my father died of colon cancer rather young; that was in 1961. All of a sudden everything changed. I missed my father very much. But even worse was the way my mother reacted to his death. Even long before he became ill, he had bought a piece of land on which they wanted to build their house together. But that had not happened. Now my mother was obsessed with the idea that she absolutely had to build the house, no matter what. Of course that was not a reasonable thing to do without my father's income. My mother asked me to drop out of my training and find a job with more money. Today I know how shortsighted my mother was. I would have earned good money after my training as a dental technician. Besides, she could have postponed her plans - after all, the piece of land would not run away. Nevertheless, at the time I gave in, and with the help of one of my father's colleagues I found a job at the Dental Health Insurance Association. Even my sister, who was three years younger, had to work. We had to give almost all of our earnings to our mother and could keep only a small allowance for ourselves. My mother was rather conservative and very strict with us girls. I was already 21 years old, but we were not allowed to go out to the movies or dancing unless one of our cousins accompanied us and kept an eye on us.

In spite of all these obstacles, right at that time I met Yunis. We walked the same way to the train, and often we just happened to meet and walk a little bit together. My mother, of course, would have never allowed me to have a boyfriend. Yunis was very charming; I liked him very much, but I was really still very naïve. After a few months during which we always met by pure chance, he once asked me where I went in my lunch break. Sometimes I went downtown with my colleagues, but he asked me if we could meet in a café. I was literally too shy to say no. So we met. Yunis was always very polite to me, and for a long time we were not even on a first name basis. He always addressed me formally as "Fraulein". For the next few weeks we continued to meet regularly on our way to the train.

After our house was finished, Yunis heard that my mother had two rooms for rent. First he asked me, then my mother; and he actually rented a room and moved in with us. My mother found him very likable because he was so charming and polite. Occasionally he complimented her, for example, when she came back from the hairdresser. On one occasion she even said: "I would not mind having a guy like him as a son-in-law. But of course he should be a German!" Not only was she very conservative, she also had many prejudices as well, like all the others in the village at that time. But I was to realize that only later.

At the time we were not yet a couple. We always met only by coincidence, talked to each other or walked a short distance together. But I liked him, and eventually it got serious and we wanted to become engaged. My mother and all the relatives, actually the whole village, were absolutely appalled: "She is going with an Egyptian!" They found that quite dreadful. Even before our engagement Yunis had moved out of our house; he did not want me to become the subject of gossip. In spite of all prophecies of doom, we celebrated our engagement in 1963 at a friend's house in another village. The friend was Egyptian like Yunis and was already married to a German woman. I was 23 by then and Yunis was 27 years old. Our engagement party took place in a very small circle of friends. I had, of course, invited all my friends and relatives, but nobody came. Not one of all these many people who had known me all my life. Not even my own mother came. What followed was a really bad time for me in the village. People gave me dirty looks and said all sorts of bad things about me. There were rumors and letters from my aunts with newspaper clippings that told of the horror stories that women had experienced after they got married to "Arabs". My mother did not talk to me anymore. After a few weeks I could not stand what was going on any longer and looked for a room somewhere else. So I moved to Freiburg. At first an aunt took me in, and after that I was able to rent a furnished room. However, my disappointment in all these people, whom I had not harmed in any way at all, went with me. Yunis continued to live in the village for a while, but for him, too, it was not a pleasant time.

When I was living at home at my mother's, she had kept practically all of my earnings. Now I had moved out and was trying to save some money. After all I would soon have to buy all kinds of things for our first household together. Yunis offered to provide an apartment and furniture. But in Egypt the bride is expected to at least provide a dowry. So I started to save like crazy. I worked at several jobs to earn money more quickly. For example, I worked for an artist who created large mosaics. I executed his designs into the mosaics, and to do that I went with him to the construction sites, too. Besides that I sewed for other people. Little by little my savings grew to a nice little sum. Each weekend I visited my mother, hoping for a reconciliation, which would have meant a lot to me, but I always heard only reproaches. So I went there less and less frequently.

Meanwhile everybody - all my relatives and friends in the village - had turned against me and in many different ways tried to talk me out of marrying Yunis. Only much later did I realize that everybody was really concerned about me. They simply could not imagine that our marriage would end well. I had not expected such concentrated resistance at all, and instead of giving up my plans I dug in my heels. I was sure about one thing: Yunis and I belonged together, and we would get married. Only my sister stuck by me, which of course put her in a rather unfortunate position between my mother and me.

Only rarely did doubts creep up on me. Was it the right thing to do to go far away with a man whom I hardly even knew? To such a foreign country, to Egypt? Yunis always told me many things about Egypt, about his family and life there. Often I tried to imagine what awaited me. But soon it became clear to me that I did not know anything about real life in Alexandria. During that time I thought a lot about my father. If he were still alive, he would certainly have traveled with me to Egypt so that I could take a good look at everything. But I was on my own, and a trip to Egypt to learn about the country was an impossible expense for me.

Shortly before Yunis finished his studies, he received an urgent message from home. His mother had become seriously ill, and he needed to go home immediately. He left with a heavy heart, and I stayed behind in Freiburg. As soon as I had the money saved for the passage, I wanted to follow. But that took almost a whole year, and during that time, I had a serious accident -- I fell from a moving tram. I had to spend several weeks in the hospital and after that some time went by until I had fully recovered and was allowed to travel.

Finally, in December 1966, the time had come. I had my whole dowry together: pots, feather beds, china, silverware and clothing. Everything I needed was stowed into two large steamer trunks. I had even bought a car, an old VW beetle, which I wanted to take with me. Then I said goodbye in the village. Their emotions had calmed down a little and in spite of everything it was my hometown. I did not know when I would return. My mother and my sister cried; I myself cried with them. It was a big journey into uncertainty on which I embarked. And I had no idea what to expect. My mother also gave me a little package that I was not supposed to open before I was on the ship. When I opened it later, I found a pearl necklace and a letter. Now, finally, at my departure we had reconciled. She wished me well. When we said goodbye, she had not told me this, otherwise it surely would have made the parting more difficult for me.

Our Egyptian friend, at whose house we had celebrated our engagement, drove me with the VW beetle to the ship in Genoa. My trunks with all my personal effects were sent by train but arrived safely and were loaded onto the same ship. Then the journey began. I had a single cabin, and the passage was very pleasant. On board I met many young people, most of them Greeks who asked me questions and to whom I told my story. So they knew that I was traveling to my fiancé, and to tease me they sometimes sang in a chorus: "Ilse is getting married, Ilse is getting married."

After three days at sea, we arrived in Alexandria. Yunis of course knew when my ship would arrive. So together with a friend who was an officer in the Navy, he set out in a small boat to welcome me. Long before we reached Alexandria, the boat came towards us; I spotted it immediately and my new friends saw it, too. "There! My fiancé is coming," I said to them, and again they sang: "Ilse is getting married, Ilse is getting married". We really had fun, and amidst cheers we came into port. Yunis's whole family had come to pick me up. There were an incredible number of people; it was unimaginably loud and all very strange for me. After a long greeting we drove home to Yunis's mother.

She lived all by herself with a maid, Azma, who was already an elderly woman and who had been living with Yunis's mother for many years. All the other children had already left their home; only Yunis still lived with her. Of course as his future wife, I lived there, too. First of all Azma brought me a glass of cool 'Lamun' (limeade). Not the sweet stuff that is called lemonade in Germany, but real limeade made with fresh limes. It tasted really good, and ever since then I have loved this drink.

Yunis's mother, by the way, had not at first agreed with her son's plan to marry a German woman. Everyone in the family was against it. After all in Alexandria there were enough daughters of marriageable age from distinguished families! At the time Alexandria was not as populous as it is today; most families knew each other. Yunis was good looking; he had studied and came from a good family. He was much sought after as a son-in-law and would have had many potential brides to choose from. But for him it was as clear as it was for me: we belonged together. Before my arrival he had already called a meeting of the whole family. Yunis made it clear to them that he would not change his mind. Since they really had no choice, they accepted his decision, and the case was already closed even before I had arrived. Then everybody was nice to me, and I felt welcome right from the beginning.

Now, we did not want to get married right away because it was Ramadan. It is better to get married after the time of fasting. So we waited a few weeks, which was very agreeable to me, because I first wanted to get used to my new surroundings. I fasted, too, and thus learned right away what it means. It was not hard for me. We were in the middle of winter, the temperatures were pleasant, and the time during which an observant Muslim was not allowed to eat was accordingly short (from sunrise to sunset). Yunis went to work everyday and did not come home until the afternoon, leaving me mostly alone with his mother during the day. In the afternoon she had her nap. She often called me and asked me to shoo the flies away from her. Those beasts were a nuisance, and she simply could not sleep with a fly buzzing around her head. She told me long stories, which I did not understand, of course. But every once in a while I picked up a few fragments of Arabic, and when Yunis came home I asked him about them. Sometimes he then told me the whole story in German. So little by little I learned the language accidentally and playfully rather than by hitting the books and cramming.

Almost every day we had visitors. I met all his relatives, although I could not memorize all their names right away. Yunis has six siblings, and in addition to them, a rather unclear number of uncles, aunts, nieces and nephews. During Ramadan they visit each other after sunset, and that often lasts late into the night. Naturally I did not understand much of the conversation, but in spite of this I bravely sat there and tried to participate. Almost all of the women spoke French; many of them had attended French schools. So at least I could communicate with them somehow. Bit by bit Yunis and I made our round of visits, too, until I had met everybody. Yunis explained to me all the connections: who belonged to whom, and slowly I got my bearings in this large family. In Egypt the family is highly important; I understood that immediately, and I liked it. Furthermore Yunis spent a lot of time showing me Alexandria. We visited the old city quarters, Montazah with the king's palace and a beautiful park, the harbor and the citadel. When my sisters-in-law learned that I liked to sew, they took me to the street with the fabric shops. I was thrilled and really felt in my element. Here one could buy almost everything, and I could continue to pursue my hobbies in Egypt.

After Ramadan had ended, we wanted to get married, and the planning for the wedding took up all of our energy. To the great astonishment of my new family, I had not brought a wedding dress with me. Not even the fabric for it. So together with some sisters-in-law I started to look for a fabric. But I disliked everything we saw; it was either too kitschy or too pompous. Finally, however, I found a fabric that I liked. The family was horrified. They thought for the most beautiful day in a girl's life it was much too plain. But I was not dissuaded and instead sewed my wedding dress from that fabric. I found the result very beautiful and would have been fully satisfied with it, but the family thought that the gown at the very least needed some sequins. I really did not want that, but we then found a good compromise. From what was left of the fabric, I sewed a simple collar, and my mother-in-law embroidered it to her heart's content with sequins. The wedding ceremony took place at home, entirely without guests. The Ma'asun, an Islamic official, came to us, and in his presence both of us and the witnesses signed the marriage contract. It was not until the next day that the big wedding celebration took place. Because we did not have that much money, the celebration took place in my mother-in-law's large old apartment. First I went to the hairdresser, who styled my shoulder-length hair, which was rather thin, by teasing it very high using a lot of hairspray. I looked almost like Marie-Antoinette. It took hours. I kept trying to comb my hair in a more natural way. But somehow the stylist prevailed, and so for my own wedding celebration I had a hairdo that I would never have chosen myself. Then he attached the veil, which, like my wedding dress, I had sewn myself. The veil, too, did not conform to what the family actually wanted. According to their taste it was much too small and much too thin. Yunis picked me up. At Zeinab's, one of Yunis's sisters, we put on our festive clothing and from there drove to the celebration at Yunis's mother's apartment. There was a lot of cheering; everybody thought I looked gorgeous. All the relatives were there, with all the children. Although the apartment was very large, with many rooms and a formal living room, it was very crowded, regardless. There was a buffet in the style of the times: a plethora of cakes, sandwiches and other delicacies. After an appropriate time Yunis and I drove to the San Stefano hotel, which at that time was one of the most beautiful hotels in Alexandria. But when I wanted to get ready for the night, I encountered a major problem and to resolve it I finally had to ask Yunis for help -- I could not undo my hair anymore. With all the hairspray and the teasing it was so glued together that it was almost impossible to loosen. In spite of our combined efforts it took us a solid hour until we could somehow free it, and the whole process cost me quite a bit of hair. Anyway, I did not forget that hairdo for a while!

The next day, after a short visit to the family, we drove to Cairo for a week. That was our honeymoon. Yunis showed me all the tourist attractions in Cairo, the museums, the pyramids, and the mosques. During those days we also took many walks, along the Nile or in the big plazas.

After our return to Alexandria, we continued to live with Yunis's mother. We could very well have moved into our own apartment, which even was ready for occupancy. But Yunis had been away in Germany for a long time, and his mother had so looked forward to seeing him. Furthermore, she was ill; various health problems troubled her. We simply did not want to leave her alone. Right from the beginning I got along with her very well. Later she once said to her eldest daughter: "Now I have eight children, and one came to me entirely without pain!" That moved me very much.

In the summer it turned very hot in Alexandria, and we were still living with Yunis's mother where we had only one single room to ourselves. In the end she finally insisted that we move into our own apartment. The day we moved she gave us lunch to go, in two pots wrapped in a large piece of cloth. So we obediently drove to our apartment. After we had eaten, we took our siesta as is common in Egypt. After that we then simultaneously asked each other: "And what are we going to do now? We will visit mother". So after only a few hours we were back at her door, which made her very happy. Although we now lived in our own apartment, we visited her regularly. Every morning Yunis stopped by at her place before he drove to the hospital. When he did not have the time for that in the morning, we went to see her together in the afternoon. About a year later she passed away, I was very sad because she had accepted me into the family very lovingly and had grown close to my heart.

I quickly settled in Alexandria; the only thing I was missing was the greenness of nature. Regrettably I could not ride my bicycle here; that simply was not done in Egypt. But the sea was not too far away from our apartment, and that was quite nice, too, although I couldn't go swimming in it. I often took long walks with Yunis. Now I have the desert and the sea; these will be my mountains, I thought at the time. The desert was not too far away either, and later on I got to know it even better.

In the meantime Yunis was able to finish his studies in Egypt and was now a physician. At first he had to work for very little money in a hospital. In Egypt one can study for free, but after that one has the obligation to do something for one's country for a few years. Anyway, Yunis's salary was not enough for both of us, and I had to earn some additional money myself. So I began to sew again; I was good at it and even liked it.

Some time later (in 1968) Yunis's employer sent him to the countryside, to a medical outpost in the Nile Delta. It was about 120 kilometers (75 miles) away from Alexandria. The only thing there was a health center with several buildings. It was not even a village, more a collection of farmhouses, and more farmers lived in the surrounding area. The next larger city and the next hospital were far away. There was a house for the doctor, a small clinic, wards for men and women, a laboratory, and a house for the nurses. Yunis was the only doctor. When we went there for the first time, I had to think of Aunt Valerie and the maggots in the plums with whipped cream. The house was swarming with bugs, cockroaches in all shapes and sizes. In the bathroom hung a beat-up old mirror. When I took it off the wall to clean it, from behind it alone hundreds of bugs emerged. Never ever have I seen as many cockroaches anywhere as those we got rid of in our first days there. Thank goodness! We had the walls of our rooms whitewashed, which made them look a little bit cleaner right away. I could not imagine how anybody could have lived in those rooms before. After an initial inspection I drove back to Alexandria to pack our belongings for our stay under these Spartan conditions. In the meantime Yunis tried to make the house more habitable somehow. We brightened up the walls with pictures: art prints and mountain landscapes from calendars that I had brought from Germany. We had to spray against vermin on a regular basis with big pump sprayers (aerosol cans did not yet exist). It was a constant battle, regardless. There were also fleas, and from the many fleabites I developed an allergy. Electricity was available only for four hours after sunset. During that time everything that required electricity needed to be done. Our water, too, was pumped up from the well into the tank during those hours.

During the day, when the clinic was open, Yunis was on duty, but sometimes people even came in the middle of the night for help. Then they clapped their hands in front of the house, which is customary in the countryside to get attention. Usually a man arrived with two donkeys; Yunis then rode with him on the second donkey. Sometimes he could drive our Volkswagen, but that depended on where he had to go, and whether or not there was a passable road to drive on. Of course, there was no emergency vehicle. Alongside the canal ran a narrow dirt path on which the people went to their fields together with their camels, cows and donkeys. Then in the evening they came back.

Soon everybody there knew us. One of the employees did my laundry, but I wanted to hang it up myself. I made sure that there was always a large sheet in the laundry. I hung the sheet first on the balcony, and then could hang the rest of the laundry without being watched by all the neighbors and patients.

Despite these basic conditions, our life was very beautiful. In an Egyptian village a doctor enjoys high prestige. The people were very nice to us and helped us whenever they could. It was the era of Nasser, and at that time the supply situation was very bad. Nothing was available in the shops; instead everything we needed came from the farmers. Yunis always worked for two weeks; after that he could take a weekend off. We often spent this free time in Alexandria, where we still had our apartment. We always brought something back from the city for the farmers, perhaps something sweet from the pastry shop. The farmers gave us home-baked bread, eggs, cheese, and butter. The relatives in Alexandria always looked forward to the food very much. Of course, we also paid for our groceries, but often they simply insisted on giving them to us as a present. So we always went back and forth with our VW beetle heavily loaded.

In the beginning the people arrived in droves to take a look at the new doctor and his wife from abroad. Soon Yunis knew all the farmers and their families. I started a garden, and Yunis had a fence of large palm leaves built around it. I could work behind the fence without being seen. Now I had my own little garden again and really felt at home. Our family in Alexandria often visited us in the village. Our house wasn't what one would call huge, but in spite of that they visited, sometimes even all together. The women then slept in one room, the men in the foyer on mattresses from the clinic. It was always lots of fun. For many of them it was a rare occasion to be in the countryside; for example, they might come for "Sham el Nessim", the Egyptian spring festival that occurs at approximately the same time as Easter. Usually they brought their own food with them, and the farmers would give us some extra food so that everybody always had enough to eat. Naturally in the countryside nobody spoke a foreign language. When I wanted to make myself understood, I had to do so in Arabic. Under those conditions my Arabic improved from week to week.

Also in our garden lived the "Diab" guy; that was his name. The wildest rumors swirled around his origin. At some time he may have had a family, and rumor had it that he had been driven away in disgrace because of manslaughter. He was around fifty years old and a little bit crazy. With his hunchback, Diab did look a little frightening, and the nurses always chased him away from the clinic. He had adopted us somehow, had built a small hut in the garden and was provided for by us. To get noticed he always clapped his hands when he needed something. Then he stood down there and held up his galabeya so that it formed a hollow. Into it I then threw what he had asked for. I gave him something to eat, tea and sugar, cigarettes, too. He also liked the sweets that we had brought from Alexandria. For us Diab was like a watchdog or a good spirit; he always watched over us very attentively. Occasionally patients of Yunis invited us for the evening. On the way there, Diab would walk in front of us with a kerosene lantern. Then, while we were in the house, he waited outside for us and accompanied us home again.

We were well-liked guests in the whole village, and everybody wanted to invite us for a meal. Most times a very strong tea -- too strong for me -- was served. Once it really made me sick, and since then I don't drink tea any more.

One of the innovations that we had brought with us was German punctuality. To actually keep to an agreed upon time is anything but taken for granted in Egypt. Each day the clinic opened at eight o'clock. To be there on time, we left Alexandria at six in the morning after our weekend off. But when we arrived, nobody else would be there. Only little by little did the other employees learn that the new doctor was always on time. Once we arrived only a little late in spite of heavy rains and extremely bad road conditions. On the way our car had skidded and it took quite an effort to pull us out of the ditch again. In this area it rains only two to three times a year, but then it really buckets down. Within a very short period of time, the dirt roads turn into dangerous mudslides. That day nobody expected us to arrive at all. But we made it, regardless, and so rather gradually German punctuality started to establish itself at the clinic.

We lived in the village in the Nile Delta for two years. I became pregnant, and in 1970 our first child was to be born. The family wanted me to come to Alexandria at all costs for the delivery. But I did not want to leave my familiar surroundings and managed to convince Yunis to let me stay in the village until the last moment. After the contractions began, Yunis was supposed to drive me to the nearest hospital, in Damanhur. That was about 25 km (15 miles) away, but the road was very bad. I had already packed my little suitcase a while ago, and I was glad that we finally could leave. But Yunis was still busy with a man in the foyer and talked and talked. That took much too long for me. I sat in the bedroom and asked myself what on earth Yunis had to talk about for such a long time. When we finally started to move. I felt every pothole in the road. After we arrived at the hospital, the doctor on duty came to me immediately. He was the same man who had been in our house just before. He had driven directly from there to the clinic. The delivery proceeded very normally. I only thought that my baby boy looked rather ugly. Later on I even asked the nurse whether or not they had switched him. But he was the only baby that was born that night. Anyway, everyone else thought he was beautiful. The next day the whole family arrived to visit us and they all thought the child was wonderful. The hospital did not meet our German sanitation standards at all. My little room had only a very small bathroom sink, and in that I had to wash the baby and myself. Not to mention the 36 cloth diapers which I fortunately had received from my mother. My son Karim had severe diarrhea and like all young mothers I was immediately very much concerned. But the pediatrician and all the nurses thought this was quite normal and it soon passed.

A few months before the delivery, we had visited my mother in Germany. She was very happy and was very nice to Yunis, too. I tried not to think about how hard she had made my life. It was supposed to be a real new beginning; everything was forgotten and forgiven. Nevertheless, she never did visit us, not in Egypt or anywhere else. I also visited friends and relatives in the village who now suddenly were quite nice to me again. Apparently they had accepted the fact that I was happy in my marriage and that Yunis was a decent man. Because I was pregnant, my mother gave me the unavoidable little jackets and hats as a present. I also received from her the above-mentioned cloth diapers, which I really needed in Egypt. At that time one could only dream about Pampers.

In 1971, we moved with the family to England. There Yunis began his training as a specialist. Within only five years we had to move five times between England and Scotland. That was part of the system because Yunis had to work in different hospitals. Our family was always assigned an apartment right next to the hospital, some of which were very dirty and first had to be thoroughly cleaned. The many moves were not particularly enjoyable but at least I was surrounded by a green landscape and mountains again. At first we did not have a car, so I could go shopping only by taking the bus. So I always waited until Karim was sound asleep, and then I quickly went shopping in the next village. I did not have a washing machine either, so I had to wash everything (!) by hand. In those years I sometimes traveled to Germany for several weeks to get some rest. Later we at least had a car; we bought an old Mercedes in Germany. During those years my husband had to work a lot; he often worked the night shift. In any case, I did not see much of him. But I was never bored; little Karim kept me quite busy. Besides that I continued doing handicrafts, or I sewed and painted. I kept doing this throughout the whole five years. Then at the end of 1971, our second son was born. Actually exactly on that day Yunis was supposed to fly to Manchester for a job interview. But the flight was cancelled due to thick fog, so he drove to Manchester by car while I gave birth to our son. However, I was very much convinced that I would have a girl. We hadn't even thought about names for a boy. Because the little one developed severe jaundice, I had to spend another two weeks in the hospital with him. Every day they asked me what the baby's name was supposed to be and for a long time I did not know what to say. After two weeks had gone by, we decided on Nadim. Right after I had given birth, I was transferred to a large ward, together with many other women. Then I was asked whether or not I wanted to breastfeed. When I said yes, I was given a private room. Besides me there was only one other woman who breastfed; she was in the room next to mine. Out of all those other women no one was breastfeeding. At that time it simply was not customary in England. During the weeks I spent in the hospital, Karim was able to stay with a woman friend of ours. How delighted I was when after two weeks, I finally could see my big boy again. Not even two years old, he was confused, of course. He was not able to understand where his mama had been for such a long time. At that time children could not be brought to the hospital; it was strictly prohibited.

In 1975, Yunis had finished his training and was now

a specialist in gynecology. He was offered a good position in Yemen. So we moved to Boreika, in the South of Yemen, approximately 100 km (60 miles) from Aden. Yunis worked in an 80-bed hospital belonging to British Petroleum. We lived directly by the ocean; there was even a quite beautiful promenade. Englishmen and Scots lived there and there were other foreign women with their husbands. I was the only German. Yunis was working as a gynecologist with four other doctors, and there were some other nurses from England. The summers were very hot, but in the winter one could plant vegetables. We lived in a bungalow, and naturally I again started a beautiful garden there, too. I planted spinach and soon was able to harvest literally an ocean of spinach, as well as tomatoes, herbs and flowers. For the children there was a small English school from Kindergarten to 6th grade in the neighborhood.

Yemen still had pretty much an economy of scarcity. There was no European clothing to buy, no white flour, no soap and so forth. Each year we were entitled to a long and a short vacation. Once a year we could bring in 100 kg (220 lbs) of airfreight. Each of the families decided for themselves what to bring in. For the British that was generally flour or confectioner's sugar for their special cakes. I myself brought in toys and books for the children, and in addition materials for handicrafts, painting, embroidery and knitting. Each year the people from abroad organized a splendid Christmas bazaar, which was visited by many people, often from far away, even from Aden. To do that each of us brought home all sorts of things from our vacations, and they were then sold at the bazaar. The money went to charity projects. We all worked very hard and had a lot of fun. Some friendships from that time have lasted to this day.

During our time in Yemen, in 1976, I converted to Islam. I thought the whole family should belong to the same religion. I did not find this to be difficult, because in my opinion the commandments of Islam are universally acceptable commandments. I learned the Islamic prayers in Arabic, and I also read the Koran. Unfortunately, to this day I can read the Koran only in German or English. I know that this is actually not quite right, but so far I have not been able to master Classical Arabic. I have tried several times; for example, when the children took classes in Arabic in Egypt. But somehow I was always very busy, and I never had the time to study enough. But Yunis had never asked me to convert to Islam. That really was my own wish. Today I wear a headscarf, too, and I feel comfortable wearing it.

In 1980 the government of Yemen took over the company, together with the hospital that belonged to it. The whole organization was changed, and for us it meant packing our things once again.

Yunis first got a job at the "Onshore Clinic" in Qatar, on the Persian Gulf. Initially, he worked as a gynecologist, but after some time he was employed as a general practitioner, because the women preferred to be treated by a female gynecologist. In the past there were many male gynecologists in the Arab countries, but today more and more women are making their way into this profession.

Our main problem in Qatar was to find a school for the children. There was no English school for the older children. We could have sent them either to a boarding school or to Doha 85 km (53 miles) away. But we did not want to demand such a long commute of them, especially given the condition of the road, which was often the scene of serious accidents. Also we could not imagine sending our children to a boarding school. We did not want them to lose touch with us. So the only alternative that was left was the separation of the family, which is still common for many Egyptians. I moved to Alexandria with my sons, and Yunis worked in Qatar. In Alexandria the children went to an English school, and during the summer break, when everybody else had left Qatar, the three of us took the plane there, and we all spent our vacation together. Each summer the children had an almost three-month long break from school, and we all enjoyed the time in Qatar to the fullest. In the winter they had another three-week break, and this time, too, we spent in Qatar. In between Yunis vacationed twice in Alexandria. Naturally during that time there was also friction; living apart is never easy. The children were at a difficult age, and it is especially difficult when the father is away for such a long period of time. Twice a week we were on the phone for an extensive time; that way we at least could talk about everything. Often Yunis was of the opinion that I spoiled our sons too much and that I should be stricter with them. That was easy for him to say from a distance, I thought. In spite of this we got through this time quite well.

In 1997 Yunis left the hospital and retired. However, he was offered an attractive position as a company physician for a large project in Qatar. By then our sons had grown up and were leading their own lives. So this time I went with him to Qatar. But first of all we had to resolve the housing problem. Yunis was supposed to live in a camp, but only men were living there so it would not have been suitable for me. The search for an accommodation turned out to be difficult. A friend of Yunis owned a container a little bit outside the city, near the camp and not too far from the ocean. We were able to rent it and soon also added a second container directly beside it. So now we were living in the middle of the desert. We had built a wall around it and had bags of top soil delivered. Naturally I had to have a garden again. We established ourselves, and I found my life there very cozy and pleasant. We had water and electricity. I worked in the garden and planted all sorts of things. There was a canopied corner bench and many, many flowers. I really liked being there - in my garden in the middle of the desert. We had everything we needed. To go shopping I rode my bicycle for about half an hour. I had already been familiar with the area for a long time and often visited friends, or they visited me.

Only later, after having returned to Egypt, did I get the feeling that the time in Qatar had somehow been uneventful. Here in Egypt, with all the noise, the cars and the many people, I had the feeling of participating more in life. Although I sometimes miss the quiet, in the long run I rather prefer to live here, amidst all the vibrant chaos.

My husband felt differently about it. He felt comfortable wherever he lived. He had his work and always made friends quickly. In Qatar he owned a little boat in which he went out to sea and fished. In the winter of 1985, he once caught 85 mackerels in one single day. It was impossible for us to eat all those fish ourselves! So we drove through the whole camp and distributed the fish among all of our friends and acquaintances. I have never eaten so much fish since as I did then.

After two years, in 1999, we returned to Egypt for good. It was difficult for Yunis to give up his work. Now he visits a nursing home twice a week and looks after the people there. Although there is a resident doctor who visits every day, the situation with the old people is the same as it is everywhere: there is still enough left to do. Sometimes he only talks to the old people. He also reads books about geriatric medicine. I almost always go with him to the nursing home. The director of the nursing home wanted the totally overgrown garden to be redone. I was immediately very excited about it, and offered my help. By now the garden is finished. Though it did not turn out exactly the way I had imagined, it is very beautiful, nonetheless, and the old people enjoy spending time in it. When we are in the nursing home, I always find something to do in the garden, and I also visit with the residents, like my husband.

We have a summer house not too far from Alexandria, of course with a little garden. In our apartment in Alexandria I use my balcony to grow flowers and other plants. A garden is simply a must in my life.

For many years I did not have any contact with other Germans here. I was much too busy with my children and the family. About eight years ago I met another German woman by chance, and she introduced me to the group called "German Women in Alexandria." Little by little friendships developed from that. I also work on the Christmas bazaar. Handicrafts and needlework are still my hobby, which practically predestines me to do the decorations.

When I met Yunis, I was still very young, and the decision to take a leap into the dark and into something entirely new was not easy for me. Although he tried very hard to describe everything to me, it was hard for me to imagine what to expect. Today I know that my decision was totally right. Our life together has not always been easy, but it has been interesting, colorful and eventful. Together we were able to overcome all obstacles. Today one of our sons lives in Cairo, the other one in Qatar, and we have three grandchildren.

Since my mother died, I seldom travel to Germany. When I do, as in former times, I enjoy nature and the abundant greenness. My sister still lives in our little village, and when I am there, I also visit our other relatives and friends. Each morning I go to the baker and buy fresh rolls. Then I have breakfast with Sophie, the daughter of our former landlord. We both enjoy this ritual, and often after that we sit in the garden, the same garden, where I liked to be so much even as a little girl.

But my home is here in Alexandria.

Chapter Fifteen
Annelies Ismail: Not Without My Husband!

As the idea for this book slowly took shape and I began doing the interviews, the other women naturally grew curious, too. "And how was it with you? What brought you to Alexandria?" Maybe my readers will share their curiosity. So this last chapter is dedicated to my own story. We have been living in Egypt for only a short time. We have had an apartment in Alexandria since 2004, but we continue to live in Germany during the summers. In our more than 40 years of marriage, I was asked quite often in Germany and elsewhere: "How did you get the name Ismail?" A blond woman with blue eyes and then "Ismail" – it doesn't add up, they were probably thinking. My answer was always the same: "My husband is Egyptian." Usually many questions followed: how did we get to know each other, what was it like being married to an Egyptian and so forth. So now here is my own story, that of a 65-year-old woman who has been married to an Egyptian for 42 years:

In the context of this book, my story, too, begins with how I met my husband. Nevertheless, I would like to tell first about how we both grew up, in two very different worlds.

Abdelmoniem Ismail, called Moniem by his friends, was born in Cairo in 1932. His father was an Islamic professor (sheikh) at the Al Azhar University (a center of Islamic learning). His father originally came from a southern Egyptian farming family. At 15 he was struck blind in an accident and could no longer work in the fields. As he was quite intelligent, his parents sent him to the Qur'an school and later to the Al Azhar University in Cairo where, despite his disability, he was able to study and then even became a professor. Moniem's mother was a housewife and came from northern Egypt. They had a total of nine children; Moniem was the eldest.

Under Nasser's government, free higher education was introduced for everyone, so almost all of Moniem's siblings were able to go to college. All of them later married, had children and spent their whole lives in Cairo. Today five siblings are still alive; three have already passed away.

Moniem studied civil engineering in Cairo. After completing his degree, he worked at first at the University and later for the government. His first contact with Germany resulted from collaboration with the German construction company Hochtief. Once Moniem had German colleagues, he grew curious and really wanted to go to Germany. At that time (1958) it was very difficult to get a scholarship and with it the precious exit visa. But Moniem was not so easily discouraged. He made an arrangement with his employer, who instead of paying him a salary gave him a written promise to support him while he sought his doctorate in Germany. Even though later everything turned out differently, he still received the necessary papers and was able to travel to Germany. Moniem was always very creative when it came to solving a problem.

So in May of 1958, he set out by ship and train for Stuttgart, because some of his Egyptian friends, who were also studying, already lived there. When he entered Germany, he presented his passport, but the official was somewhat annoyed by it. A whole list of names was written in the passport, but it was not clear which was the last name and which were the first and middle names: Abdelmoniem Mohammed Ismail Hammouda Achmed. Moniem's full name is actually even longer: Abdelmoniem Mohammed Ismail Hammouda Achmed Schihata Achmed El Dali. In Egypt it is customary to string together all the first names of the father, grandfather, great-grandfather, et cetera. El Dali is his actual last name; however, that name was not in Moniem's passport at all. But to explain all of that to the official was too complicated; therefore, on the spur of the moment, Moniem selected the name ISMAIL as his last name, and it has stayed that way all these years. Moniem's brother, by the way, had the same thing happen to him upon entering England, but he chose the name HAMMOUDA. Now the two brothers just have different "official" last names.

When Moniem arrived in Stuttgart, he did not speak any German at all--only English. Then it turned out that before he could get his doctorate, he had to get a German degree, because his Egyptian bachelor's degree was not officially recognized by the German university system. But even in the face of that hurdle, he did not let himself get discouraged. In the space of only six months he wrote his thesis. A German friend helped him with the language. Moniem's thesis was accepted; he received his German degree and went in search of a doctoral advisor for his PhD. It took a little time, but eventually Moniem was accepted in Karlsruhe. There he rented a room with a very nice family. That family, and above all his landlady, Lotti, contributed very much to the fact that he felt so comfortable in Germany. She helped him with the German language, mothered him, and cooked for him. He became familiar with German cuisine and with German customs and traditions. On top of that, along the way he quite casually picked up very good German, not a regional dialect. Also during that time he began to get interested in music, which had not been part of his life in Egypt. In later years, Lotti often took care of our children while we were away. She used to bring along her dachshund, Sissi, and the children accepted her enthusiastically as a surrogate grandma. Today we are still in touch with Lotti's son, Michael; unfortunately she herself has already passed away.

After three years Moniem was able to complete his doctorate; he earned the designation magna cum laude. With that he had achieved his intended goal in Germany, and he could have felt free to return to Egypt. But Moniem had other ideas.

Even while he was working on his doctorate, he had done some programming on a 'Zuse' computer at the Karlsruhe Institute of Technology. That first forerunner of our modern computers filled two entire rooms and consisted of huge cabinets containing all sorts of circuits and wiring. Originally Moniem only wanted to save himself the cost of a programmer, but after a while he found he was enjoying this work more and more. Before he went back to Egypt, he wanted to gain a little more experience, so he tried to get a traineeship at one of the computer companies. At that time only three or four companies even manufactured computers. One of the advisers at IHK (the chamber of industry and commerce) said of IBM: "I am not sure, but I think they make only typewriters." At first, Moniem had no luck with his applications. While he was tutoring an acquaintance who wanted to improve his command of the Arabic language, Moniem happened to mention to him that he was interested in working with computers. As it turned out, Moniem's "pupil", in addition to his position as a professor, had good connections to the supervisory board of IBM. As a result, Moniem got to work for IBM for three months as a student trainee. He enjoyed the work, and when the three months were up, they offered him a job in the IBM computer center. Moniem stayed there four years and wrote computer programs for statics (civil engineering) at first. At that time they still wrote programs in machine language, which today seems incredibly complicated to us. Moniem thought so, too, so he developed a kind of translator (a compiler) that changed mathematical equations into machine language on its own. Later another computer language, FORTRAN, was developed to do something similar, but at that time Moniem's program, MOPSY, was something very new. He proudly presented it at an IBM conference in Heidelberg and people were very impressed. The head of IBM systems programming in the development lab in Böblingen noticed Moniem and offered him a position right away. So Moniem started working there, in the same department where I myself had already been working for four years.

I was born in 1942 in Berlin as the second of two children. My father had been in the war, and at the end of the war he was released from an American prisoner-of-war camp and came back to us. During the war, my mother fled with us to her sister in Stuttgart. My Aunt Lis lived in

Stuttgart-Degerloch with her husband in a stately old villa; anyone who belonged to the family found shelter there during the war. People were constantly coming and going. Our apartment in Berlin had been bombed out and completely destroyed, so we stayed in Stuttgart after the end of the war. My father had originally worked as a clerk in a bank. After the war he started working at a publishing house as an accountant. On the side, he began to write articles for the same publishing company, and as soon as he could support his family with that work, he became a fulltime journalist and writer. My mother was a homemaker. As things slowly improved financially, we moved to Stuttgart-Oberaichen, where I grew up.

After I finished school, I completed a training course as a lab assistant in Isny in Allgäu. It was important to me above all not to do what everyone else did. Almost all the girls my age wanted to become teachers, so that was out of the question as far as I was concerned. My first job was at IBM in the so-called testing laboratory. There transistors around 3/8 of an inch in size were put together and tested: a job that deeply bored me. I was able to get myself transferred from the testing laboratory to the new systems programming department. That was a great stroke of luck because I started out as a programmer assistant, and I really enjoyed that work. Except for me, everyone had a university degree, so they were all older than I was. I was just 20 and effortlessly compensated for any missing expertise with my speed. At that time there was no college major in computer science anyway; all of my colleagues were career changers, who had perhaps studied physics, electrical engineering, or mathematics. But everything that had to do with computers we had to teach ourselves through experimentation and with the help of manuals. For me that was just the right thing, and I felt very comfortable there. I still lived at home with my parents; besides my work only books and music interested me. I liked to go to the opera or to the theater.

So Moniem and I met in the office, but at first it seemed a budding romance was out of the question. Moniem was used to having women in Germany go after him. That certainly had to do with his appearance; in Germany he seemed very exotic with his dark eyes and black hair. But it did not work with me. I did like him very much, but I would never have dreamed of running after him. We were colleagues, after all, so it was just out of the question. Moniem came into my office every day and we chatted a bit , but that was it. I did not notice that he was coming by just because of me. It wasn't until six months later, at a Mardi Gras event at IBM, that we finally got together. It is a wonder that it ever happened at all. First of all, I had to go alone. I was very uncomfortable with that and it cost me quite an effort. I bought two admission tickets so no one would notice that I was going alone; it would have gone around the whole company right away. That afternoon I realized I did not have a costume. I decided to go as Cleopatra; that would make Moniem sit up and take notice. I wore a black wig that I styled myself and I put on make-up in what I imagined to be the Egyptian fashion. Still everything almost went wrong; as Cleopatra I could not wear my glasses, of course; how would that have looked?? Well, without my glasses in the great crowd of people, I could not spot Moniem. If our mutual colleague, Willi, had not recognized me and guided me to the right table, everything would have probably turned out very differently. But once I had reached the right table and was sitting happily with Moniem and a group of other colleagues, it turned out to be a fantastic evening. We had a great time, laughing and dancing a lot - of course, only with each other. From that evening on, it was clear: we belonged together.

A few weeks after that evening we made a contract. By chance I came across it recently, and to my amazement I realized that I would not add or change a thing -- our agreement is still valid today! It reads as follows:

Sindelfingen, the 13th day of March in the year 1965

Contract between

Annelies Will and Moniem Ismail

1. We pledge in all conscience to abide by the following principles:

2. To be VERY good to each other

3. To be faithful

4. To be honest, "lies are forbidden on principle"

5. Not to be petty

6. To forgive each other's mistakes gladly and quickly. This refers to forgiveness after a quarrel.

7. Not to be afraid of the future

8. To practice mutual tolerance. Each has command of his or her own free time. But a peaceful compromise will always be sought.

9. Not to care about the opinion of others.

10.To respect equal rights

This contract can be expanded with approval of both parties and at their discretion

Annelies Will Moniem Ismail March 13, 1965

In the more than forty years of our marriage, there were of course a few stumbling blocks. But all in all we have held to these principles.

Before we got engaged that April, I brought Moniem home to introduce him to my parents. Upon greeting him, my father said: "You are the first Egyptian in my life." They liked each other right away. We got married in August of 1965 at the marriage bureau in Stuttgart. My parents were happy for me, but Moniem's family had no idea he was married. He was not a particularly good letter writer and had let the correspondence peter out. The family naturally thought he would come back to Egypt. However, Moniem had other plans. He liked it in Germany very much. He thought that later, in Egypt, he would miss the freedoms that are part of daily life here. In Germany, one could travel without restrictions and there was more variety in nature than the endless sand in the Egyptian desert. So one could say that Moniem fell in love with the country even before he met me.

For me, Egypt has always been a fascinating country that had intrigued me long before my first meeting with Moniem. I had, of course, read "Gods, Graves and Scholars" by W. Ceram as well as other books about ancient and modern Egypt. Now I began to read more about Islam, because I assumed it could be important for me. I bought myself a Koran in German translation and got started. I myself had been baptized and confirmed as a Lutheran, but in my parents' house the church did not play a big role. Neither of my parents was religious and later I found out that even my grandfather had left the church. Of course Moniem grew up as a Muslim. His father was a scholar of Koranic studies at the Al Azhar University. Now you might think that religion could have led us into some tough discussions. But it never did; on the contrary, we were able to exchange ideas easily and we soon realized to our astonishment that we were not that far apart in our views. Concerning religion, Moniem never tried to influence me in any way.

During the first few years of our marriage, we both worked as programmers at IBM. The department was expanded further and many workers came to Böblingen from all over Germany. We drew together quickly as a group, and there was always something to celebrate: an engagement, a wedding, later the births of the children. Many of those friendships are still active to this day, and now we tell each other about the grandchildren. I remember that at one of our parties, seven women were pregnant at the same time, including me.

In October of 1966 our son Achmed was born, and I stopped working. There was no leave of absence for child-rearing then, only six weeks before and after the birth as maternity leave. Afterwards one had to either go back to one's job or give notice. To go back right away full time was out of the question for me, so I quit. But soon thereafter I was able to get a small project as a freelancer, so that I never entirely lost the connection to my occupation.

By 1960, Moniem had already applied for German citizenship; he was that certain that he wanted to stay in Germany. However, it took ten years before he received his German passport. When we married, he was still an Egyptian, and he could travel hardly anywhere with that passport; he needed a visa for everything. Usually his passport was renewed for only about three months, because the Egyptian government was very interested in having the well-educated young people return home again to Egypt. At some point the renewal of his passport was denied altogether and the passport was taken away. Instead, Moniem received a German alien passport; that was in 1966. At least he was able to take some business trips with his alien passport.

In 1967, IBM offered Moniem a position in the United States. He remained an employee of IBM Germany but received generous cost-of-living payments while we were in America. We did not hesitate long, and went to New York on the ship "Bremen" in May of 1967. Friends of ours, Norbert and Gudrun, were also being sent by IBM to the United States and traveled with us on the same ship. Traveling by ship was very pleasant; I have very fond memories of it. The passengers were quite elegant, and when we went to dinner, a babysitter came to our cabin to look after Achmed. During the day we enjoyed the fresh air on board and played with our child. Our arrival in New York was full of suspense; all of our suitcases were opened at customs and a tall African-American customs officer thoroughly searched through them.

We were all supposed to go together in a big rental car to Endicott (in New York State) where the men would report for work in the development lab. Moniem generously agreed to be the driver. At first there were a few abrupt starts and stops with the brakes, but after that everything was fine. The car had an automatic transmission, and Moniem had taken the brake for the clutch! Nevertheless, we soon left New York City behind us and arrived at our new residence around three hours later. We spent the first weeks in a hotel; later we moved to a rented apartment.

During those years in the United States, we did very well financially because the benefits from IBM were very generous. We liked the surroundings in upstate New York, too. We quickly made friends with Americans and some Germans who lived in the same neighborhood. Once a year we flew to Germany for home leave and visited family and friends. In November, 1968, our daughter Mona was born in Endicott, NY, USA.

Early in 1969 we returned to Germany. We moved into an apartment again. Moniem was working in the IBM development lab in Böblingen, and I soon got programming projects again as a subcontractor for IBM. For the housework, I had someone who came every morning to help. I worked mornings at IBM; afternoons I was home with my children. I was very satisfied with this arrangement; I could work and still spend plenty of time with my children.

In 1970, we bought a house in Gechingen (near Calw). We lived in it happily for almost 30 years. In that same year Moniem finally received his German citizenship after a ten-year waiting period. At the same time both our children were naturalized. Our daughter had had American citizenship since her birth in the USA, but up until then

Achmed had only a German alien's passport like Moniem's. Luckily the alien passport was never a problem during our two-year stay in America.

In 1971, there was a job opening from IBM for Moniem in Egypt. The offer from Cairo seemed interesting, and we really wanted to live for a time in Moniem's homeland. As a first step we went to Cairo for a survey trip. That was customary so that the family could get an impression of the country where the husband wanted to relocate. First contacts were arranged, schools were checked out, and sometimes there was even time to look at apartments, too.

By then, Moniem had not seen his family for many years and they still had no idea he was married. On our first day there, I let him go alone to his family, who did not even know he was in the city. They were very surprised and of course happy to see him again. How they reacted to the news of his marriage, I do not know. In any case they all wanted to meet me right away. So Moniem brought me along the next day. Hussein, the quarter where Moniem's family lived and where he himself grew up, is one of the oldest quarters of Cairo's Old City. Even though some of the houses have been torn down since those days, there are still many houses that are exactly as they were then: with many, many storeys connected by old staircases and often with several generations living in one house. Moniem's family lived in such a house, too. I met everyone and was very warmly received, although I could not keep track of every name at the first meeting. There were simply too many. Moniem's father, who as I have mentioned was blind, touched my face very slowly, then kissed my hand and embraced me. Moniem's mother kissed and embraced me very affectionately, too. She seemed very happy that her eldest had found a good wife. Unfortunately, we could not communicate with each other since neither of them spoke English, and I could yet not speak Arabic. But Moniem's siblings spoke English, so I could at least converse with them. Then a constant coming and going ensued. All of the neighbors were informed immediately, and all of them came to see Moniem.

I was very warmly greeted, too.

We stayed a few more days in Cairo while Moniem had his job interview, and we even looked for a suitable apartment. Moniem showed me his old haunts and led me through the narrow, crooked little alley-ways of Hussein with the certainty of a man who knew it blindfolded. Of course, we also went to the pyramids and to the Egyptian Museum. For me everything was entirely new and very exciting. With my blond hair I stood out immediately everywhere. In 1971, by the way, one saw very few women with a headscarf; most of the younger women dressed as I did, in summer dresses with short sleeves, a little bit low-cut because it was, after all, very hot. The few women with headscarves or even veils seemed very exotic. Moniem explained to me that they were probably from rural areas.

I felt very good about Cairo right away. The people were friendly and often came up to us to speak to us. At that time there were not as many tourists as there are today. The Egyptians are inquisitive by nature and anything but shy.

Upon our return to Germany, IBM informed us that unfortunately the position had already been filled by someone else. We were very sorry to hear it -- we were both already really looking forward to Egypt.

Shortly thereafter Moniem again received an offer from the United States. We knew the area already from the last time and did not have to think it over very long. He accepted, and in the summer of 1972, we moved for the second time to Endicott in upstate New York.

Moniem flew ahead and bought a furnished house. Then he came back and we flew together with the children to the United States - our new home. Some of our friends from the last stay were still there, so we settled in quickly. Our neighborhood was near the university so we came in contact with interesting people and some genuine friendships resulted that have outlasted the years. The children went to a regular American public school: Achmed began with kindergarten; Mona went to nursery school. Mona was four years old and doggedly refused at first to learn English. After a few weeks she vehemently maintained that the boy next door spoke German. That cannot be, I thought and went off to check things out. I quickly realized that she had picked up so much English on her own that she was completely convinced it was German. She was learning the new language subconsciously and all by herself. Achmed was already six and could clearly distinguish between the two languages. Sometimes he came home with other children, and they had me translate a few words, for Achmed into English and for the other children into German. With time the communication worked better and better.

We stayed in Endicott for three years this time and felt very comfortable there. We had many friends and I was soon able to work again: I got a job as a programmer in a hospital. The children went to school and did not come home until 4 o'clock. The school was even nearby, so they could walk. We were members of a club, so we could go swimming any time we wanted to. Public swimming pools are not common in the United States unless one lives in a complex that has a pool available to residents. The club had dozens of activities like judo, ballet and "summer day camps". They had activities there during vacations where the children were taken care of for the whole day, coming home only to sleep. Both of our children really liked to go to summer camp; they spent a good part of their summer vacation, which in the States lasts almost three months, there. In addition we visited Germany in the summer for a few weeks.

In 1974, we traveled to Egypt with the children for the first time . They became acquainted with Moniem's homeland and met all of the many relatives. Moniem's father had already passed away in 1972; he was 80 years old. But of course Moniem's mother and all his siblings had to meet the children. Mona was six and rather overwhelmed by all the people. Every time the door opened and someone new came, she asked somewhat anxiously: "Do I have to kiss them, too?" That is how it was in Egypt with family, neighbors and friends: everyone - and especially the children! - were embraced, hugged and kissed, even if it was the first time they had ever seen each other.

Afterwards we spent two weeks by the sea in Alexandria, where our children quickly made friends with the Egyptian children who lived in the apartment below us; they even picked up a little Egyptian Arabic. For example, they all played a card game together that, although I did not understand it, did not present any problem at all for the children.

Our last year in the States just flew by, and in 1975 we returned to Germany. Actually, I would have liked to stay in the United States, and the children would have, too. We really felt good being there. But Moniem was drawn back to Europe; he did not want to live permanently in the States. He especially liked the cultural diversity in Europe: after just a few hours' drive, one is already in another country with a different culture. There is so much more to experience there. Also, our children's education was important to us, and we thought the German school system was better for them.

So we came back to Gechingen, and the children went to the German elementary school. In the beginning there were some difficulties, but with time everything sorted itself out. Achmed started at the Gymnasium (high school) in 1977 and Mona in 1978. Most of our friends still lived in the area, and with the children one or the other friendship had survived the long separation. Moniem was working again at IBM in development, and I got programming work there as a freelancer again. Although I could still arrange my own hours, the circumstances were not nearly as good as in the States. The children never came home from school at a regular time. Sometimes they were already at the door at noon, then another day not until 1 o'clock and sometimes later. One of them even came home once at 11 in the morning because a teacher was sick. Schools that ran all day did not yet exist. Mothers were expected to be home and to take care of their children; mothers who worked outside the home were unusual. It worked out reasonably well for me, but for most women it was practically impossible to work. Moreover the shops were already closed by 6:30 in the evening, so I never had enough time to go shopping. In the States shops were open around the clock even then, and I often went shopping in the evening, without being rushed, after Moniem had come home and the children were in bed.

Nevertheless, we quickly got used to our new rhythm and were actually quite content. It was only Moniem who soon desired another change. In 1979, he accepted a job offer from IBM in Saudi Arabia. We seriously considered moving with the whole family, although the children were not exactly thrilled. They had just about halfway settled in again, and now they were supposed to move to another country. Regardless, I went with Moniem to Dhahran, and we even looked at houses and schools. We really liked the American school, but then we realized that we had a legal problem. The school could not accept our children because Moniem is a Muslim by birth. In Saudi Arabia, Muslims are required by law to send their children to an Arabic school. That meant a move to Dhahran was not possible for us as a family, since we really did not want to demand that of our children. I was even a little bit relieved myself that it had not worked out. My life there would have been very restricted; I would not have been allowed to drive a car or to work, and my daily life would have probably taken place completely within a gated foreigners' compound.

Just a short time afterwards, Moniem was transferred to Paris. The IBM headquarters for the Middle East are located there, and his job was to organize IBM conferences for decision-makers in Saudi Arabia. Of course, he had to travel a lot, but he spent the majority of his working hours in Paris. Paris - that was a very different story from Saudi Arabia! There was a German school, and during the vacations we would be able to travel to Germany at any time. Our suitcases were soon packed, and after a totally rained-out vacation in Normandy, we arrived at our new apartment in a suburb of Paris. We stayed in Paris for two years, and the children later described that time as the best of all. They felt very comfortable at the German school and formed many friendships, some of which they still maintain to this day. I myself did not work during those two years. First of all, I set about polishing up my school French, and after a few courses, I was quite proud of my progress. Then I attended several courses in French cuisine. My family was especially pleased with that, because at the weekend at home I tried out the dishes that I had learned in my classes. In the rest of my free time, I enjoyed everything Paris had to offer: I went into the city, to museums and to parks and took a look at everything that interested me. Of course, we always had visitors from Germany, as well. Only towards the end of the two years did I gradually begin to miss my job. To be better prepared, I began to familiarize myself with the French vocabulary for computer technology. But before I was finished with it, it was back to Germany again.

In retrospect, it strikes me that I have perhaps presented that unsettled time with all the moving a little too smoothly. In reality, it was not always so easy. Moniem worked for almost two years in Saudi Arabia and during that time he came to Germany only every six weeks. The situation put a big strain on our relationship. The children were still of school age, and I had to cope all alone with their needs, the household, and my job. When Moniem was finally home, we got into arguments because of little things, and everything was different from what we had hoped for. I thought that in Paris we would get along better. We actually did, but in spite of that Moniem began an affair with a French woman. Of course, at some point it all came out. I was stunned and seriously thought of separating from him. But in the end I stayed with him. He always said he did not want a separation, and for both of us our children were the most important consideration. Today I am very glad that I endured that time and that we got our relationship back together, because afterwards we experienced very beautiful years together again.

In 1981, we returned to Germany where the children continued to go to school and got their diplomas. Afterwards, Achmed fulfilled his alternative civilian service (instead of military service) with the Red Cross and studied medicine. Mona went directly to the United States for just under a year. Through a student exchange program, she had established ties with California and lived in San Francisco together with a girlfriend. As she was born in the United States, she had American citizenship and could enter the country without any problems and could work there. We thought at first that Mona would study at an American university, as well. But then she decided to study the advertising industry and advertising technology at the Technical College in Stuttgart-Vaihingen. She even lived with us again for a while. After college, Mona found a job with a publishing company in international marketing.

Moniem continued to work at IBM, I got programming jobs again, too, and we continued to live in our house in Gechingen --- so far so good. In 1984 someone approached me about giving training courses for software. I decided to just try it out, and gave some training courses for IBM and also a few courses for adult evening classes. This was an entirely new direction for me, and to my amazement I discovered that I really enjoyed it.

With my training courses as a first pillar of support, we founded our company, Ismail Computer of Calw, in 1986. We bought a big old house in Calw, renovated it and hired some employees. At first ICC was my company; Moniem was still working at IBM. But a year later he took early retirement and joined ICC full time. Practically immediately we became IBM Business Partners, meaning we could market IBM computers and software. In addition, we gave training courses, wrote programs and marketed networks. It goes without saying we were always state-of-the-art; we were after all used to nothing less from our experience with IBM. In the best of times, we employed twenty people. My purview was the training courses; I developed courses and traveled to the customers to provide the training. Moniem usually worked on site in Calw; he negotiated with the customers and did programming. It was an interesting, exciting life. During that time we worked extremely hard, but we enjoyed it.

In 1993 a general stagnation in trade caused us a lot of trouble. Fewer computers were sold and fewer training courses were requested. We were about to give up the company when we got a new order from IBM. It had to do with the development of a program for administering tests and managing test results - of course, complete with the necessary services like database management and updates. We did not know it at the time, but this program was to occupy us for many years and more or less determine our lives. For the first time Moniem and I did the programming on a big project together. After some initial difficulties, we worked amazingly well together. It is probably about the same as when a couple builds a house together. Either it brings you closer together, or you end up divorced. Fortunately for us, the former was true.

In only four months from the IBM order, we were able to bring the first version onto the market. At the push of a button, test questions could be generated by a random generator. The test could be completed online, and all the results were stored in our data base, retrievable at any time. IBM soon utilized the program worldwide in all sorts of areas: for certification, at assessment centers and so forth. Data management as well as the compilation of statistics was in our hands, too. Between 1994 and 2001 our staff was constantly traveling around with all the technical equipment, presenting the program and administering tests. Moniem and I traveled to conferences in Istanbul, Paris, Lisbon, Warsaw, Tokyo and many other cities. It was really exciting. We kept developing the software further, and after several years we programmed everything all over again, completely from scratch and again state-of-the-art. During those years Moniem and I worked very closely together; usually we traveled together, too. We were practically Siamese twins.

Since many of our customers were located in the United States, we bought a house in Atlanta, founded a company there, and began spending a good part of the year there. About the same time we sold our house in Gechingen and finished off the attic of the house in Calw, where our business was, to create an apartment. Whenever we were in Germany, we had only to go downstairs and we were in the office. In our office in Atlanta we had only one employee, and we tried to promote sales for our product from there. Everything looked very promising. In 2001 we had new contracts in the States and were negotiating with a university that wanted to utilize our product throughout the whole country. The plans for the pilot project were already complete and available. We were virtually raring to go when something totally unforeseen occurred that undid all our high-flying plans. On September 11, 2001, Islamic terrorists hijacked four passenger planes and steered two of them into the World Trade Center in New York. There were thousands of dead, and apart from the human tragedy, it ultimately destroyed our business. For the next year none of our contracts were renewed. We did not get any new contracts either. All of our contacts left us stranded. No one returned our calls, letters or emails. Some of the assassins were thought to have been Egyptians who had lived in Germany. Suddenly we were under suspicion by association; no one wanted to do business with us anymore. It was a very strange feeling suddenly to be so cut off; one does not want to believe what is happening. We tried for quite a while to save our business. We did not give up for good until 2003, although it was very difficult for us. We had put our whole heart and soul into that project, and through no fault of our own we had lost everything. In 2004 we sold our house in Atlanta and left the United States for good.

In our almost twenty years with Ismail Computer of Calw, we had become more and more absorbed in the company, worked very hard, and become very busy. Sometimes almost too busy. Both of our children had taken up their professions long ago and had married at almost the same time. In 1996, within three weeks, we had two grandchildren (two boys, Tarik and Simo). In 1998 a little girl (Paula) and a boy (Musa) arrived, and in the year 2000 we got our little "Millennium-girl" Meryem. So today we are the very happy grandparents of five grandchildren.

But the family was not yet complete! The big surprise came in 2002, actually out of the blue. A young woman named Isis, 20 years old, called from France and presented Moniem with the fact that she was almost certainly his daughter. She was born in Paris in 1982. Her mother was Catherine, the woman with whom Moniem had an affair. Her name, Isis, implied she probably had something to do with Egypt. Her mother had already died, in 1993, without ever telling her who her father was. She was sent to live with a foster family, and only as an adult, while rummaging through her mother's papers, did she chance upon Moniem's address.

I did not notice her first call to us. Moniem was probably rather shaken; he did not know how he should handle the situation and what he should say to me. Shortly thereafter we went on a trip to Egypt with friends. In Egypt it seems that every other temple is dedicated to the goddess Isis; there are images and references to Isis everywhere. Well, Moniem was walking around among all these Isis inscriptions and was probably wondering what he should do now. As for me, I noticed nothing and did not find him changed in any way. Such a trip is always very exciting and for Moniem even more so because he was, as it were, the host in his own country and felt responsible for everything.

When we were back in Germany again, another call came from Isis, and this time I happened to answer the phone. I thought it was a customer and gave Moniem the receiver. After a while he hung up the phone, took me away from my book, and informed me he had something to tell me. I was puzzled because he never made highly official announcements in that way. After I had heard the whole story, I was certain immediately that this young French woman had to be his daughter; I did not doubt it for a second. I knew too, that her mother had already died. My first thought was that we had to see Isis right away. I was struck by the thought that she had grown up with foster parents when actually we could have taken good care of her here in Germany. Moniem called her back immediately and arranged to have her visit us that weekend. Before this first meeting, Moniem and I had very long talks, but it was way too late for recriminations. It had all happened such a long time ago, and in the meantime we had had such a good life together - I had forgiven him a long time ago. Our relationship had survived the crisis at the time, and today we understand each other perhaps even better than at the beginning of our marriage. The only thing that is incomprehensible to me to this day is how Moniem was able to keep the entire story from me for three whole weeks, when we were traveling together and were also together every day for almost 24 hours, and we always told each other everything else. It was naturally a load off Moniem's mind that I took everything so calmly

Then the weekend came. Moniem picked Isis up at the airport in Stuttgart. Out of the whole crowd that came through the gates, Moniem recognized his daughter right away. They looked at each other and there was no doubt about it -- they had to be father and daughter. In the meantime I was sitting at home on pins and needles and could hardly stand the suspense. When they finally arrived, I took Isis in my arms, and she even cried a little. It must be an overwhelming feeling finally to find one's own family after such a long time. She was very happy that we received her in such a friendly way, and we simply sat together a long time and talked. Isis talked about her mother, about how she had grown up, about how they had lived. The two of them always had very hard times financially because Catherine could not manage money at all, and yet she was too proud to ask for help. So her family in Paris (mother, brother and sister) had never known how bad it was for her. We felt very sorry about that. Isis's mother died of hepatitis C, but Isis had learned that only a few years ago. When she died, Isis was only eleven years old and was sent to a foster family that lived in the country. Isis went to school and passed all the necessary exams. But she never did feel really comfortable in the foster family, who did not treat her as they did their own children, starting with the food and clothing she got. Isis had married young, when she was only twenty; her husband, Omar, came from Morocco. Moniem had already spoken to him on the telephone. The two of them normally speak Arabic with each other, and it seems a little bit as if things have come full circle.

The next day I called our children and told them about Isis. Both of them were quite nonplussed but wanted to meet Isis as quickly as possible. That same day we visited Mona, who then lived with her family just about an hour away from us. The whole family accepted Isis very warmly, especially the grandchildren, who did not have a problem at all with a new aunt who had appeared out of nowhere. Mona said: "And I always wanted a sister; now I finally have one!" Achmed and Isis met later at Christmas. The whole family was together: Achmed with his wife and children, Mona with her husband and children and Isis with Omar. Communication occurred in up to four languages. Most of our family speaks German with each other, but Achmed's wife is Turkish and speaks Turkish with their children. Omar does not speak German, so he speaks Arabic with Moniem and with the rest English or French depending on whatever is easier at the moment. After that weekend, our heads were swimming with the Babylonian confusion of tongues.

Of course, that kind of exciting news has to be announced in an appropriate setting, so I invited all my friends for a kaffeeklatsch (coffee afternoon) and ceremoniously told them the whole story. They were very surprised and fascinated. I still remember the comment of one of my friends, Isolde: "Just like Rosamunde Pilcher!"

In 2003 we officially adopted Isis, so she has the same rights as the other children and really belongs to the family now. In the meantime, she has visited for longer periods of time with both siblings. She was at Mona's in the summer for six weeks and worked in a company there; she even stayed at Achmed's for three months. Her German was already good, but during the long visits in Germany it got even better. In the summer of 2003, we took her with us to America, and on this and some other trips we really got to know her well. She strongly resembles her father, perhaps even more than the other two children.

After we sold our house in Atlanta in 2004, our primary residence became our apartment in Calw. But soon we began to consider whether or not it might be nice to spend the winter in Egypt. All those years we had been in Egypt again and again but only as tourists. Moniem had organized several trips for us and our friends to Cairo, to the pyramids and to the temples in southern Egypt. Almost all of our friends have visited Egypt with us at some point. In May of 2004, the two of us flew to Cairo to look around. I thought right away of Alexandria on the Mediterranean because I had always loved it there. One of our nieces and her husband went with us to Alexandria and we looked at different apartments. At first we tried rental apartments, but there was nothing that we liked. Then we looked at three apartments which were for sale. The second apartment was it. We looked at each other and agreed immediately. It had a view of the sea from the bedroom. The apartment was supposed to be auctioned off. The auction was scheduled so that we could participate; shortly thereafter our flight was leaving for Germany. The auction proceeded; we were full of suspense. At first there were only a few people in the room but then gradually it began to fill up. Moniem was supposed to take over the bidding; I sat way in the back and only heard Moniem's name repeated again and again. At some point it was over. He came to me, gave me a kiss and said: "We got it." Later he told me there had been a second bidder who kept raising the bid. When the price approached our upper limit, Moniem looked at the man and said: "If I do not get this apartment, I will never come to Egypt again!" The man was so taken aback that he stopped bidding.

First of all we had to organize the renovation. Moniem's family contacted an engineer for us who was very experienced with renovations. But even more important, he knew all the craftsmen and how to deal with them. So the renovation went along quite smoothly and by the end of October, 2004, we were able to move in. But all our household goods were still in the cellar of our house in Atlanta -- we had fortunately been able to arrange that with the new owner. From Egypt we now had to organize the transportation of our things from Atlanta to Alexandria. With the help of email, internet, fax and the support of good friends locally in Atlanta, it worked out without our having to go to the States again. The arrival of our furniture was scheduled for an afternoon at the end of October. So we sat in our apartment and waited. The afternoon turned to evening, but no furniture arrived. Around ten o'clock we decided to go to bed. The furniture would come some time—so we hoped, anyway. And indeed it did: at midnight the doorbell suddenly began ringing like crazy; the furniture was there! In only two hours everything was in its place. Four men had carried up everything that could not fit in the elevator--furniture, lamps, bed linens, blankets, and all the kitchen appliances. And nothing was broken. Around two in the morning we were sitting on our couch with the feeling we had been "beamed" from Atlanta directly to Alexandria. It was somehow unreal.

We settled in quickly in Alexandria. We go almost everywhere on foot, by bus, tram or taxi. We do not need a car here. Many Egyptians are surprised at that, but we do not miss the car one bit. We live directly on the 15-mile-long waterfront promenade, the Corniche. We often go shopping at one of the big markets. We have our favorite merchants, who already know us very well, as do many people in the area. Whenever we come back from Germany, they always ask us where we were for so long.

Arabic is Moniem's native language. That language had not played much of a role for me until now, because when we met, Moniem already spoke very good German. I already knew simple things like the names of vegetables, fruits, and meat in Arabic. But I wanted to learn more, so I registered at the University of Alexandria for an Arabic course for foreigners and steadfastly persevered for two semesters. With me in the class were young students from Japan, England, Canada and Sweden. As expected, I found it very difficult. Four days a week at two hours each, and then tons of homework. Without Moniem I would have surely given up quickly. First he taught me the Arabic script. Actually, that would normally have been part of the first semester curriculum, but in my class, everyone but me already knew it. Although I found it very hard, I still enjoyed it, and I learned a lot. Now I can read Arabic and understand it to some extent, although speaking is still very hard for me. I can shop, read the signs and hold simple conversations. I like best to speak to children; with them I have the fewest inhibitions.

Moniem is happy to be living in his homeland again and enjoys being able to speak Arabic with everyone. But in the 46 years abroad (Germany, America, France) he has changed a lot. He is hardly a typical Egyptian any more. Probably he never was; otherwise, as a young man he would not have had the desire for freedom that brought him to Germany. Now we are both trying to get used to the Egyptian mentality. Much is simply unfathomable to us: why do Egyptians not keep their appointments? Why does no one consider it important to keep things clean outside the apartment, as well as inside? Our beautiful old house (more than sixty years old) positively screams for someone to clean and polish the marble floors and columns in the entryway. It is a crying shame the way the streets look, too. But once we have been in the country again for a few weeks, we get used to it and simply enjoy the surroundings, the nice weather, and the friendliness of the people.

Alexandria even has an opera house, although operas are almost never performed there. Instead there are often concerts: classical music, Arabian music or concerts by ensembles from other countries. In the past few years, I have even become somewhat used to Arabian music.

At one of the concerts, we met a German woman who sat in front of us with her Egyptian husband. Even before I could speak to her, she turned around and spoke to us. Since then we have been friends, and our husbands get along very well, too. Through her I have met many German women and other women from other countries. Without that encounter this book would not have evolved - she opened a new world to me, and I am very grateful to her.

Of course, we spend time with Egyptians, too,

through Moniem's family and with others. I find it very difficult to converse with most Egyptians, though. There are simply very few topics of conversation in common once the subjects of family, children, and grandchildren have been exhausted. I'm sure my insufficient language skills have something to do with it. However, my German friends in Alexandria, some of whom speak very good Arabic, say the same thing. I hope that will improve, and we will soon get to know Egyptians, too, with whom we can have a good conversation.

Whenever we are in Egypt, after a few months we look forward to our return to Germany. In Germany we have a large circle of friends we have known for years. Naturally we want to see our children and grandchildren regularly; that is very important to both of us. But when we are in Germany, we are soon drawn back to Egypt again, especially when the weather in Germany is cold and gray. In Alexandria we have friends now, too, and we enjoy our life. Like all Egyptians, my husband loves his country very much. Sometimes he grows melancholy. It is hard for him to understand why many things are so complicated here, when they seem much simpler elsewhere. There are so many intelligent people here, but often they cannot do what they would like to do and what seems obviously right to us.

The constant change between Germany and Egypt demands much flexibility. One learns to appreciate many things more when one does not have them all the time. In Egypt we enjoy the beautiful weather, the friendliness of the people, the fresh fruit and all the other food that we cannot get in Germany. We appreciate the dependability of the people in Germany, the nicely kept small towns and the beauty of nature. We will definitely always have a home in Germany, but right now we love Egypt just as much.

Wherever we go, one thing is clear for me anyway: "Not without my husband!"

In Conclusion

What struck me with all the stories was the spontaneous willingness of the women to talk about their lives. Some seemed truly relieved finally to be able to talk about everything and to meet with understanding. Their stories just spilled out, and it was not always easy to recount all the information in a structured way. For that I have my daughter Mona Gabriel to thank who worked with me to put the stories in coherent and readable form in the original German. From all the life stories in this book, a shared pattern emerges in the end. As different as the women and their stories may be, they have much in common. Almost all of them experienced in their immediate environment in Germany that friends, relatives or parents reacted rather coolly even took offense at their decision to marry an Egyptian. In the end they not only followed through with their decisions despite all the prophecies of doom, but also were happy with their choices. Within this group of women there is an amazing feeling of togetherness. What connects them is not only friendship but also the awareness of being able to cope with all the difficulties in Egypt. The others managed after all. Over the years they came up against all sorts of problems. The most striking is probably the poor provisions during Nasser's time when everyone suffered more or less. But there are many other things that are not so obvious, yet just as difficult. Family always comes first in Egypt, and many found the strong influence of the parents or siblings on their husbands annoying. For an Egyptian man parents always come first. In Europe we see things differently; there the wife or the children come first.

These women, therefore, have far more experiences in common than is usually the case for women friends in Germany or in other countries.

Almost all of them talked about the jealousy of their husbands. Of course there are jealous men in other places, too, but in Egypt it is the norm. That is the way the society is there. In their eyes jealousy serves as protection for the woman. It is astonishing how tolerant most of the husbands are when it comes to religion. But I assume that a certain tolerance is necessary in this regard as a prerequisite for a man's marriage to a non-Muslim woman from another country. A fanatic Muslim would certainly never think of marrying a Christian.

We women in Germany consider ourselves emancipated. But does that always have advantages? We have to think and act much more independently; that can be very stressful. When we have families, we wear ourselves out between profession, children and household. Most husbands support their emancipated wives - only in theory - one seldom catches them actually doing housework. When women do the shopping, they subsequently lug the heavy bags all by themselves into the kitchen.

In Egypt hardly anyone talks about emancipation. The woman is always considered weaker than the man. One helps her so that she does not have to carry heavy loads. That goes for shopping but otherwise, too; the people in Egypt are much more helpful than in Germany. Within the family the brother takes care of his sister, and of course the children take care of the parents.

When an accident occurs or someone falls on the street, everyone rushes to the scene to help. Sometimes that becomes more of a hindrance because if too many people are involved, they begin to discuss first what should be done.

We have all observed the change in Egyptian society over the years. What was once an open, joyful country where hardly any woman wore a headscarf, is today a land with ever more extreme tendencies. No one really knows why this has come to be. How these changes will develop is the subject of many discussions. We do not know anyone personally with fanatic or extreme views. Up to now apparently different standards have applied to foreign women from those for Egyptian women. Nevertheless we watch all of these changes very carefully.

It is our wish that this book will contribute to greater tolerance and understanding among religions and cultures.

Annelies Ismail Alexandria, February 2009

Appendix A
Egyptian Cuisine

Almost all of the women featured in this book mentioned Egyptian cuisine at some point in their stories. No matter who we are or where we live, food is an important part of our daily lives and everyone has an opinion about it. From some of the women I even got recipes. You can't get all of the ingredients in Germany, but most of them are available in the United Kingdom and the United States. This appendix contains a few of the recipes I gathered in the course of working on this book. You can easily find more on the Internet. Two good sources are: www.touregypt.net/recipes for English speakers, and www.lamiz.de/aegypten-reisen-rezepte for German speakers.

First a few basic observations on Egyptian cuisine. In general, the food in Egypt is not hot and spicy; to our palate it seems almost mild sometimes. Egyptian cuisine uses some spices that are rare in Germany but can be found in the United Kingdom and the United States in Indian and Mexican cooking:

Cumin (in Arabic Camun) is used in meat dishes. This spice is also an ingredient in curry, which is a mixture of spices. Use this spice sparingly because it has a very intense flavor. Ground cumin is available in most supermarkets and definitely in Indian or Middle Eastern shops. In Turkish it is called *Kimyon.*

Coriander Seeds (in Arabic Cusbara) are also used to season meat. One sautés the coriander seeds with garlic in oil and uses the mixture as a condiment for soups at the table. Coriander is available at the supermarket. Fresh coriander, known as cilantro in the United Kingdom and the United States, looks like Italian parsley and is used in salads and with grilled meats. Often fresh *Gergir* is served with fish and meat. It is the same as Arugula or rocket. In Egypt, it is eaten with one's fingers.

Egyptians eat a lot of vegetables and many legumes,

like lentils or beans. They eat rice, too, and noodles in many shapes. Potatoes are usually used in stews. In general they eat less meat than we do because meat is relatively expensive.

Lettuce is cut into very small pieces and usually flavored only with lime. In Egypt one also calls dips „salad;" an example is eggplant dip *(Babaganough)* and sesame dip *(Tahina).* These are served at every meal without fail. One eats them with a flatbread that is similar to pita bread and usually before the main meal.

Many vegetables are familiar to us in Europe and the United States: eggplant (aubergine), zucchini(courgette), carrots, leeks, green beans, peas, cauliflower, and broccoli. In addition there is okra or ladies fingers *(in Arabic Bamia),* which looks like a thick green bean and is well known in the South of the United Kingdom and the United States. It is usually cooked with tomatoes and meat and is characteristically a little slimy after cooking. The Egyptians really like the finely chopped green leaves of Molokhia (mallow leaves, botanical name corchorus olitorius), which are cooked in a meat broth. One eats them with bread or rice. They, too, have a slimy consistency. All the Egyptians love it, although many foreigners have difficulty getting it down.

The usual way to prepare a stew is as follows: First sauté onions and minced garlic in clarified butter, and season it with coriander, cumin, salt and pepper. Then add pieces of meat. Let it all steam for a while, and then add some vegetables, such as carrots, zucchini, and potatoes. At the end add the tomatoes (in Egypt they use soft, fresh tomatoes). Simmer until the meat and vegetables are soft and then season to taste. Serve with rice or flatbread.

Ful Medamis

Ful Medamis is a typical Egyptian dish served at breakfast. In Egyptian hotels one sometimes sees puzzled tourists standing in front of the brown, cooked beans (fava beans). I have often shown foreigners how to prepare them. All Egyptians love them. There is evidence that these beans were part of the diet during the time of the Pharaohs. Today Ful Medamis is sold on the street from large copper kettles. In the morning you can see workers and other people getting their breakfast and eating it in the street. Once you eat a serving of it, you do not need anything else for the rest of the day. You can cook Ful Medamis yourself, but it takes a long time. In some cities in Germany and UK you can buy Ful Medamis in cans just as you can buy canned fava beans in the United Kingdom and the United States.

Preparation of the dried beans

Wash 500 grams or 1 lb. dried fava beans. Add enough water to cover beans (2-3 quarts) and 1 teaspoon baking powder. Cook on low heat for 6-9 hours.
Another way is to cook the beans slowly in a covered clay pot (Römertopf) in the oven at 250 F. Now and then check that there is enough water in the pot. The beans are tender when they have absorbed all the water. Makes around eight portions.

Serving the cooked beans

For each serving, place the warm beans in a deep dish. Add olive oil, some lemon or lime juice and season with salt, cumin and cayenne powder to taste. If you like, add chopped onions, tomatoes and cucumbers. Everything is mixed together and eaten with flat bread.

Shorbet Ads (Egyptian Lentil Soup)

This is another typical Egyptian dish. It is still eaten often today and is very healthy.

Ingredients: (serves four)

1 cup red lentils (Ads Asfar)
1 onion, chopped
1 carrot, peeled and cubed
1 zucchini, peeled and cubed
1 tomato, peeled and cubed
5 cups broth or water
1 teaspoon freshly ground cumin seeds
Salt
Lemon juice to taste

Preparation

Cook the lentils with the broth and vegetables for about 30 minutes until they are soft and almost fall apart. Press through a fine sieve. Season to taste with cumin, salt, and lemon juice. The soup turns yellow after cooking.
Serve with **Taleya** (Garlic sauce)

Ingredients

10 cloves of garlic
1 teaspoon of ground coriander
1 tablespoon oil
Salt
Pepper or cayenne pepper

Preparation

Crush the garlic in a mortar and mix with salt, pepper, and the coriander. Toast 3 minutes in a pan until golden. Sprinkle over the soup.

Kosheri

After Ful Medamis and Ads, Kosheri is the next most popular dish in Egypt. It is served in small, simple restaurants. Usually it is served in tin bowls and eaten with a spoon. It is very easy to make, and I do not know anyone who doesn't like it. We have it whenever there is no time to go shopping. Every home almost always has the ingredients on hand.

Ingredients (serves 4)

2 cups brown lentils (Ads Iswid)
1/2 cup small noodles e.g. small elbow macaroni
2 cups rice
5 cups of water for macaroni and rice
8 cups of water for lentils
Some tomato sauce (should be spicy with chili and cumin)
Oil

Preparation

Fry the macaroni in a pot with some oil until they take on color. Add the rice and toast it, too. Add 5 cups of water and salt. Cover and cook on low until the rice is tender, and all the water has been absorbed.
At the same time bring the lentils and 8 cups of water (enough to cover) to the boil in another pot, and simmer until the lentils are tender. Check if water needs to be added. Drain any leftover liquid. Mix everything together.
Serve with the hot tomato sauce and fried onions or Taleya (garlic sauce).

Tameya - also known as Falafel

Tameya is also often available at hotel breakfast buffets. It is not just an Egyptian favorite, but is found all over the Middle East. It is made from the same beans as those in Ful Medamis, except that they are peeled. In other countries the Falafel is made from chick peas.

Ingredients

200 g/ 1 cup dried, peeled, fava beans
1 bunch of Italian flat parsley
1 bunch of cilantro (coriander)
1 onion
1 teaspoon salt
1/4 teaspoon cayenne pepper
1/4 teaspoon baking powder
Sesame seeds
Vegetable oil for deep-frying

Preparation

Soak the peeled beans in water for 24 hours.
Grind the beans in a blender. Add onion, parsley, cilantro, cayenne pepper, baking powder and salt. Mix in blender to make a firm paste. Let stand about 1 hour.
Form small balls from the paste, press a little flat and roll them in sesame seeds to cover.
Deep fry in the hot vegetable oil. Tameya tastes best freshly fried.
If you do not want to fry them right away, it is best to prepare the dough and fry them as needed.

Eggplant Casserole

Ingredients (serves 6)

8 middle-sized eggplants
3 red peppers
3 green peppers
3 large onions
6 garlic cloves
Oil
Salt, pepper
1 can peeled whole tomatoes 500 gr (1 pound)
Filling:
40 gr (1 ½ oz) margarine
500 gr (1 pound) ground beef
2 onions
2 garlic cloves
Salt, pepper
Wash the eggplants. Cut into 1 cm (½ inch) thick slices, salt on both sides and let drain in a sieve for about 10 minutes. Pat dry on both sides. Clean the peppers and cut into 4 cm (1,5 inch) slices. Peel the onions and cut into thin rings 5 mm (about ¼ inch). Peel the garlic cloves and cut them into small slices.
Heat the oil and sauté the eggplants, peppers and onion rings well. Drain on paper towels.

Filling

Melt the margarine and sauté the chopped onion and garlic cloves. Add the ground beef and fry well. Season to taste with salt and pepper.
In a large casserole dish, layer half of the eggplants, peppers and onions. Sprinkle with salt and pepper. Stud with half of the cut garlic. Spread evenly with the beef filling. Spread evenly with the remaining eggplant, peppers and onion rings and the rest of the chopped garlic. Crush the tomatoes well and pour over the casserole. Bake for a good hour at 180 C (355 F) in the oven until soft. Sprinkle with parsley and serve with rice.

Kosbareya - Fish a la Alexandria

Kosbareya is the local way to prepare fish in Alexandria.

Ingredients (serves two)

500 gr (1 lb) fish filet
1/4 teaspoon cumin
1/4 teaspoon coriander seeds
3 onions
1 small can of tomatoes, 14 oz (or 1 lb fresh tomatoes peeled)
1 tablespoon tomato paste
2 garlic cloves
Salt
Pepper
Flour

Preparation

Using a pestle and mortar, finely grind cumin and coriander seeds with pepper and salt. Wash the fish and rub with a minced garlic clove and the spice mixture from the mortar. Let stand about 30 minutes.
Slice onions thinly and sauté until golden brown. Add the tomato paste and sauté for a minute. Add the tomatoes and season with pepper and salt. Simmer for a few minutes.
Coat the fish with flour and fry golden brown on both sides. Drain the fish on paper towels.
Put half of the tomato sauce in an ovenproof baking dish. Place the fish in the dish and cover with the other half of the tomato sauce. Bake in the oven at 180 C (355) for around 15 minutes. Serve with rice or flat bread.

Tahina Sauce

Tahina is a paste made of ground sesame seeds. It is available already prepared in Indian and Middle Eastern shops as well as most supermarkets in the United Kingdom and the United States. One can make a tasty dip from the paste. It is always served in Egypt with the usual salads as an appetizer.
Ingredients (serves 4 as an appetizer)
1 cup of sesame paste (Tahina)
3 garlic cloves
1/2 cup water
Juice of one lemon
1/4 teaspoon ground cumin
1 bunch parsley, chopped fine
Salt
Preparation
Place the sesame paste in a bowl. Press the garlic as fine as possible and stir into paste. Add water and lemon juice until the consistency is creamy. Season with the remaining ingredients. This dip is usually served with flat bread.

Baba Ganough Eggplant Puree with Sesame Paste

Baba Ganough is one of the salads often served before the main course. It is also a side dish for roasted or fried meat.

Ingredients (serves 4 as an appetizer)

2 middle-sized eggplants
1/2 cup lemon juice
1/2 cup tahina(sesame paste)
Salt to taste
3 garlic cloves, chopped fine
2 tablespoons olive oil
1/2 bunch flat parsley, chopped

Preparation

Prick the eggplants in several places and bake in the oven for half an hour. The eggplant must be very soft. Cover with a damp cloth and let cool. Scoop the soft eggplant out of its skin with a spoon.
Mash the eggplant with a fork and beat with a puree beater or puree in the blender.
Mix in the remaining ingredients and season to taste.
Garnish with paprika, some parsley and olive oil.

Busara / Puree of dried Ful Beans

Busara is also a salad served before the main course. It can be a side dish for roasted or fried meat. It is a very old recipe which is not often prepared today. It is not difficult to make and very healthy.

Ingredients (serves 4 as an appetizer)

Half pound (250 gr) of dry ful beans without shell
Salt to taste
Cumin, cayenne (chili powder)
3 garlic cloves
2 medium sized onions, cut up in pieces
1 bunch of flat parsley , cut
1 bunch of cilantro (coriander), cut
1 bunch of dill, cut
2 tablespoons oil
2 medium sized onions, chopped (for the topping)

Preparation

Cook the ful beans with the greens and 2 onions and garlic in water until everything is soft, about 40 minutes
Season with salt, cumin and cayenne (chili powder)
Beat with a puree beater or puree in a blender
Pour into small bowls

Fry the chopped onions until golden brown and put on top
Let stand to cool, the puree will be firm when it is cold
Eat with flat bread, bread sticks or vegetable sticks (carrots, cucumber, and celery)

Om Ali (dessert)

Of the many Egyptian desserts and sweets, this is just one example.

Ingredients (serves 4)

2-3 dried, day old rolls or slices of bread (cut in roughly 2cm (¾ inch) cubes)
30 gr (1 oz) ground nuts (hazelnuts, walnuts or almonds)
20 gr (3/4 oz) coconut flakes
30 gr (1 oz) raisins
30 gr (1 oz) sugar
2 cups milk
½ cup whipping cream

Preparation

Warm the milk with the sugar and pour over the bread cubes.
Mix in all other ingredients and place in a baking dish.
Pour the cream on top
(or whip the cream and put aside to serve with the bread pudding when it is almost cool)
Bake for around 15 minutes at 220 C (425 F)
Serve slightly warm.

Appendix B

Chronology of Recent Egyptian history

1917-1922	**Egypt** under British occupation (with Sultan Fouad as the highest Egyptian representative).
1922-1952	Independent Kingdom of Egypt (first under King Fouad, later under King Farouk).
1945	Egypt is a founding member of the United Nations.
1952	Revolution of young military officers and coup d'état of General Naguib. King Farouk is forced to abdicate.
1953	Egypt becomes a republic, with General Naguib as its first president. A year later he is deposed by Gamal Abdel Nasser. Nasser becomes Head of State.
1956	Nationalization of the Suez Canal by Nasser and beginning of the Suez Crisis. Military intervention by Israel, France and Great Britain. The UN intervenes and settles the crisis. In addition: introduction of women's right to vote.
1958 - 1961	United Arab Republic **(UAR),** through a political union with Syria and North Yemen.
1961	Break-up of the United Arab Republic
After 1961	Socialist government under Nasser.
1967	Egypt loses the Sinai Peninsula to Israel in the Six-Day War.
1970	Nasser dies, presidency assumed by Anwar el Sadat.
1973	Yom-Kippur-War against Israel, expulsion of the Soviet military advisors. Sadat opens up the country, numerous restrictions are relaxed.

1977	Beginning of the peace process between Egypt and Israel. Egypt becomes increasingly isolated in the Arab world.
1979	Withdrawal of the Israeli troops from the Sinai Peninsula.
1981	Assassination of President Sadat. Hosni Mubarak becomes his successor. Emergency law is imposed. President Mubarak continues negotiations and tries to act as a peace broker in the Palestine conflict.
1995	The ruling party is confirmed in parliamentary elections. In spite of a few set-backs the peace process in the Middle East continues. This leads to an increased militancy among Islamists, who are suppressed with the help of the emergency law imposed in 1981.
2005	For the first time several candidates run for the office of President in the parliamentary elections. President Mubarak is re-elected for a fifth term in office.
2007	Reform of the Constitution.

More on the History of Egypt on the internet under www.touregypt.net